DRAGONBAND
SAGA

CROSSROADS OF DRASTON
TALES – VOLUME ONE

Aaron Wulf, Anna Warkentin, Jack Gabriel and Joel Norden

Knights of the Northwest, LLC
NAPOLEON, OHIO

Knights of the Northwest, LLC
Napoleon, OHIO/43545

Publisher's Note: This is a work of fiction. Names, characters, places, and incidents are a product of the author's imagination. Locales and public names are sometimes used for atmospheric purposes. Any resemblance to actual people, living or dead, or to businesses, companies, events, institutions, or locales is completely coincidental.

Cover art by Jamie Noble.
Edited by Joel Norden, Aaron Wulf and Jack Gabriel.

Crossroads of Draston/ Joel Norden -- 1st ed.
ISBN 978-0-6927135-3-2
Library of Congress Control Number: 2016917384

Acknowledgements

First and foremost I'd like to thank my siblings. Jacob and Gigi, your names will forever be branded on the foundation stones of the Dragonband setting.
A special thanks to Charles Beason and Aaron Wulf for helping with world building among other things. Nilstria Archmagus, Heather and SOR for giving me the courage to bring this project to the light and also for helping out with the forum back in the good old days.
To the writers who contributed to this anthology, I am truly grateful to have gotten to work with you. You helped me breathe air into this fascinating project and create a vibrant setting.
Finally, to all the family, friends and fans who have encouraged Dragonband forever onward. I am truly blessed to have you along in this adventure. Without all of you I'm afraid this novel wouldn't have happened. I am enormously in your debt, so again, I say thank you!

Joel Norden

The Librarian

By Jack Gabriel

604 AM Age of the Dracon-esti

Wiggum pushed his cart through the Great Library of Evesburg, shoving books back where they belonged. The books were carefully arranged in the order of the elven alphabet, on the insistence of Athrar, the Lord Head Librarian. A strange thing to insist in the library of a human city.

Re-shelving was Wiggum's least favorite

duty. Not because he hated the manual labor – he was well used to that – but because every book he picked up called out to be opened. His gnomish hands would grip the history of a lost country, or find a translation of an epic poem he had never read, and before he knew it he'd be lost in the words and hours would pass. What should have taken him a few hours often took all day, meaning he'd not only gain a scolding from Athrar, but also run out of time for his own studies.

Today was different. One book, in particular, was holding his attention.

Among the brightly bound and freshly published books on his cart was one to which he could not stop his eyes from wandering back. It was a book bound in rough leather with frayed stitching and stamped with faded runes. A book that once sat on the shelves of the long-destroyed Library of Mythalis. A book that his hands itched to open.

For the hundredth time since that morning, Wiggum cleared his head of the temptation and turned down an aisle. He parked his cart, checked the numbers and letters on the spines and found their corresponding shelves. He made quick work of dashing up the ladders or clambering along the shelves to find the necessary gaps and plug them with books. He was making good time with this floor, though he knew it would take longer to shelve when he reached the third floor, where the huge reference tomes were kept. There, also, was the room where *that* particular book belonged: The Sealed Section. This section was usually under guard, for the books inside could be dangerous in the wrong hands.

"Gnome!"

Wiggum, dragged from his daydreaming, peered down from the ladder where he was perched to see a man standing by the cart wearing a silver-hemmed travel cloak and sword. He had a clean, straight chin and bright eyes. An adventurer, maybe, Wiggum thought.

"Yes?" Wiggum said, as politely as he could muster.

"I wish to learn about the dargrash," the man said, flourishing an arm into the air and flapping his cloak.

Wiggum assessed the man as he slid down the ladder. His hair was slick and red, a trait common in human nobility. Wiggum remembered reading that in certain circles among the upper classes of Glandstone society, young males would assert their worthiness by traveling outside the city and bring back a trophy to prove their stories were true. Heads of various beasts were common, as were tiny captured creatures, brought home and given to a younger sister as a pet. Sometimes the young men returned with a foreign wife. Sometimes they returned years later, a haunted hood over their eyes. Sometimes, they never returned. But no matter what their fate, or how their story ended, it always began the same way.

With fresh-muscled arrogance, the handsome young human watched Wiggum descend to the floor. "Just point me in the right direction," he commanded.

Wiggum wished he'd stayed up the ladder now. "What do you want to know?" he asked.

The youngling stared bravely into the middle distance. "I wish to know their habits. How they might be hunted and killed."

Wiggum sighed. "Grasslands Fauna is next floor up." He pointed at the lavish central stairway. "Turn left at the statue of Dunarth."

Wiggum watched after the human as he bounded towards the stairs. Soon the young hero would read eyewitness accounts of dargrash patiently ripping a man into six equal portions to share evenly around their family.

Humans were funny creatures. Of all the races Wiggum had met and read about, humans were the most varied in their habits. Some of them had an almost gnomish desire for knowledge and were second only to the elves in their contribution to the Library's collection. Others only drank and fought.

Wiggum focused again. He grabbed more books from the cart while he was down. He told himself it was accidental when he brushed his fingers against the tattered spine of the ancient book. He wondered vaguely what was inside. What kind of book was worth keeping all these long years?

Suddenly he had grasped it in his hands. He gasped when he realized he was already pulling it from the cart.

"Wiggum!" a voice snapped.

He dropped the book like it was hot and it slid down, hidden among its sisters on the cart again.

"Athrar!" Wiggum squeaked. He hadn't even noticed the approach of the Head Lord Librarian's clicking heels.

The elf's long legs force him into the aisle of books. "Wiggum," he stated, like a child pointing to an animal.

"Yes, Sir?"

Athrar's sharp cheekbones were pulsing. He was grinding his teeth. "The University has commissioned us to prepare a series of lectures on the beasts of the tundra."

Wiggum's shoulders drooped. "Can't Libbin do it?"

Athrar did not respond.

"Alright," Wiggum moaned. It was hardly a challenge, researching beasts of the tundra. All giant fluffy white things with lots of teeth. He hated tedious work, but it had to be done if he was to afford the rent to live so close to the Library.

"By tomorrow morning," Athrar added.

Wiggum shrugged in agreement. The University always wanted things urgently. It was the worst-kept secret that the University's urgent requests were thin covers for the military. The lectures would be attended by stocky soldiers, ordered to be there by their captains so they could learn about the creatures or peoples they were about to encounter. The army must be secretly preparing to move north for some reason.

Wiggum wondered, as he often did, how much that valuable piece of information would be worth.

"One more thing, Wiggum."

"Yes, Lord Athrar?"

Athrar's steel eyes narrowed at the cart of books. "The Sealed Section, on the third floor. A book is missing."

Something stopped Wiggum's tongue from replying. He could see, if he dared glance, that the ancient book was hidden from Lord Athrar's sight. A sudden need took over him. A need that outweighed his morality and his duty.

"I've not seen such a book," he said.

"Watch for it," Athrar snapped. "Bring it directly to me should you find it." As he glided away, Wiggum heard him mutter, "I hope that fool Libbin's not found it."

Wiggum's hands itched for the book, but he made himself concentrate and set to re-shelving again.

Faster than ever before, he had completed the ground floor. He took the cart to the winch, climbed the stairs, then turned the stiff handle to raise the cart up the vertical tunnel. He concentrated harder on this floor, but the old book in the cart was always drawing his eyes.

The young man he'd helped earlier was also on the same floor, sitting cross-legged in an aisle, pale-faced at the illustrations and accounts of the dargrash spread out before him. He was whimpering to himself, biting his nails, and hardly registered when the cart rolled past.

When he'd finished that floor, Wiggum took

the cart to the winch again. He cursed the speed of concentration. It meant that the third floor was coming closer, and soon *that* book would be the only one left to put away. Then what would he do?

Heaving and stacking, Wiggum almost wished for an interruption to delay him. But he'd threatened his job with daydreaming and distraction in the past, and he needed the money. Evesburg wasn't a cheap place to live. Rent drained him almost dry each month, and even the small amount of food that he ate was all he could afford. One thing to be said for humans: they knew how to take your money.

When he finally reached the third floor, Wiggum found himself hiding the old book under others as he trundled up and down. The labyrinthine building had many corners and alcoves, and it wasn't long before he was pausing in these out-of-sight spots. Before he knew it, he was picking up the book, but only to look at the cover.

The book had been branded with symbols Wiggum didn't recognize. A kind of elvish, by the look of the flowing runes, but he couldn't make out the words. Of only one thing he was sure. It was a book from before the fall of Tenthrolen.

It was the law that such books could only be held by elvish hands. Some were enchanted to cause great pain to any other. It sent a shiver down his spine to think he'd picked it up so casually when he didn't know what it was. He could have been dead in an aisle if it were the wrong sort of book. Still, Wiggum knew he could be banished from the Library for touching it, and that was bad enough, especially since he had denied that he'd seen the thing.

The book lay open in his hands.

Wiggum gave a quickly-stifled shout. He didn't remember opening it. Peering carefully around the corner of the window-bay in where he was hiding, Wiggum listened out for the tapping of Athrar's shoes, before looking down again.

The pages that had opened before him contained strange diagrams and the same types of runes as the cover. There was a scribbled illustration of a creature in the corner. Wiggum focused on the letters. If he stared at them long enough, they began to make sense. It was as if the runes wanted to be read. They seemed to be instructions of some kind.

Suddenly, meaning snapped into place, and Wiggum found himself proudly reciting the words out loud.

Two things occurred to him then. The first was that the book began to feel chalky in his hands, as if the pages were crumbling. The second was that he had not considered how Athrar had known that a book was missing from the Sealed Section.

There was no room for the last thought. The book crinkled and turned to ashes as if burnt by an invisible flame. Its remains sifted through his fingers and piled up on the tiles between Wiggum's feet.

"Dunarth's beard!" he whispered.

The ash pile started growing. Particles tumbled down the side as it heaved upwards, like something was pushing up from inside.

"No, no." Wiggum held his hands out, uselessly hushing the ash pile, which now towered over him. It would soon rise above the stacks of shelves. "Please stop."

It slowed down, but its edge was still pushing him towards the stained window, where Dunarth proudly held his Scrolls of Knowledge and scowled down.

Wiggum desperately tried to remember what was written on the rest of the page he'd tried to read. He scratched at the corners of his memory for some kind of reversing spell.

And it was a spell, wasn't it? He bit his fingernails at the realization that he had just performed magic. That's why the meaning of the runes had fallen into place. The book wasn't written in elvish at all. Those runes had been the language of magic.

As a rule, humans did not trust magic. The Magi had been cast out of the cities long ago. Their towers burnt, left to ruin. The Tower of Red Robes was now their only sanctuary.

Nobody would like that a little gnome had performed magic. He would be banished from the city unless he could reverse it. Maybe he could get past the guards of The Sealed Section and find how to fix it in another book, if only he could keep this ash pile under control.

The gray mound finally stopped moving. For a moment, everything was silent, except for the half-imagined click of Athrar's heel.

The ash pile exploded apart like a dragon's cough, spraying all over Wiggum, filtering through the surrounding shelves, dimming the sunlight.

When Wiggum opened his eyes the ash pile was gone.

Looming before him was a dark creature stretching out its great leathery wings, its furry snout snarling, tapping the cold tiles with its hooked talons. A shroud of black mist swirled and eddied with its movements.

Wiggum held his hands out and backed himself against the window. The snorting nostrils of the phantom creature followed him. Blank white eyes stared. Windows into the Elisus, a realm that mirrored this one, where all was decayed and withered. Populated with twisted creatures such as this. Shadowspawn.

"Oh dear," Wiggum panted, his brain racing. The shadowspawn was watching him. He knew he had to figure something out fast before it could do some proper damage. He imagined what it could do in this Library alone, let alone if it escaped.

Too late.

With a shriek, the shadowspawn raised a mighty leg and kicked in turn at the two bookshelves flanking it. The shelves toppled away like splash ripples on a pond. Shouts of alarms began to ricochet around the Library. The shadowspawn looked panicked, then its empty eyes rested on Wiggum.

He ducked when the shadowspawn came at him, flapping its great wings and screeching. But the shadowspawn leapt over him and crashed through the ancient stained glass like it was paper.

Wiggum watched numbly as the shadowspawn soared over the city of Evesburg, trailed by a wispy cloud of darkness. All over the thatched roofs of the island city washed waves of fear. Warning bells clanged from brown stone towers, horses whinnied and broke from their harnesses, the city's birds swarmed and squawked.

The shadowspawn alighted neatly on a spire in the center of the city, not too far away from the Library. Below were broad avenues, parklands and crowded squares, filled with people now all in a hurried panic. Wiggum often ate his lunch at the markets directly below where the creature now rested. He imagined the horror of biting into his favorite meat-on-a-stick and looking up to see that thing.

The clink and beat of the City Guard began to filter through the screams. They were efficient, the King's Own.

The shadowspawn snorted again and let out an ear-screech. The clouds of shadow around it shivered and lashed. The creature's limbs extended, its wings spread, and its torso puffed up.

Absently, Wiggum wondered if it would eat people.

On cue, the shadowspawn leapt from its stoop, folded its wings like an eagle and swooped towards the ground. It was out of his sight for a moment, then swept back into the sky.

Wiggum almost vomited. In its talons, the beast held two halves of a man. Off balance, it crashed back into the spire, sending the masonry tumbling into the quickly evacuating square below. When it regained its balance, kicking more stones away, the shadowspawn bent its head and began feasting on the man.

"Dunarth's beard," Wiggum whispered.

A series of telltale shoe clicks on the tiles behind him made Wiggum wince. He wished he had a halfling's skill and could vanish from sight.

"You found the book then," Athrar drawled.

Wiggum held his hands up. "I didn't mean to! I swear it. It was the book." It felt ridiculous to say it. "The book did it!"

"Gnomes are such curious creatures," Athrar said. He sucked in air through his teeth, raised his eyebrows at the scene outside. "Just look at what you've done."

The shadowspawn dropped the man's remains and began licking its talons clean. Wiggum hoped desperately that it was not still hungry.

The creature leapt down again, plucked a screaming woman from the street, settled back onto the crumbled spire, and set to feasting on her.

Unhinged terror gripped the city below, and Wiggum stared uselessly down at it all from the safety of the third floor of the Library.

"Come here," Athrar said.

Wiggum found himself turning from the

chaos and walking on reluctant feet towards Athrar's outstretched hand.

A dark pallor washed over the elf's face as Wiggum approached him. The Head Librarian, always tall, seemed to loom higher now by another foot at least. The steel eyes that had always patronized him were now molten and full of fury. A frozen horror took hold of Wiggum. He dared not disobey, and before he could stop himself, he was standing before Athrar. He felt the elf's hand rest on his shoulder, burning cold.

"What are you-"

The Library tore into shreds. Reality swirled and danced, and the broken shelves and scattered books restitched themselves suddenly into the dank bricks of an alleyway.

Wiggum fell to his knees and dry-retched on the cobblestones. Athrar had somehow transported them here from the Library. A skill possessed only by very powerful Magi.

The alleyway opened up to the now-empty Market Square in the center of town. The shadowspawn, now grown to twice its original size, was brooding on the building opposite in a nest of simmering black flames. A discoloration had begun to seep out from the place where it sat. A sort of rot was spreading, turning paint to flakes, crumbling wood and cracking stone, causing trees and plants in the square's gardens to curl and dry. The decay of the Elisus was leaking out into this realm.

"Look at it," Athrar whispered, awestruck.

"How do we stop it?" Wiggum wailed. He hoped the thing didn't move anywhere else.

The shadowspawn quickly clambered to its feet. It chugged its massive wings and took to the sky. A triumphant shriek split the air, setting Wiggum's beard hairs bristling. The shadowspawn began moving north, towards Three Bridges, where the richest merchants lived.

Athrar's hand slapped onto his shoulder again, and Wiggum realized with a sickness what was about to happen. His body folded and churned through space. When he popped back whole again, pieces of him felt out of place still.

"An excellent viewpoint," Athrar announced.

They had appeared at the meeting point of the three bridges that gave the area its name. The few people that were rushing by didn't even notice the sudden appearance of an elf and a gnome. A well-tended and large triangular courtyard spread before them, the three-story villas of influential merchants lined around its edges. And there, trailed by dark swirls from another realm, was the shadowspawn coming towards them. It swooped along avenues and churned the city below into a chaos of despair.

"What are we doing? It's coming this way!" yelled Wiggum. "Are you going to fight it?"

"Not me," Athrar said. His nails dug into Wiggum's shoulder.

Streaking bands of blue, red and white crashed into the courtyard, ending in an explosion of flames that burnt away to reveal color-robed figures. Two white, two blue and a red.

"Magi," Wiggum hummed in astonishment.

"And five of them," Athrar muttered, pleased with himself.

Wiggum looked back at Athrar, and a pit opened in his stomach at what he saw.

The elf had shed his disguise now. His skin was coal, his hair white as snow. A dark elf.

"You did this," Wiggum said. He wished he could get away, but the elf's grip was tight.

"No, no," Athrar cooed. "You did this."

The shadowspawn screeched and crashed into the row of luxurious houses. It was a clumsy beast, learning to use its ever-growing body. It snorted down at the five Magi.

"You see, young gnome," Athrar whispered into Wiggum's ear, "my colleagues and I have been trying to flush the Magi out of hiding for years. There are so few left now. They are becoming hard to find. The Tower of Red Robes will be their only stronghold soon, and there we will destroy them utterly."

Wiggum shook, the only movement his paralyzed body allowed. Athrar, the Lord Head Librarian, was a renegade sorcerer.

"As soon as you denied seeing the book I knew you had found it. Your curiosity is greater than your will. I'm impressed with the page you chose. Albeit accidentally, I'm sure. Not even I knew what to expect, but this is wonderful, isn't it?"

"Why?"

"Humans are stupid. I'm sure we can both agree on that, at least."

Wiggum shrugged. He had a point.

"It is their doing that the Magi were driven into hiding. Humans destroyed the Blue Tower because they didn't understand what it represented. The humans fear what they don't understand. And they hate what they fear. I mean to show them genuine fear. If they refuse to accept a peaceful relationship with the Magi, then they will be ruled by us."

"How will this monster make that happen?"

"The creature was summoned by magic. The people will see the danger of magic. These five

Magi have been exposed. They will have no choice but to retreat to the Tower of Red Robes. It doesn't matter if the beast kills them or if they kill it. By the end of this day, people will remember only that magic caused destruction and death. I am feeding their fear of magic users."

"But why me?"

"Many old books hold strange magic. The grimoire you found could not be used by me. Some enchantment, blocking anybody who meant to use it for evil. I figured that a curious gnome, who only cares for knowledge, may be a way around the spell. Seems I was right."

Then Wiggum found that he was responsible for this after all. He was ashamed. Angrier at himself than he was at Athrar.

Then, something struck him as odd. For all its terror and power, the beast was still clinging to the roof of the fancy houses. The Magi below were frozen in their ready stances, each a point of potential power. Energy crackled in the air.

What were they all waiting for? When was the shadowspawn going to attack?

As if Wiggum had commanded it, the creature roared and descended on the five figures. It flapped open its wings, talons writhing as it swooped.

The Magi answered with bolts of light that

struck the creature and sent it crashing into the rows of houses. The Magi advanced, sending bolt after bolt at the screeching black abomination. They were pummeling the creature with so much power that Wiggum wondered if it would escape at all. Perhaps this would be the end of it.

All at once, from the cloud of rubble and dust, emerged the shadowspawn. It burst soaring into the sky, traced by bolt after bolt of light from the five Magi.

Wiggum frowned and stroked his beard. There was something about the way the shadowspawn was acting. When he thought of it escaping the library, it did. When he thought of it eating people, it did. When he had been distracted by Athrar talking, the thing hadn't moved at all.

With a sickening thump to his stomach, Wiggum realized that *he* had been controlling the shadowspawn this whole time. It reacted directly to his thoughts, whether they be positive or negative. If he imagined it doing something, even if it was a horrible thing, the shadowspawn did it.

Trying desperately not to give away that he understood this new information, Wiggum looked back. Athrar was watching the shadowspawn turn great circles in the sky, grinning. The dark elf surely didn't know that Wiggum controlled the creature.

Many books held magic so strange that even a powerful Magi may not know how it worked.

Wiggum had to test the theory without killing anybody else. He focused on the shadowspawn and put all his thought into a command.

"Land," he whispered.

The shadowspawn dropped like a rock, slamming into the flagstones of the courtyard. It turned to him and snuffled, those white eyes staring. The Magi, tired now, surrounded the creature. They were not attacking. The beast was still.

"What is it doing?" Athrar snapped. Wiggum kept his face blank. Gnomes were known for their empty expressions. It made them hard to beat in betting games. But behind his round cheeks and sparkling eyes, his mind began to control the shadowspawn like a puppet.

The thing roared at Athrar. It folded its leathery wings and started stalking towards them, talons clicking on the cracked flagstones.

"Stop!" Athrar commanded.

The Magi flanked the shadowspawn as it walked, hands raised should it turn on them and attack. The Red Magi pointed at Athrar and exclaimed.

"It was the dark elf that summoned the creature!"

Athrar cursed in elvish. He had forgotten to cloak himself in the guise of a wise gray elf. He was losing composure. Wiggum felt the grip loosen on his shoulder, and he took the opportunity to scurry out of the way. Athrar's hand snatched after him, but he did not follow. Wiggum found a hiding place behind the statue of the god Glowt, whose grin greeted those who entered the city from the north.

The shadowspawn screeched again, and Wiggum concentrated hard. He needed to make sure it stayed focused on Athrar. He didn't want it to attack the other Magi.

The creature's neck swung to the side suddenly as it lunged at the Magi. It was met with flashes and bolts of light, but it was too late. The shadowspawn's large claws had swiped one of the Blue Magi and sent him sprawling across the cobblestones.

"No!" Wiggum yelled. He had to be careful what he thought, even the hope that the creature would not do something would cause it to act.

Attack Athrar, he thought. He put all his concentration into it. Wiggum did not appreciate being used for anyone's plan. He felt the anger bubbling inside as he thought of every scowl he'd received from the Lord Head Librarian. What made him even more furious were the shelves of books that had been destroyed. All that knowledge lost. Wiggum knew he was not entirely free of blame, but the book was enchanted. He had been hypnotized by it. He was nothing more than a pawn in Athrar's plan. Athrar the dark elf.

His anger funneled down into one thought-command: Attack Athrar.

The shadowspawn turned away from the Magi, who still danced on their feet, and back to Athrar. The Head Librarian backed away. He raised his arm, and a dark flash crackled into the shadowspawn. It reared at first, then shook off the attack and advanced.

The Magi watching yelled in wonder at the impotency of Athrar's attack.

The shadowspawn paused for a moment, then its entire body pulsed. It grew in size, gaining at least another two feet in height and wingspan. It kept coming forward.

"No!" Athrar screamed. Still backing away, he held his hands together, and a black ball of sparkling energy grew between them. He threw it at the shadowspawn, which took the blow on the chest, absorbed it, and kept walking.

"It cannot be defeated by your magic, dark elf!" yelled the White Magi.

"You are only feeding it!" a Blue Magi added,

laughter in her voice.

The beast pulsed again, and grew in size once more. It was almost upon the dark elf now.

"But why does it attack me?" Athrar screamed. Then, a sick realization swept over his face. He turned to find Wiggum watching the scene from behind the statue.

He had worked out that Wiggum's mind was linked to the creature. "How?" he yelled.

"Many books hold strange magic, Lord Athrar," Wiggum whispered.

The shadowspawn grasped Athrar in its talons. In simmering anger, Wiggum could only think of one thing for the beast to do with its prize.

He looked away, but couldn't cover his ears from the wet crunching that followed.

"Now let yourself be banished from this place," he said.

The concentrated blasts of the Magi lit up the river surrounding Three Bridges as the Magi cast the shadowspawn back to the realm of Elisus. Wiggum tried not to think about it. That was the only way it would stay still and allow itself to be destroyed. Instead, he watched the kaleidoscopic colors dance as the water lapped at the bridge supports, swaying the boats and caressing the banks of the city of Evesburg.

Darkness began to creep into the side of his eyes. He wondered for a moment whether it was suddenly night time. The bridges and the water and the boats all swirled and shifted. His legs felt tired and he sat down. A great weariness gripped him. He leaned back against the statues and closed his eyes. Only for a moment.

Wiggum woke in a soft bed.

"What?" he said.

Tapestries hung from stone walls all around him. A soft breeze and birdcalls filtered through the room. A mug of water was by the bed and he drank from it thirstily. When he lowered the cup he glanced out a window and almost spat everything out. He could see for miles. Forests and plains stretched out before him, far below.

"You're awake," said a dark-haired human at a heavy door. She was dressed in plain cotton and leather, but a blue stone on a chain around her neck betrayed who she was.

"You're Magi," Wiggum said.

"And you, young Master Gnome, have read enough to know an awful lot about us." The woman smiled, tucking the stone away.

"What happened?"

She sighed. "The shadowspawn is gone. Once it destroyed the dark elf, we managed to banish it back to the Elisus. We found you soon after it was all over. You were unconscious, but we knew somehow you were linked to the beast. You summoned it, didn't you?"

Wiggum nodded, ashamed. "It was a mistake."

The woman stroked his head with her huge hand. "Dark magic is seductive. It uses you, not the other way around."

Wiggum looked out the window again. "Where are we?" he asked, though he suspected.

"After the beast was gone, people gathered in the courtyard. They didn't care that we'd saved their city. They only knew that magic had brought the monster. Magic is still feared. And ignorant voices will always be loudest. We five had to abandon the lives we built in Evesburg. You, too, have the mark of magic on you. There is no return for us."

"Us?"

"You've awakened a power within you. Rare for an Arcadium gnome – or any gnome at that. We fear dark magic has a hold of you, and you must stay here. We can help you guard against it taking you. You must learn the ways of the Magi, Wiggum the gnome."

"So we're...?"

"In the Tower of Red Robes."

Wiggum gulped. He suddenly felt very alone.

In a tower full of outcast Magi. Associated with those who use magic, he was banished from Evesburg, the city he'd called home for years. He could never return to the Library. Tears began to well. "What must I do?"

"Well, to start with," the woman said, "the Tower of Red Robes needs a new librarian, if you're interested."

A Vicious Cycle

By Joel Norden

631 AM Age of the Dracon-esti

Cyren Oaktrue breathed heavily as he leaned against the trunk of a massive burr oak. The Eltharian elf was grateful for the large branches that forked out above him. The tree's large lobed-shaped leaves protected him from the sunlight.

He was exhausted. Sweat poured down his face and covered his body. Cyren had been a blacksmith for most of his life. The muscles in his shoulders and arms proved he was no stranger to bringing hammer to anvil all day. But as physically built as Cyren was, he was not used to running.

Granted, Cyren had enjoyed his trek through the forest. He hadn't been able to help staring around in sublime child-like wonder at the mighty oak, hickory, and maple trees standing tall and proud. Raccoons, fourri goats and axis deer scampered through the forest. Cyren had never seen any of these animals in the rolling hills that lay north of Elthar.

Around him, a group of Eltharian commandos searched the tall grass for any signs of the orcs they pursued. The elves had been hot on their trail since early that morning.

Parentha spoke, jogging Cyren from his thoughts. "Found the tracks! The orcs went this way." Parentha pointed to boot prints in the dusty earth. "I'm certain there are only six. One of them is perhaps injured or carrying a small deer." He gestured to blood on the blades of grass.

They had been tracking the foul orcs with relative ease, despite the ground being hard and crusted with the summer heat. The elven commandos had been gaining quickly on the creatures from what Parentha had said. Cyren, who was just out of his first century of life, was excited to bloody his sword and rid Harthx of a few orcs.

"Seven. There are seven, I am *certain* of it," Landia Arginièr replied, standing behind Parentha.

Cyren marveled – not for the first time – at Landia's silver hair. It glinted in the waning rays of sunlight intruding the clearing. It was unusual for a Eltharian elf to have such hair, but the house of Arginièr was known for such rare genes. She was stunning, even in the camouflage tunic and muddy face-paint that the elven commandos wore.

Cyren shook his head chuckling, and his long blond hair fell over his face. Landia and Parentha had been at it since the squad had crossed the great Brinfal River that bordered the elven country of Elthar. At first, Cyren had thought Landia and Parentha as merely two good friends making good-natured jabs at each other. But after a few hours they started to bicker. Their arguments became harsher. They didn't argue much in front of the others in the squad, but didn't always check to ensure all were out of earshot.

The rangers moved forward at a signal from Landia's hand. Seven in all. Cyren wasn't even sure what the names of the others were. He just knew

Landia was his commander and Parentha the second in command.

The small group spread out and slipped through the forest like phantoms. Not for the first time, Cyren wondered if these orcs stood a chance at all. Most of the elves in the group had leaves bound to their clothing or dirt rubbed on their skin. The camouflage worked wonders for the commandos as they slipped from tree to tree. It reminded Cyren of the tales his mother used to tell his sister and himself before bed about wilder elves.

It was odd. Eltharian elves were known for their fancy silk garments. Elves higher up in society commonly wore velvet, taffeta, or damask clothing – things only human royalty wore. To see them with leather tunics, covered in soot and leaves like typical human rabble, was almost unthinkable.

Parentha was in the center of the seven elves, Landia right next to him. They jogged along quietly, bows in hand and arrows knocked. Parentha's keen, electric blue eyes never left the trail left by the orcs.

Not even an hour had passed when the rangers reached the crest of a large hill and entered a clearing. The sounds of animals disappeared entirely, replaced by an uneasy silence. At the other end of the hilltop the earth dipped down into a deep valley. A long, wispy trail of smoke snaked from the valley into the blue sky.

"An orc village," Parentha said knowingly.

"A vile splotch in this beautiful land. Even the animals know to avoid this place." Contempt was thick on Landia's tongue.

Cyren nodded. The evil creatures needed to be eradicated.

"Firin and Qualin, go down there and scout out the situation. I want numbers of warriors, women, and children. Be swift!" Landia still managed to look beautiful as she sternly gave orders.

Parentha stood next to her, his eyes studying. Again, Cyren wondered if there was something between the two. There was undeniable chemistry between them, despite the arguing. Parentha met Cyren's gaze with a hard look. As if guessing what he was thinking.

"The rest of you set up a perimeter around this clearing. Be sure we are not ambushed by these beasts," Parentha said, stepping forward to the remaining three elves.

"As you wish, sir," Cyren replied with a nod. He started off for the south end of the clearing where Firin and Qualin had disappeared. He took up a spot next to an ancient maple tree, his bow on his lap.

Cyren was curious. He had never seen an orc, only heard of the terrible stories of plunder, murder, and rape that their race had inflicted against the elves since the beginning of time. Would orc blood run upon his sword this day? Would his arrows fly true and pierce the flesh of evil?

Cyren had never killed anything before. Not a living humanoid anyway – Cyren had only hunted animals. Not for trophies, as he had heard many humans did, but out of necessity. Tasar the Golden Archer, god of nature, had put animals on Harthx to be cared for and respected. But also as a food source.

Late evening rolled around. The sun had dipped behind the tree line, leaving a dusky pink glow in the sky. A few more hours and darkness would be upon them. No sign of orcs or elves. The animal noises had picked up, though much quieter than normal. Landia and Parentha whispered in the clearing, possibly arguing.

A shrill call echoed through the woods – a screech owl. The elves had returned. Cyren answered the call, acknowledging them. The two elves appeared from the underbrush below and nodded as they passed Cyren.

It wasn't long before they were all called back to the center of the clearing. Landia and Parentha both looked pleased.

"Fifteen orc males, seven females, and eight children. This isn't a small village, most likely just a hunters' outpost. The scouts report shoddily-made deerskin tents and hurriedly-built structures. Even more shoddy than normal orc craftsmanship." Landia was obviously pleased with the detail Firin and Qualin had supplied.

"They most likely don't know how close to our borders they've built their homes," Parentha chuckled.

Landia nodded. "And the scum will pay for their mistake. We hit them at nightfall. Then we can use our sharper vision to our advantage."

"What about the women and children?" Cyren asked without thinking.

Landia turned, her icy blue eyes staring at him coldly. Cyren knew the answer before she spoke.

"Orcs are creatures of Valendek. Therefore they are evil. If any survive, they will inevitably breed and raise their children in hatred to attack us. They must all be killed," Landia replied simply.

Cyren looked at the ground, nodding his head. The thought of killing women and children of any race sickened him. It had never occurred to him that he would be asked to do such a thing – even if it was for the greater good.

Finally, the sun's glow had all but disappeared in the darkening sky. Cyren's gut clenched. He couldn't shake his nervousness.

The elves slipped quietly down the hill. As they approached the hunters' camp, Cyren could see the light of a large bonfire through the silhouettes of trees.

As the elves came to the edge of the tree line bordering the hamlet – Cyren wasn't even sure he could call it that – he saw a roaring bonfire. Orcs stood around it as a deer cooked on a spit. Most of the orcs grumbled in their brutish language.

Cyren was instantly disgusted by the creatures. In the firelight, Cyren could see their green skin, pig-like snouts, and jutting foreheads. He shivered at the sight of one of the orcs eating, tearing into the meat with large tusks that jutted from its lower lips. It ate like some kind of animal, chewing loudly and smacking its lips. Cyren could hear it from where he crouched.

The seven rangers split up, surrounded the camp silently, and waited for Landia's signal. Cyren tried to ease his breathing. Tried to calm his nerves. The adrenaline from bringing down a large buck was bad enough, he thought. This was almost over-bearing.

Next to Cyren crouched Parentha, his bow at the ready. Then the signal came, an owl's hoot. There was silence for a moment as Cyren raised the bow in what seemed like slow motion, taking aim at the closest of the male orcs.

The quiet was broken by the twang of bow-strings and the zing of arrows. Cyren's arrow struck his target in the small of the back. The orc screamed in surprise, before another arrow hit it in the wind-pipe.

Parentha chanted as he shot his arrows. Cyren had never seen an arcane archer in action. It amazed him. Each arrow Parentha shot was guided by mag-ic, twisting and turning until it struck its foe. One orc hid behind a large log and one of the magical arrows zipped over its head, missing it. But the ar-row swerved upwards and returned to the orc, stick-ing it in its piggish red eye. Causing it to screech in its harsh language.

At the sight of Landia moving in with two twin daggers on the opposite side of the encamp-ment, Parentha motioned an advance. Cyren quickly slung his bow over his shoulder and drew his sword.

Cyren charged the closest orc to him, sword raised high. The feeling was exhilarating. Blood rushed to his head as he waded into the anarchy. He had one thought: kill as many of these abominations as possible.

The first orc Cyren attacked had large tusks protruding from each side of its mouth, and bits of slobber rolling down its chin. At the sight of Cyren, the orc pointed and shouted in its guttural tongue.

Cyren ducked under the first swing of the orc's rusty bastard sword. As the orc realized his mistake, Cyren's short sword slashed into its thigh. It didn't have time to do anything else because one of Parentha's arrows had found its heart.

Cyren, without hesitation, swung his sword to the right, feinting, causing another orc to halt its charge and hesitate. To Cyren's surprise, it was a woman, incredibly ugly even by orcish standards. Like the males, two tusks protruded from her jutted jaw. Greasy coarse hair clung to her neck, and she held a pitchfork. Cyren hesitated for an instant. In her eyes was not bloodlust or excitement for the kill. The look in her eyes was desperation to protect her family.

That moment of hesitation was a mistake, Cyren realized, as she raised the pitchfork. Her blow never fell though. Qualin sprung from the darkness, impaling the woman orc. Her eyes went wide and even wider still when Qualin twisted the blade.

Cyren looked around in shock. There were small battles all throughout the camp as the orcs fought with no formation. One male orc slipped behind a large deerskin tent.

Cyren surprised himself as he charged in after it. To his astonishment, another beast jumped from the doorway of the tent-like hut.

The orc punched him in the chest and attempted to wrestle Cyren's weapon away from him. With trained agility, Cyren slipped out of the orc's grasp. In one smooth motion, Cyren spun and struck the beast in its neck. The blow landed a grisly upward slash to the orc's throat. The male orc gurgled as he fell backward.

Breathing loudly, Cyren looked into the hut. His breath caught in the back of his throat. Two young orcs huddled in the back of the tent near a slit that had been made from the outside. On the other side of the slit, a large male orc stood.

The large orc ripped the slit more and stepped into the tent, standing in front of the two children.

Cyren's hand clenched tightly around his sword hilt as he took a step forward. But he didn't take another. The faces of the two young orcs would haunt him for the rest of his days. For now he saw the truth.

The truth was not pretty. Within their eyes he saw horror, shock, and sadness. The same look that elven children would have made if it were orcs attacking.

The thought made him sick to his stomach. Perhaps these orcs weren't much different than elves. Maybe they were just a race misguided by hatred. A hatred that had been built over centuries of elves slaughtering orcs. And orcs, in turn, killing elves.

Did it honestly matter who had started the bloodshed? These orc children would grow to hate elves, and perhaps hunt them. It was a vicious cycle, a wheel of never-ending violence.

In that moment Cyren decided he would no longer take part in it. If killing women and children was the will of the gods, they were no gods he would worship.

Cyren lowered his sword. The male orc stared at him suspiciously, waiting for Cyren to advance.

"Go. Now, while you can," Cyren said in common, hoping the orc would understand.

The male orc's eyes widened. He turned and said something to the young orcs – a boy and and a girl. They both disappeared through the slit in the wall.

Before the large male slipped through, he turned to Cyren. He nodded, though a glint of anger and shock still dwelled there. Then the three orcs were gone.

Perhaps someday that orc would realize what Cyren had done and in turn not slay another elf. There was no way of knowing.

Cyren turned to leave the hut but stopped in shock. Parentha stood there, eyeing him coldly. The moments slipped by slowly before Parentha finally said something.

"Why did you let them flee? They will grow, then come for our ears as trophies," Parentha said angrily.

Cyren said nothing, but met Parentha's gaze. He had made a choice. A choice opposing his society's beliefs, and he would pay the cost.

"I will not kill children. I will take no part in it."

"And the male orc? If Landia finds out about this, you will be tried as a dark elf. Do you still stand behind your actions?" Parentha asked, anger still fresh in his voice.

"I do," Cyren replied quietly.

"A shame. You fought well. I went through the same thing when I joined the rangers. A female orc. But I still drove my sword into her. I regretted that for so long. Until one day on the outskirts of Elthar, I saw one of our villages that had been raided." Parentha shook his head sadly.

"They impaled all the men on stakes, the women they raped… Even some of the younger girls." Parentha's words shook with disgust. "All of them had been farmers, blacksmiths, and tradesmen. Simple folk. After that, I never again hesitated to kill an orc."

"But don't you see? It's a cycle, we raid the orcs and in return they raid us. Someone needs to break that cycle, or it will never end," Cyren argued.

"This is the way of the world, Cyren. Nothing is fair. I kill each one of these creatures in hopes of saving an elf. Tell me, you don't honestly view an orc as an elf's equal?" Parentha spat.

"No. But maybe not all of these creatures are evil. What if, because of our own hatred, we helped them choose the dark road they walk on?"

"We could argue and philosophize all night. You will not change my views, Cyren. And neither will you change society. As I said, I've seen what orcs are capable of, and I care not what our races did to each other in the past. The present is all that matters to me."

"But-"

"Enough. I will not tell Landia of this, but you will resign. Tell her you don't have the guts for it." Parentha wiped blood from his face and walked away.

Cyren stayed a while longer. He truly didn't have the guts to kill innocents. A wrong for a wrong doesn't make a right. He would speak to Landia now. Get it over and done with.

Cyren left the tent.

As the flames consumed the huts around him, he contemplated the cycle. Maybe it was too late for the cycle to be broken. Still, he would try.

*****

The dryphon's call echoed out over the mountains of Rhoben. If anyone happened to be looking up from within those mountains, they would have sworn they were looking at a griffon. But they would be mistaken. Though dryphons did have the head, wings, and front legs of a giant eagle, just like the common griffon, dryphons had the body of what seemed like a young dragon instead of a lion.

On the back of this dryphon rode Parentha, leaning forward in the saddle and peering at the ground below. The elf's blond hair whipped behind him wildly as they soared over summits and dived into gorges.

Parentha blinked tears from his eyes as he looked forward into the wind. Something had caught his eye.

Do you see that to the right, Thunderbolt? In that valley there, is that smoke?

So it seems, Eltharian. Shall we take a look?

No words were exchanged between rider and mount, the conversation was held completely telepathically. Parentha wasn't sure he'd ever get used to speaking to the dryphon with his thoughts, and he had grown up with the animals.

Thunderbolt dipped down on the other side of a mountain peak with insane speed and agility. Parentha clutched the saddle and squeezed his eyes shut, praying for the ride to end. Abruptly, the dryphon spread its winds and landed on a ledge.

Parentha jumped from the saddle and landed gracefully on his feet.

I absolutely hate when you do that, Thunderbolt. I fear one of these days my heart will burst within my chest.

The creature stared into the valley below, its hackles raised.

Orcs.

Parentha's breath caught. Thousands of creatures moved down below. Smoke rolled from cooking fires and smithies. Giant foundation stones had been laid.

This was no camp. This was the creation of a city. Stone walls were being erected around the many buildings clustered in the valley. The city was strategically placed. A large river flowed through the valley, providing an excellent source of water. Much of the southern portion of the valley was covered in thick woods, which would be needed for smelting ore and building.

An orc horde was forming in the mountains of Rhoben. This was more of a threat to the mountain dwarves than the elves of Elthar, but the news was still troubling.

His mind drifted back six weeks ago, when they had slaughtered the small hamlet of orcs. Had Cyren been right? Were these more than just thoughtless evil beings? Orcs had always been known to be barbaric and animal-like. But now, here before him lay the seeds of an empire. What could have made the orcs band together so?

Parentha mounted Thunderbolt and took off. They flew to the east, to Qustia, capital of Elthar. The King would need to hear this dire news directly.

In Search for a Soul

By Aaron Wulf

654 AM Age of the Dracon-esti

Ryddle leaned on his walking staff as he stared into the Redwood Forest through his long black hair. After crossing vast hilly plains for two days, it was daunting to see such a massive dark forest before him.

The sun had sapped much of his energy, but his sense of smell was still much higher than the average human. His nostrils flared at the sweet aroma of pine needles, and a mustiness which he figured was mold. He cringed, and looked towards the open sky in search of reassurance.

"Father, Mother," he cleared his throat. "I barely know your faces these days. I know I have no place with you in the afterlife. I turned to the darkness many years ago. But somehow I…" His lips quivered. "I believe I can make it right again. I have found a man who is very skilled in the work of magic. It is said that for a small price he can return a dark one's soul and make him human again. I do not wish to live as this shell of a man any longer."

Ryddle sat down in the grass for a moment and glanced behind him. A flock of sparrows flew up beyond the hills about a mile south. Something urged him to leave the plains and enter the Redwood Forest. He had a compelling feeling that he had been followed from Renhet, but he ignored it.

Reaching out to his parents once more, as if to resurrect himself from his path of evil, he cried his confession to the sky, though it was to himself he was really admitting these faults.

"I have betrayed the will of the gods and turned to the dark ones, the vampire. I was blinded by greed and the promise of immortality, so I sold my soul to Wesif. Now I live a life of unimportance.

The others don't see it this way. They see it as a gift. But I have been living on while all my family dies, and now I wish to die myself — a mortal death — and enter the afterlife, instead of dying a prince of darkness and dissolving into an abyss of nothingness, void of soul.

"Many years ago, I heard stories of a sorcerer in these woods who can return a lost soul. If you were still alive, I know you would help me find this man who can cure me. Please guide me on my journey, as I hope to meet with you once more. Please forgive your son."

Bird's wings beat overhead and disrupted the quiet morning. Magic flowed in their flock; with it came a feeling of uneasiness. One by one, the little brown birds landed on a stone a few feet away from where he sat. Beady black eyes stared at him.

Ryddle stood up, his knees buckling. It had been a whole day since his rations of human blood had run dry. He wanted to quit. The taste had grown sour after three hundred years. But he could not continue on without the strength it gave him, especially with the sun draining him.

Then a bird spoke.

"We give you an offering. Please accept it with great humility. Be it the last mortal blood you feast upon." The bird's wing outstretched, pointing towards the vast forest.

The vampire, stricken with shock, fell back into the tall grass.

"What are you? A shapeshifter?"

The speaking sparrow was not like the others. His chest shined crimson, and he stood an inch taller than the rest. The bird cocked its head. "Perhaps what I am is not as important as the question of what you are? You appear to be a dark one, yet I sense something more than that within you. Perhaps the hint of a soul?" The bird hopped from the rock, came through the thin stalks of bronze grass, and pecked at the vampire's boots. "Bah! Others of your kind do not radiate this essence I see around you."

Ryddle, confused, inspected his arms and legs.

"Don't be a fool," the sparrow chattered, throwing his wings about. "Quit looking at yourself like that. Your aura is not visible to you. For you, my friend, see only death. That is what I was taught to believe, but is it entirely true? Perhaps you occasionally glimpse beyond death. Now, you see, there are much more tantalizing answers afoot than what I am."

"I…my apologies little one." Ryddle found his balance again among the knee-high grass. "But I must ask you one more question: What is this offering you speak of? Are you insinuating that I feast on your feathered friends here? Pardon my ungratefulness, but I don't see much good in their blood. You see, I need a human to fully satisfy my bloodlust."

"Ah, you're a rather peculiar sort of vampire, aren't you? And dumber than I took you for." The sparrow began to flutter his wings and rose to the level of Ryddle's face. "Follow the path of these fine birds. They will show you to the offering we have uncovered for you. It will fulfill you for the remainder of your journey. Be it the last taste of mortal blood you ever indulge in, or you will forever be a slave of the dark god Wesif. Your choice, my odd vampire friend."

The flock of birds flew towards the opening of the forest in single file, the crimson-chested sparrow in the lead. Ryddle quickly descended down the sunlit hill and into the mossy redwoods. With the lack of direct sunlight he could feel his powers returning. His boots stomped against fallen pine needles and moss. His hands brushed against soft bark as he glided past trees. The trunks of the redwoods descended from the canopy like the legs of giants, plunging into the soft ground and claiming their place in the world. Here they would stand for the rest of their days.

"Pardon me, O Feathered One. What shall I call you? How about Crimson for now?" Ryddle licked his dry lips with each stride. "But how am I to trust a talking sparrow?"

Crimson flew back to where Ryddle was walking. "I have seen into your past, dark one, and I believe you are the one to be questioned on the matter of trust. Allow me to tell you what I know of you before your dark years."

"I'd rather you not."

"I have seen a warrior. As a human you were brave and fought valiantly for your beliefs. You took a wife, Ismha, who gave you all that she had. Even her own soul, so to speak. You did not have many riches, but you had each other, and that was enough. Then came the secret vampire wars. Your small army invaded the Grottos of Collapse, but you were not fast enough. The legion of dark ones descended upon you all, claiming every last soul for the dark god Wesif. You discovered new-found strength, power, gold, sexual pleasures, and blood-lust. But best of all, you were shown the truth of immortality. And you just had to bring Ismha along for the ride, didn't you?"

"Stop this!" Ryddle clutched his face.

"No, I must go on for you to see the true nature of your existence."

Ryddle pulled his hair. He hated remembering his past.

The bird continued. "You took your wife's soul so she could indulge in the life of immortality, or that's what you told yourself. In truth, you wanted one love to remain with you, while all others died. After over three hundred years of marriage, you grew tired of Ismha, though she still loved you. You became distant. You missed your parents, and others, lost forever. That's when you left Ismha in search for an end to your condition. And here we are. Now tell me, if you cannot still trust me after all you have done to Ismha, then I shall turn my back on that once-great warrior and declare you the ignorant dark beast you've become."

An intense sensation of anger sparked in the vampire. His eyes clenched shut. He bit his lip so hard that it bled. Ryddle was trying to ignore the darkness that still resided in him. Then he opened his eyes, much calmer now, and saw Crimson sitting on a fallen branch not more than ten yards away. Ryddle took a deep breath and strode over to the sparrow.

"Your anger will be the death of you, my friend. It will end the last love you ever have," the bird spoke somberly. "There is no afterlife for an angry death." Crimson spread its wings and gestured down an ancient path amongst the fallen pine needles. The path declined into a foggy ravine where Ryddle saw a huge stone overhang. The stale smell was strong down that path — the same smell he noticed when standing between the forest and the plains.

"Down this path is where you will restore your strength," the crimson chested sparrow spoke for the last time. "Stay away from the sun's rays. You will still need your strength before you reach your journey's end. Life be yours."

And with that, the sparrow flew into the treetops, its fellow birds following suit until their beating wings were inaudible. Ryddle clenched his walking staff and hesitantly made progress into the ravine. As his heart thumped, yearning for mortal blood, his black eyes stared into the canopy. The trees seemed to grow taller. He searched within his heart for the courage to fight once more. Shadows crept behind the massive trunks, darting quickly out of sight. Ryddle walked faster. He began to jog, and then run. Strange sounds encompassed him now, piercing his brain. Sounds of the underworld.

The evil noises screeched around him, penetrating his ears. Ryddle began to feel disoriented. He tripped every other step. He spun around, eyes rolling into the back of his head, but he fought and regained control of his consciousness. A dark evil was in these low levels of the forest. Something stronger than vampires. Something not native to the open lands above.

He slipped and fell over sticks and brush, and landed heavily on a pile of dirty pans and discarded trash. Ryddle gazed upon an old camp site, long abandoned. There were three off-white tents to the far end of the site, and in the tent to the far right the vampire caught a whiff of something he yearned for desperately.

"Blood," he whispered behind his fangs.
He looked up to where he had fallen from and sensed a dark creature creeping closer. Ryddle pushed himself up and sprinted to the tent, flinging open the flap of fabric. He gazed lustfully upon a bloodbath that must have taken place no more than a day ago.

Cold blood was not as fulfilling as warm blood, but it would give him a sufficient amount of energy to replenish his powers one last time.

Two men were lying on the floor. One was a Renhet soldier, clothed in bright gold armor detailed with red accents. The other man seemed to be a prisoner. His clothes were ragged and his forearms were still confined by manacles. The prisoner was gruesomely beaten and tortured. His open wounds suggested that it was his blood painted on the canvas. As Ryddle looked over the soldier, he did not see any open wounds. He pondered what the cause of death might have been, but decided it was not important. An offering such as this, in a desolate location such as this, was a one-time opportunity too precious to pass up. Ryddle kneeled, and delicately removed the soldier's gauntlets and arm braces, uncovering his flesh.

Ryddle scrutinized the dead soldier's face. It seemed so serene. Ryddle felt unusual compassion toward the human, despite the apparent murder the soldier had committed before his death.

"I thank you, stranger, for this feast. May it be my last." The dark one opened his mouth and revealed his fangs. His black eyes swelled and glossed over in hope of putting this damning life of immortality behind him. He brought the man's forearm to his mouth and sunk his teeth into the stiff wrist. Stale blood cascaded down his throat, coating his esophagus. Though Ryddle's body always felt cold, his insides now radiated warmth as the blood painted the interior of his body.

Ryddle stood up from the cadaver. He felt some strength return to his body. Energy now coursed through his being. His senses were now up to half his potential and his ears were picking up movement outside the tent. His eyes grew blacker, his lips parted, and blood-stained fingers clenched in a fist. He had company outside. It was likely he was followed all the way from Renhet.

Reluctantly, Ryddle stepped outside the tent. He reached over to where he left his walking stick, but once Ryddle grabbed it, he felt the movement near the rear of the tent. The air high above the forest was still. No branches moved with the wind. But the air in this ravine seemed to swirl, almost pushing out the air of this world and replacing it with the dark, putrid air of the Underworld. Ryddle took his walking staff and walked past the three tents to the foot of the overhang, which created a shallow, cave-like hollow. Foolishly, he explored the hollow.

The semicircular area had a depth of thirty feet, rose twelve feet high, and offered one dark tunnel into the dark earth. Ryddle felt the harsh musty air being pushed out of that opening. After a few moments, he turned to exit but was barricaded by a row of dark beasts at the entrance.

Ryddle cursed under his breath.

Three sets of glowing eyes stared back at the vampire. Three figures stood upright with dark bluish-grey hair all over their bodies. They looked like wolves but stood like werebeasts. These creatures had no human affiliation, however, for they were creatures of the dark caverns of the Underworld. Ryddle had heard tales many centuries ago about the barghest and how they had escaped the Underworld in search of easier meals. Ranking a low threat in their realm, these creatures still served as worthy opponents to even an experienced vampire.

Ryddle froze, plotting his next move. He couldn't die a vampire. He was so close to finding the cure that could make him mortal. After the re-transformation, he knew he could finally die in peace. At that time, he would have his soul returned to him from Wesif and be freed of his curse. But until then, he would use his curse as a gift, a tool to fight his way out of this darkness and back into the upper levels of the forest.

He often reminisced about the time before his heart went cold. He was a mighty warrior. He fought for his kingdom, his parents, and the gods who wished for the good to rule the land of Draston. But once darkness overcame the continent, so did it overcome his birthplace. That was when his parents were killed, and he left his home to take revenge on the vampires. During that very attack is when he was bitten by a vampire named Dregan, but he did not die. Dregan took Ryddle in as one of his own, and soon they added Ismha to their coven.

The darkness had never left Ryddle. As he stood before the three creatures, he knew he was mentally stronger than these wolf-like beasts whose fangs shone sharper than his own. Ryddle's mortal past still lived somewhere inside his soulless vessel. He searched for the warrior within. He thought of his wife, Ismha, and began to regret leaving her behind as he did. He knew once he reversed the dark curse he could never return to Renhet, nor could he show his face to her again.

But his emotions were pushed aside. Ryddle dropped his staff.

Two of the barghests charged.

*****

The sun rose over the city of Renhet. The streets were filled with merchants selling jewelry, selling slabs of meat, fresh fish and produce. Peddlers lacking the proper permits were being hauled off to an overcrowded prison. Most of the city's buildings were made of oak and stone, but at the center stood the extravagant red walls of Lord Hayward's palace, the highest building in Renhet. He had taken a liking to the view of the hilly landscape north of Renhet and demanded to be built a home like no other in Draston.

The majority of the palace was supported by stone, however all of its five storeys were elaborately crafted with redwood. Flying buttresses and arches were carved from single trees, as were the three towers which encompassed this impressive effort of human craftsmanship. At the very highest floor, in the center of the building, was a room that was an almost perfect circle. Here, Lord Hayward conducted his most critical business, and any other matter that dealt with large sums of money.

Inside this room, Hayward sat at one end of a long table, with his council of fourteen men seated on either side, ready to advise. At the opposite end of the table sat the captain of the guard, severely cut, bleeding all over Lord Hayward's redwood table. As the apologetic captain pleaded about some recent event, Hayward was almost asleep with boredom. Then a door burst open and Rhazien stomped into the room.

"My apologies," Rhazien hissed. "I didn't know there was a gathering. So sorry to interrupt. But I must speak to Dregan, if it is fine with you, my Lord."

Dregan was Lord Hayward's right-hand man, a man he secretly feared. Hayward met Dregan's eyes, glaring daringly back at him. Hayward then looked casually at his wrist, resting bandaged on the table.

"Yes," Lord Hayward interrupted the captain's mumbling. "You may steal my old friend for a few moments." He stared at Dregan, not breaking his gaze. The Lord continued, "Or however long you wish to see him for."

Lord Hayward became flustered as the two men walked out of the room. Rhazien and Dregan heard the captain shouting something about an escaped prisoner as the heavy door slammed behind them.

"This better be good," Dregan warned Rhazien.

Rhazien was hesitant but looked fearless, as any vampire of a high-class society would. "We tracked him all the way to the Redwood Forest. He was only about a half mile ahead of us, but once he got inside the forest, we quickly lost him." His whisper was so faint that Dregan demanded he repeat himself.

Dregan opened his eyes wide after hearing this news. His pupils expanded until both eyes were completely black. His fist clenched while his other hand grasped Rhazien's throat and pinned him against the wall. Rhazien's face remained blank, but his body trembled.

"This coven was established over five hundred years ago, young one." Dregan ground his teeth and flashed his fangs at Rhazien. "You may be new to the family, but I still desperately want to rip out your heart and sink my teeth into your face." The old one let the young vampire down. "This particular vampire you and your group were chasing is a liability to our legacy. He is a brother of old, but is confused these days. I put my trust in you and you fail to deliver?"

Rhazien picked at old wounds on his arm. "Maybe he won't come back. He may not be a problem."

"Are you willing to bet the future of this city?" Dregan folded his arms behind his back. "We have control of Lord Hayward, and with him cowering from our presence, we also have control of the city."

"What would it matter if he returned to Renhet anyway? Nobody would ever believe him that vampires live inside these walls."

"We cannot take that risk. If we have control over the Lord and the city, then the docks remain in our control as well. Remember, that is the whole reason we are here."

Dregan ran his fingers through his silver hair and walked down the hall towards the elegantly carpeted stairs. "Stay here, I am putting my trust in you to watch over Hayward and the other humans. I don't trust them. I sense Hayward is growing weaker and will unveil our presence soon, if Taos doesn't return first. They must not discover our plan. Well, enough of that, I suppose you can handle that little task. Now, as for Taos-"

"Ryddle," Rhazien interrupted. "He is now going by his mortal name."

A vase shattered on the wall behind the young vampire. His eyes red with anger and bloodlust, Dregan broke several other items in the hallway in a fit.

Rhazien stepped aside, understanding the blasphemous act Ryddle had done. A painting flew past Rhazien's head, almost severing his ear.

"Master, if I may suggest calming down a bit? You really must be leaving, shouldn't you?"
Dregan could not hear the young one over his temper tantrum, and he stomped down the stairwell shouting curse words so foul that Rhazien covered his ears. As sinister as vampires can be, it is still common courtesy to maintain a civil vocabulary.

On the third level were housing quarters for the Lord's Council. There were fourteen doors spread throughout an array of hallways. All were painted gold, as were the chandeliers hanging over the red tapestry lining the center of the hallways. Standing next to a shelf stood a man, shocked to see that an angry vampire had made its way into the palace. Dregan stopped right before the man, heart thumping in his chest, eyes bulging.

He bit into the man's neck, feasting on the mortal to fuel his dark powers.

Dregan calmed down a bit as his vampire attributes slowly faded back to a human-like appearance. Dregan was not only right-hand man to Lord Hayward, he was also the leader and founder of the vampire coven in Renhet.

The coven master entered his quarters. Each home on this floor of the palace was twice the size of the average Renhet home, each room decorated with gold and riches.

Dregan lifted up an old, woven rug to uncover a trap door. The dark one descended into a secret room within the walls of the first floor.

"Why have you fools come back when you should still be out searching?" he demanded as he entered a room where six vampires were sharpening their blades. "Wipe those dumbfounded looks off your faces. You've all let me down." Dregan sighed and rubbed his face with his hands.

"What shall become of Taos when we find him, Master?" one of the vampires asked.

Dregan paused before he answered. "Taos is already dead. But it will not be long until Ryddle is dead too. He's already made his decision to leave the brotherhood. Once he transforms back into a mortal, we kill him."

A woman sat in the corner of the room reading an ancient book on magic. When she heard the name of her husband, she looked up from behind the tattered pages. Her face was gentle and kind, her hair black and shoulder-length. She put the book down and approached Dregan.

"Dregan, I know Tao would never sell us out. What he is doing has nothing to do with us. It has to do with his future. Can't you just let him be?"

"You're right, Ismha, this has nothing to do with us. That's why he left you behind as well, to live out eternity without him. If he doesn't care about you anymore, he won't care about what happens to us." Dregan never looked Ismha in the eyes, but instead prepared for his departure.

"Please." Ismha clutched his shoulder. "He still loves me, just as he did before when he was mortal. He is just confused. I know in my heart he will return."

Dregan whipped around and shook the woman. "Maybe he will come back for you, but not us. Honestly, if he still loved you, don't you think he would have taken you with him? Look at the truth. A vampire and a human cannot share a life together. Now let him stay out of your life forever, or I will kill you right after I am done with him!"

Ismha cowered back. She had been sensing that Ryddle had been distant. He had begun to speak of his parents often, and about his past. She felt his love still. It was there. She had to find him and let him know she would always be there for him. Ismha sat back in her corner to create a plan. Right after Dregan left, she would set out on her own in the hope her husband was still alive.

Dregan walked towards a wooden chest and opened it. The other vampires stared in sheer horror as he pulled out a blade made from dragon bone. Aside from silver, dragon bone was the only other material lethal to vampires. Dregan had a glimmer in his eye and a smirk shining on one fang. To the relief of the other six, he sheathed his weapon, walked passed his brothers of darkness and right through a wall.

One of the vampires, still sharpening his blade, simply stated, "I wish I could do that."

The journey to the Redwood Forrest would take two days by horseback if Dregan were to ride. But time was of the essence. If Ryddle were to retrieve his soul and surrender his dark powers, he surely would not stay put for long. A deed this selfish could not go unpunished. No. Ryddle had to die along with Taos. Dregan closed his eyes and withdrew the energy he needed from his body to perform the task he desired. The vampire began to float as he stood outside the palace wall. He dematerialized until he was nothing but smoke, rapidly charging towards the giant redwood forest.

If it were not cloudy, the sun would have been directly overhead as the sinister smoke flew over the hilly plains. Into the Redwood Forest Dregan flew, following his intuition. Fueled by rage, he came upon a peculiar site in the woods. Within the circumference of eight redwood trees was a clearing. The vampire descended and materialized back into his physical shell of a body. His lips curled, his brow turned inward. Candle-filled jars were strung from tree to tree. The forest floor was swept free of pine needles. Carved into the massive tree trunks along the perimeter were shelves stocked with glass bottles and wooden boxes. A few cages lay around filled with various forest animals and insects. A few cages housed brownies, looking confused and disoriented. As Dregan took everything in, something caught his eye that made him furious. He tried his best to remain calm, for his own safety.

"Hello, Vibus," Dregan spoke daringly to a figure standing in the clearing. "You have a visitor arriving shortly. After you're done with him, he's mine. Understand?"

The renegade sorcerer challenged the vampire's stare but said nothing in reply. Vibus's red beard trembled at the dark one's presence. But behind wise eyes, the mage knew he had to bargain. He took off his old brown hat and held it against his chest.

"Anything for a price, dark one."

*****

One of the barghests rammed into Ryddle's shoulder, leaving him disoriented for a moment. The second came up behind the vampire and dug grimy claws into his back tissue. Ryddle screamed in agony and spun around faster than a tornado, slashing the second beast repeatedly in the face with his talons. He landed on his feet and turned to the other barghest.

Ryddle ran into its hairy chest with such speed that the barghest landed on his back, winded from the blow.

The other two barghests yelped with anger and flanked the vampire on either side.

Ryddle was much quicker on his feet now. His powers were restored, and he was desperate to leave this battle alive. Ryddle screamed and charged between two of the barghests with his arms outstretched. His razor sharp talons shredded through the shadowy flesh. But both barghest's grabbed hold of his arms and slammed him to the ground.

The three were ready to feast upon their kill. The leader of the pack knelt down, his fangs dripping over Ryddle's face. The cold saliva landed on his cheek, and right as the open mouth was about to clamp down on Ryddle's throat, the vampire reached his arm into its throat and ripped out its tongue.

A tremendous shriek echoed through the shallow cave, and the walls began to rumble, stones fell all around them. The overhang was starting to collapse. The wolf-beast went mad with pain. Blood dripped from its mouth, and it ran out.

Ryddle was the only one who took notice of the stone overhang beginning to slide off the cliffside. He darted between the two barghests standing before him. They both turned toward each other to chase the vampire. The slab began sliding faster. Ryddle staggered closer to the entrance, away from the two beasts. Dirt scuffed Ryddle's chest as he slid under the slab right as its edge slammed into the ground, trapping his left foot.

Ryddle cried out in agony as the massive slab crashed down into the cave, instantly killing the barghests.

Pain shot through Ryddle's nerves and muscles as he frantically dug the dirt away from underneath his leg. When he pulled it out he knew there were broken bones, but was surprised he still actually had a foot at all.

Walking proved difficult, especially since he had no way of knowing where to find the magician in this forest and would surely die of starvation before he made his way out of the ravine. He would have to pull himself back up.

Ryddle was too close to death, yet too close to salvation. He had to remain in the lower levels and find the answers he was looking for.

The small ravine was deep, with tree roots protruding from earthy walls too steep to climb. The rounded walls began to straighten up towards the northern end of the forest, creating a thin walkway between walls of earth. Ryddle limped through the ravine, making haste down the mystifying passageway. The walls were only four feet across but stood nearly eighteen feet tall. The ground was gradually sloped downward, and about eight hundred feet down the path, the walls grew shallow, and the land flattened out into a new level of the forest.

The trees here were spread much farther apart, and the natural sunlight was beginning to shine through in a few areas. Ryddle studied his surroundings, and his vampire intuition pulled him west. Dragging a bad foot took a lot of time and effort, and sweat poured down his pale brow, clinging his black hair to his forehead. He was beginning to feel that his journey had been in vain when he spotted an odd sight in the distance.

With a new spark of energy in his step, he limped towards a clearing. Here Ryddle saw clutter spread throughout, shelves carved into trees, and lighting fixtures made of jars and candles on string. In the middle stood an old man. His robes were worn by years of use, but were maintained. A smile peeked from behind his red beard as he removed his pointy hat in a welcoming gesture.

"Glad you could make it!" The man was brisk in his step as he got closer. "Oh my, how awful you look! Here, lay down over there and I will clean you right up. Taos is the name, is it not? Wait, my apologies. Ryddle. That's it."

Ryddle sat on a bed under a makeshift roof made of branches and leaves. The sorcerer placed his warm hands onto the injured ankle and Ryddle could feel heat jolting up his leg.

"Only a temporary fix for now, I'm afraid. Why have you come? How is it that you have found me? Have you had breakfast today? How long have you been cursed as a vampire? Will you ever speak up? Well, go ahead, speak!"

Ryddle tried to answer all the questions the old man had rattled off, but the magic the sorcerer had worked on his ankle was making him dizzy and faint. He felt about to slip under as he pointed to his chest.

"My… soul…" Ryddle stammered. "I wish to regain my soul."

"Well, why didn't you say so, my boy!" The sorcerer jumped with glee. "I only ask for an offering worthy of redemption. Gold, perhaps? If you wish for me to retrieve your soul and destroy the vampire blood within you, I want to obtain payment so that I may gain something as well."

"Staff," he said under his breath.

"Calf?" the old man questioned.

"No, the walking staff."

"Talking cat?" The sorcerer began to grow irritated.

Ryddle pointed to his walking staff, leaning against a tree close by.

"It's not much," he forced words out. "But it has served me well and is all I have from my mortal life. Please, take it."

The sorcerer scratched his belly while he stared at the staff. He looked at Ryddle.

"Young man, what do you know of a soul?" The man's voice was calm now, and suddenly soothing.

Ryddle began to close his eyes, trying not to pass out as the magician continued to speak.

"Your soul is not something that can be easily returned, my friend. Even a god cannot have full control over a force as powerful and reckless as the human essence. Fragments of your past linger around you. It's in the air. It flows through your hair and across your skin and with the wind over the land. Your mortal life rests with a god of dark power. However, with the fragments of your soul that dance in the realms of the dead, let us draw a map to once again find your source of life and restore it to you. The gods of neutrality work with me on this process, and together with the language of magic, we just may be able to steal back your soul." The sorcerer continued to ramble as he fiddled with jars of black liquid, boxes of feathers, and other substances to perform the art of magic. Ryddle was paying no attention to him. He began to fall into a deep sleep just as the sorcerer started to chant his spell.

"Ajcoth, be hatax va torae. Di Kareth-ja-torae va undar vi olae. Xarthnek vha harglei xi vardai xi un."

The darkness behind Ryddle's eyelids lit up in spectacular radiance. His body began to vibrate from his head to his toes, yet he was unable to move. Every muscle flexed. Sound as intense as a waterfall overcame him, so loud it was almost unbearable. He felt himself begin to spin. Faster and faster, he felt his body turn around and around. Ryddle heard himself fly past roaring waters, too intense to properly comprehend.

Then, it all ceased to be. Noise vanished, movement stopped. Time stopped. Ryddle slowly raised his heavy head, and noticed he could feel movement once more in his body. He sat up and noticed the sorcerer was nowhere in sight. Hours must have gone by, for the sky was now dark. Candles lighting the clearing were much lower now, and shadows danced eerily across the tree trunks.

The young mortal stood up and tried to find his balance. To his astonishment, his foot had healed. There was no more pain, though he did feel utterly exhausted. He slowly adjusted his boots and had started to stumble around to find the sorcerer when he was stopped cold in his tracks.

Dregan lurked in the shadows of the forest with rage in his eyes. The canopy above creaked inward towards the clearing as if bowing in respect to the dark one. Tree trunks bent as wood cracked, the candle jars swayed ferociously in the wind, one falling and smashing into a hundred pieces.

Flames leapt onto the dry forest floor and set it ablaze. Dregan's black eyes reflected the embers flying about. He began to walk amidst the inferno straight for the horror-stricken Ryddle.

Ryddle was afraid. It wasn't fear of death. He now realized his mistake in leaving behind Ismha. He so desperately wanted her here right now by his side, even if he was about to die. He knew what he'd done was unforgivable, and scoffed at his selfish act. Now he would die without telling her how sorry he was.

He had no vampire abilities to defend himself with now. The fire was growing fast and the heat was intensifying with the increasing winds.

Ryddle found that odd. Wind inside a dense forest. He looked past the smoke, and right before Dregan could dig talons into his chest, Ryddle's heart sank into his stomach.

Vibus stood among the trees, spell book in hand. He spoke in tongues as the winds raged.

"Vibus!" Ryddle yelled. "Stop!"

Dregan roared. "Shut up you bastard, I paid him more than you did." He tore into Ryddle's chest and threw him across the burning wreckage.

"Please, Dregan, let this be over. I'm too weak," Ryddle pleaded.

"Weak?" Dregan laughed. "That is your own doing. I gave you eternal life, and you threw it away. What a fool to think I would show you pity after you gave up such a wonderful gift?"

"At least allow me a fair fight. Let me recover!" Ryddle looked around the fire, hoping to see Ismha one more time.

"You gave me no warning before your sudden disappearance, so as far as I knew you could have come back to sell us out. Curse you. Now Wesif frowns on us both."

"You've been blinded by your many years of darkness," the mortal cried. "We were brothers! Kin! You can trust me."

"Just like you trusted me? Bah! You acted like a coward and fled to your long-dead mother and father. The mirage you are running to is gone forever. You knew the truth after years of living as a vampire that they were gone! And yet you deny the truth right before your face. It's lunacy!"

"Don't you see? Wesif has been using vampire souls to feed his own being! He is a god of evil, Dregan. He does not love us nor care for us. He-"

"Blasphemy!" Dregan spit on Ryddle's face. "I could have killed you while you slept. I could have murdered you in cold blood any moment if I knew you would betray us. Now here you lay, on the ground, slandering the great one who granted you the eternal life on Harthx that so few are granted. You curse the name of Wesif and the name of our coven. If you were a stranger, your throat would already be pouring with blood into the depths of-" Ryddle catapulted himself into Dregan's torso. The vampire fell hard onto his back, but evaporated into a plume of black smoke that mixed with the smoke of the fire.

"Vibus!" Ryddle cried. "I could damn well use your help! Are you with me or against-"

Dregan appeared behind Ryddle in full vampire form and smashed him into a pile of burning wood. The vampire unsheathed the dragonbone blade and stabbed Ryddle in the gut, just missing his stomach.

Human blood flowed in little pools away from Ryddle as he was butchered. Vampires were known for clean kills, but this was a murder fueled by hate, not bloodlust.

"Ajcoth, be hatax va torae!"

Bright light, brighter than the fire they were engulfed in, blinded the two beings. Ear-piercing shrieks were met with those of Dregan, who grabbed his neck and withered in pain.

"Di Kareth-ja-torae va undar vi olae. Qu Mari Tetha Foru char-tun."

The screams and flames rose high as the mysterious voice spoke louder. Ryddle's eyes began to roll back into his head. Dregan screamed and punched and clawed at the air as if he was fighting off an invisible creature. The forest was white, a blank canvas. Energy swirled around them.

"Xarthnek vha harglei xi vardai xi un," the voice spoke out.

Everything became silent. Dregan lay still on the ground, no longer in full vampire form. The flames were gone. Ryddle's beaten body throbbed, but the pools of blood suddenly came rushing back into his body. After several minutes, his wounds closed up, his bruises faded, and his color returned. Among the great redwood trees lay Vibus and his hat, next to an open spellbook stained with the sorcerer's blood.

The forest was still.

Not even an undisturbed crypt could be this still.

The sun peeped out between breaks in the canopy. No forest animals made themselves known, no birds chirped, no insects crawled. Hours went by like this. The forest started to darken, then night fell upon this peculiar scene.

Out of the silence, Ismha and Rhazien approached the bodies.

"You're right! They're both still breathing!" Rhazien put his ear to Dregan's nostrils. His nose twitched, and he shot a concerned look to Ismha. "Why do I smell so much mortal blood? Dregan's skin, it is warm. What did you do?"

Ismha glanced away at the fallen renegade sorcerer. "That old man wouldn't help Taos. Ryddle. I couldn't watch him die, not like that."

"You mean you..." Rhazien studied the vampire in astonishment. "You used magic?"

"I dabble." Ismha examined Ryddle's body. "I read a chapter out of the sorcerer's book. Through my personal studies, I've come to understand much."

Rhazien stood back in disbelief and awe at her power. "And what exactly happened?"

"These two men laying here are both mortal, and free of any injury. That means Dregan is no longer one of us. You better stay with him. When he wakes up, he will not be happy." Ismha pulled up a wooden cart they had brought, and she lifted Ryddle onto it with ease.

"Where will you go? Are you not coming back to the coven?" Rhazien propped Dregan up against a tree.

"No, I have a feeling I will not be accepted for what I did. I cannot stay. I am sorry." She stroked the sleeping face of her loved one. "I owe this man my life. And I will make sure he lives out his own with me."

Rhazien inhaled the sweet fragrance of human flesh emanating from Dregan. His lips were moist as he licked them. The blood pumped fresh inside the new mortal.

Ismha picked up the handles to the cart and bid the vampire farewell as she departed.
"What kind of magic was that?" Rhazien asked himself as he felt the pulse in his leader's throbbing neck.

Rhazien pushed Dregan's sleeping head aside and sunk in his fangs, succumbing to the call of blood.

Ismha pushed Ryddle north out of Redwood Forest. Where they were headed, she did not know. It would still be many hours until Ryddle awoke from the healing spell she cast upon him. In the sky ahead of her flew a flock of sparrows. The largest one, in the lead, occasionally looked back at the two to make sure they were following. Ismha didn't know why, but she felt a strong urge to follow the flock.

No matter where they headed, she knew now that Ryddle could live out the rest of his life with her, and finally die a mortal death to meet his parents in the afterlife.

Magic Within

By Anna Warkentin

660 AM Age of the Dracon-esti

Smoke. That was the first sign that something was wrong. Alaya urged her horse up the final hill. A knot grew in her stomach as she laid eyes on her home for the first time in three weeks. Like ants running around an overturned anthill, the villagers hurried to and fro, toting buckets of water and thick blankets. Clouds of smoke billowed from several of the straw-thatched houses, staining the sky in intrusive contrast to the bright white clouds. Somewhere in the village, a child was crying as if the world had come to an end.

Whinnying nervously, Rascal sidestepped as Alaya's hands unintentionally clenched the reins. The acrid smell reached the horse's sensitive nostrils, and his rider was doing nothing to help calm him.

Breaking out of her trance, Alaya took a deep breath, laying a comforting hand on Rascal's neck as they both descended the rocky slope. Ahead, the girl saw a familiar flash of orange hair. Her heels touched Rascal's sides as soon as the path flattened out, and he broke into a quick canter, sending Alaya's own ginger locks bouncing on her back as they clattered into town.

Before her horse had come to a full stop, Alaya slipped down and headed for the granary at a sprint. The village was quiet, but not a comforting quiet. It was the lull of an archer's last breath before the arrow's release.

"Papa!" Alaya called, skidding to a stop in front of the blackened walls of the storage barn, her eyes wide. The harvests would have been brought in only days before she returned, the same harvests that would feed the small village through the winter.

The man with orange hair and a scruffy beard looked up from a tight group of men and women. Seeing Alaya, he instantly strode to her, wrapping her in strong arms. She returned the hug with nearly equal strength, clinging to her father and thanking every deity in existence that he was safe. Burying her face in his chest, she took a deep breath. The familiar scent of soot, flames and metal grounded her a little as the panic within her settled.

After a moment he pulled back, hands on her shoulders. His eyes searched her face, the lines of his brow a worried frown. Alaya looked up into her father's deep brown eyes and the pain sparking behind them.

"What happened?" Alaya asked softly, chest tightening as she saw tears begin to gather in his eyes.

He pressed his eyes closed. His rough, calloused hands weighed heavily on Alaya's young shoulders. She had only seen him cry twice in her life. Once, in joy, when her little sister was born. The second time was mere hours after the first, in utter heartbreak, when the midwife delivered the news that his wife had passed away due to the childbirth.

"Bandits," he began, taking a deep breath to force back his shaky voice. "Nomad bandits. They swept in and…took some of the women and children."

Alaya's head spun. She frantically searched her memory for any image of the young girl with raven hair – her mother's hair – flitting around the village to help attend to the grieving families. Nothing.

"They took Terra...they just snatched her up. It was over so quickly…"

Alaya expected to feel grief, shock, fear perhaps. But instead, rage began burning deep within her. The bandits raided their homes, burnt their food, stole their families. Stole her sister, Terra. Terra who had always been sweet and kind and selfless. Who would have fed them if they ever came to her hungry. Who would have dressed their wounds if they were injured.

Alaya brushed a kiss across her father's rough cheek. Perhaps it was a goodbye. He looked up, already knowing what she was going to do.

"Alaya. No. I've lost one daughter today. Don't make it two…" his voice trailed off with a defeated sigh.

"You have your mother's eyes. I've seen that light in them before. There's nothing I can do to stop you, is there?"

"Not a chance," Alaya said, a near-feral smile dimpling her cheeks.

"Then go, my darling. And may Jarak bless you." He touched her cheek softly, studying her. "You have become a strong young woman, but you are reckless. Don't let it be your undoing."

"Can you tell me anything about the bandits, Father?"

He sighed deeply, passing a hand over his eyes, thinking. "Ah... red. They all wore red robes and scarves that covered their noses and mouths. They rode white horses that flew across the ground like demons. Tails like banners, streaming out behind them as they swept through the village. That's all I can remember. That and fire. And Terra screaming." With that, he stepped back.

Alaya turned, mind racing. She started walking slowly, but picked up speed until she was sprinting towards the other end of the village, coming to a stop by the butcher. She was in luck, he was there.

"Renbard!"

She stepped into the dim, cool shop, her slight frame blocking the light he was using to hack apart a leg of lamb.

"I see you're too busy to help the village recover from the raid," Alaya said in a cold tone, walking up to the counter.

"I see you were too busy gallivanting across the entire gods-forsaken country to help defend the village," he replied with a sneer, planting the blocky butcher's knife into the lamb meat with a thunk. "What do you want?"

Pulling a small pouch of coins off her belt, Alaya counted out a few and set them on the counter.

"Whatever's cheap and ready to go immediately."

Studying the few coins that glinted in the twilight of the room, Renbard swept them into one of his massive hands and emptied them into his rust-stained apron pocket.

"Heading out in pursuit, are we?" he mocked as he turned into the back room to rummage through his stock.

"Aye," she replied shortly, uninterested by his goading.

"Good luck catching them. They were armed, and many. Besides, they have a good two days on you already."

"How? The fires are new."

Renbard re-emerged, a smug smile on his face. "The granary smoldered before catching fire again today, and it spread before they could douse it again. Some are saying it was magic."

Alaya's stomach dropped. If the raiders had mages among them, it would be much harder to rescue her sister.

Renbard's ugly smile grew as if he could read her thoughts. "Aye," he said, leaning on the counter and adopting a nonchalant tone. "It appears that the little rescue mission you're going on is going to be harder than you anticipated. Even deadly, perhaps." Renbard's small, yellowish eyes glinted slightly.

"How are you – practically a child, untrained in combat or magic, the daughter of a nobody – going to defeat them before they kill you. Or your sister?"

An image flashed of Terra, her beautiful black hair fanned out around her, crimson blood trickling from her throat, staining her skin.

Alaya leveled a glare at Renbard. "Just give me the meat and get back to the only bodies that can stand to be around you," she spat, catching the package he tossed her.

"Fine. But remember, farm girls don't become princesses, and the daughters of blacksmiths don't become heroes." Renbard wrenched his knife out of the lamb and raised it above his head. Before he could sink it into the meat once more with a sickening squelch, Alaya had swept from the store.

After slipping the package of dried, seasoned meat into her saddlebags, Alaya quickly mounted Rascal. As she adjusted the reins, a young man came sprinting out of one of the houses.

"'Laya!" he waved, a fabric bundle under his arm. He stumbled to a stop beside her, puffs of dust rising from his feet.

"Hao, what are you doing?"

He panted, his skin a sickly pallor in the bright sunlight. "Mama said you were going to rescue Terra." He raised his teary eyes to her, offering up the bundle like a sacrifice. "Please. Bring Nori back too. Please, 'Laya."

Alaya's face softened. "I will do everything I can to bring her home." She gestured to the bundle. "What is this?"

Hao raised it higher, urging her to take it. "My bow. I pray to Glowt it will assist you in bringing my promised back to me."

Alaya hesitantly accepted the gift. She would likely need it before her venture was through.

"Thank you, Hao. Fear not, you will wed Nori come spring." She gave the man an encouraging smile, which he returned unsteadily. "Watch over my father while I'm gone, please. I fear losing Terra may have broken something inside him," she whispered.

Hao nodded like a soldier given a mission. "I shall."

Alaya lashed the bundle to her saddle, then turned Rascal's head to the north, where, she could tell from silent gestures, the bandits had gone. Determination flooded her mind, tempering the rage within her into steel with which she would cut the bandits down. With an angry, wordless cry, she urged Rascal into a fast canter out of the village.

The stallion tossed his head, snapping the reins in her hands, pulling at the bit as he strained to unleash his speed within. Alaya allowed him, and his strides stretched into a gallop. It wasn't until the village was out of sight behind them that she reined him back, not wanting her steed spent before their travels had even begun. Rascal gave a faint, breathy nicker, but slowed to an easy, mile-eating canter. The cobblestone soon faded to a well-worn dirt road, and she could now see a pair of deep ruts, so far unaffected by wind or rain. The bandit's caravan.

As she rode, observing the ruts every once in a while, she pieced together how the raid must have occurred.

The caravan would have gone ahead, cumbersome and slow moving as they were already loaded down with previous slaving success. It would have circled around the village to avoid suspicion. Once it was far enough ahead — half a day or more — the horsemen would have circled back and swept through, stealing away wives and children, sisters and mothers. Terra, Nori, any who would catch a fair amount in a large city. And from there, once sold…

Alaya shook the thought from her head. It would not reach that point.

As the sun began to set, she pressed her legs to Rascal's sides, desperate to get another mile in before dark.

*****

The sun kissed the horizon, streaking purples, blues, oranges, and pinks across the sky. A final flare of yellow flashed onto the canvas of clouds before darkness appeared, like ink bleeding into paper. As the first stars winked into view, the road forked, both trails pocketed with holes, hoof marks, and heavy wagon ruts. Alaya stared in dismay, unable to discern in the dying light which way the caravan of slavers had gone.

She dismounted Rascal, who happily stayed in place as she knelt to examine the dirt. But the sun had disappeared completely now; the light was too dim for her to investigate anything properly.

Admitting temporary defeat, she led Rascal off the road, built a small fire, and rolled out her sleeping mat. One disappointing meal of tough meat and dried berries later, she stretched out on her side, watching Rascal graze and huff where she had picketed him.

"I'll find them," she whispered, rolling onto her back and looking up at the speckled sky, patches of darkness swaying as a mild wind danced through the leaves. She reached a hand out, and the stars seemed to shrink away from her grasp.

"Mother, will I ever get to see the world?"

Looking up through younger eyes, Alaya saw her mother in her memory.

Her soft face blurred, but her dark green eyes still sparkled as she pushed a strand of curly red hair out of her daughter's face.

"Of course you will, my little adventurer."

Young Alaya stuck out her bottom lip, pouting. "Hao says none of us will ever leave the village. We'll all live here until we die. And Renbard says I'll never amount to anything because I'm just the daughter of a blacksmith."

She said the last word angrily, stomping her little foot.

Her mother swept the young girl up in her arms, pulling her onto her lap and stroking her head.

"Darling, the daughter of a blacksmith is no meager thing. You are the child of fire and metal. You are stronger than that metal and sharper than any sword. Heat will not harm you, and you will come out of the fire stronger than ever. Flames are trapped in your hair, steel in your heart." She rested a hand over Alaya's small heart, looking her in the eye. "My little adventurer, you will find your way to the ends of the earth, and when you have seen all there is to see, you will dance among the stars."

*****

Alaya blinked her bleary eyes at the pre-dawn forest. Her fire had gone out in the night, the coals still glowing a dark red, occasionally shifting to release a puff of sparks into the chilly morning air. The smell of pine and dew mixed with the tinge of smoke clung to her clothes. A few feet away, Rascal tore small mouthfuls of grass from the earth, munching slowly.

Weariness still pulled at her limbs and cobwebbed her mind, but Alaya forced herself to her feet. Gathering a few dry twigs, she stirred her fire back into a weak flame. As she crouched by the sputtering warmth, Rascal's head shot up, eyes wide and ears perked forward. Alaya instantly looked towards the road, frozen in silence as she listened, trying to sense what the stallion heard. Seconds ticked by, horse and girl completely still, the forest quiet. Waiting.

Footsteps.

Alaya slipped a hand down to her boot where she kept a hunting knife. Her heartbeat quickened as the sound of cracking twigs and crunching leaves sounded once again. It was someone heavy, but alone.

What if the slavers knew she was on their trail?

What if they had sent someone after her?

Breath caught in her throat. Alaya slowly began drawing her dagger. The grating of metal on metal as it crossed over the steel band at the top of the sheath was deafening.

Several footsteps. Shuffling, quick.

Alaya moved to a standing crouch, ready to spring into action. A few leaves shifted beneath her feet, betraying her movement.

The bush to her right, a yard or so in front of her, began rustling. Every muscle in Alaya's body tensed.

A dark shape poked out, and with a war cry, Alaya sprung forward. A surprised yell mingled with her own, and she collided with the figure, her knife struck metal and glanced off. Alaya quickly raised her left arm to protect her head as she bowled into her target.

The two hit the ground, the figure dropping like a rock. Alaya managed to roll away into a rotting log, pain spreading through her shoulder.

"What in Owe's name d'ya think ye're doing?" the figure roared, struggling to his feet. Alaya looked at the figure from her defensive crouch, jaw dropping slightly.

Before her stood a stocky, well-built Daignar dwarf, who also happened to be fuming as he stared at her, rage in his deeply wrinkle-framed grey eyes.

Alaya stood, rubbing the back of her neck abashedly as she studied her shoes.

"My apologies, master dwarf, you caught me unawares."

"Unawares? Unawares! Ye nearly took me head off ye knife-happy Alkonost!"

His face – or what face could be seen between his bushy beard and low helmet – was red in the weak morning light.

"I… I'm terribly sorry. I didn't expect anyone to stumble upon my camp…"

"Stumble upon? Ye're only a dozen bloody steps off the main road ye daft cu-"

"Oi!" Alaya yelled, interrupting him. She pointed at him with her dagger, eyes narrowed.

"I've been through bloody enough without you coming in here and frightening and yelling at me at," she paused, glancing at the sky, "four in the gods-damned morning!"

The dwarf settled, indignant.

"Well it wasn't exactly a pleasant experience for me either," he grumbled.

Alaya passed a hand over her face, leaning down to sheathe her knife.

"Listen, just... I don't know. Take your piss or whatever you were going to do."

She waved her hand dismissively and trudged back to her camp.

Footsteps crunched behind her, and she turned, sighing.

"What do you want?" she asked, resigned.

The dwarf tugged on his beard, glancing away.

"Well ye see, lass, I barged in because me waterskin ripped on the road this morning, and I was hopin' to buy a patch off ye..."

He trailed off, grumbling under his breath.

Alaya rolled her eyes, jerking her head towards the log on which her saddlebags rested. "Come on you grumpy little half pint."

She left the dwarf sputtering as she walked over to her bags.

The sun pulled itself over the horizon, the sky turning to the grey-blue of morning. Birdsong bounced among the trees.

Rummaging through her pack, Alaya took out a patch and sewing equipment, then gestured for the dwarf to hand over his waterskin.

"I'll repair it if you provide breakfast for me," she offered.

The dwarf considered this, then agreed with a shrug. "I'll bring me pony around."

He led a shaggy tan pony with large packs on its back into the clearing. Seeing Rascal, the pony whinnied happily. Rascal looked up from his grass, stretching his neck to tower over the small, stocky creature. As the dwarf tossed Alaya the waterskin and stirred the fire to life once more, Rascal leaned down to inspect the pony. Looking up at the much larger horse, the pony bravely touched her nose to Rascal's, dark eyes sparkling as she nickered softly.

"What's your name, master dwarf?" Alaya asked as she lined up the patch and threaded the thick needle.

"Skarin," he replied. His chin rested on his chest as he tended to the fire, beard covering his mouth.

"I'm Alaya," she continued pleasantly, stitching carefully. "I come from a farming village on the edge of the Aryan Desert, east of the L'jeer River. What about you? I haven't seen a mount like that before."

"I'm traveling from the ruins of me people's home. Looking for someplace to settle." Skarin's voice was deep and gruff, his eyes fixed on the fire.

"What skills do you have to offer a new home?" Raising the waterskin into a patch of sunlight to inspect it. Alaya nodded, proud of her handiwork.

"I'm a sword for hire. I can track anyone. Defend any person. Cone and I can help on farms when we're not working as soldiers."

"Cone? That's an unusual name for a pony."

Skarin grumbled something under his breath, causing Alaya to lean forward, resting her elbows on her knees.

"What was that?"

"Me niece thinks she has the coloring of a pinecone. Let her name her as a birthday present."

A grin stretched across Alaya's face. "That's very sweet."

"Aye," he replied. "She is."

With that, Skarin took the bacon he had been cooking on the fire. He stood to retrieve two small, dense loaves of bread from his packs. He tossed one to Alaya, who drew her knife and sawed through the bread. After receiving permission from Skarin, given in the form of a grave nod, she gingerly lined the inside of one-half of the bread with the hot bacon strips, sandwiching them with the other half. The two swapped conversation as they ate, Alaya sharing her mission with the dwarf, who turned out to be a surprisingly good listener.

"May I ask one more favor, Skarin?" Alaya asked once she swallowed her last bite, handing his waterskin to him.

*****

Skarin and Alaya broke through the tree line onto the road as the sun became fully visible. Leaving their mounts to the side of the road, they moved to examine the various ruts and marks that scarred the dirt. Skarin knelt, studying carefully, while Alaya peered up each branch of the fork as far as she could see, searching for any sign of the slavers.

"North," Skarin grunted, standing and stretching to his full four foot six inches. He pointed down the right branch of the road. "A large caravan passed by here a few days ago."

Alaya nodded, hurrying to Rascal and mounting up.

"Thank you, Skarin. I must make haste. Good luck in your ventures."

She turned her horse, facing down the northern road.

"Oi, lass. Hold up a moment."

With a grunt, Skarin pulled himself onto his pony, who took his weight sturdily.

"I canna let ye go alone," he grumbled. "Not one like ye without a scrap of armor or even a sword."

"I have my hunting knife and bow!" Alaya sputtered.

"Ye're a village girl, ye canna go up against those bandits and expect to come away unharmed. Besides, the roads be a nasty place for a lonely traveler."

"Aww, Skarin, you care!" Alaya put a hand over her chest.

"Now don't make me take it back, ye cheeky lassie!" He gave her a glare, wagging one finger, his bushy beard hiding the twitch of his lips. "Let's just get going, aye?"

"Aye!" Alaya agreed, unintentionally mimicking his accent, earning her another sharp look. She smiled, adjusting her grip on the reins as Rascal shifted. "More seriously, though, can you and Cone keep up with us? I have to catch them before they reach the city—"

"Worry not, young lass," Skarin patted his pony's neck, grinning proudly. "We'll keep pace with you. Now enough talk! The day is young, but we have far to travel."

Cone whinnied in agreement, and the four of them set off at a quick canter.

The two swapped conversation when they could, but it seemed no matter what questions she asked or prying looks she gave, she couldn't get as much as a last name out of him. Eventually, Skarin seemed to catch on to what she was doing, and descended into sullen silence, apparently upset. This wasn't what she wanted. She was trying to get to know him, not make him clam up on her.

"You know," she began, loosening the reins and letting Rascal steer himself as the pair slowed to a trot. "When we were growing up, Terra and I spent a lot of time together. Since mother passed away, I was the one who took care of her. And Terra, she tells these stories that she just makes up out of her own head. They're incredible. I remember dozens of times she'd be helping with chores, and she'd just start talking, then suddenly there would be a little crowd all around us. Once I was doing laundry by the river, chatting with some of the women there, and Terra began telling baby Ryu a story. It was about a shadow who wandered the plains at night, cold and alone and never able to meet any friends because everyone went to sleep. Then, one day, he saw a girl. She was too afraid to sleep because her nightmares were so bad. The shadow was scared, he had never met a human before, but went up and said hello. Soon they met every night, and she ended up telling him about her nightmares. He told her if she allowed him into her home he would keep the nightmares away. She agreed. And so she was able to sleep the night away, he was warm and had a friend, and the two of them went on many adventures on the nights she stayed awake for him. The children loved it, she told it many times for them."

Skarin grunted, about to reply when a large dodo darted out from the bushes, running almost directly under Rascal's feet. The horse let out a scream, rearing suddenly, the whites of his eyes showing in fear. The dodo immediately froze, staring up at the horse about to cave its skull in. As Rascal began descending, the bird screeched. The loud, ear-bursting noise turned Alaya's stomach. Not expecting this, Rascal shied hard, leaping to the left and jostling Cone, who nipped back in return.

Skarin yelled wordlessly, pulling Cone away, and Rascal attempted to bolt. His left front leg caught a dip in the road, causing him to fall. Alaya only just managed to leap out of harm's way before the 1500-pound horse slammed onto the ground.

She rolled twice, bouncing from the velocity. As soon as her head stopped spinning, she leapt to her feet. The world wavered around her.

Skarin was a few yards away, trotting Cone in tight circles as he spoke to her, trying to calm the mare down. Her eyes then darted to Rascal, who was struggling to stand. A long gash appeared on his leg as he moved, blood matting into his chestnut fur.

"Rascal!" Alaya ran to his side, skidding onto her knees by him as he lay on the ground, panting, eyes rolling in fear.

"Hey, hey, it's alright, you're alright boy," she cooed, stroking his neck, one hand resting gently on his nose. The stallion's breathing slowed as long seconds ticked by. Skarin appeared behind her, still on Cone.

"There's an odd tower structure a little ways up the road. I'm going to try and get help," he said, voice low and urgent.

Alaya knew how bad a leg injury was for a horse. If they didn't manage to heal it, Rascal wouldn't be rideable. He wouldn't even be able to stand. And if that were the case, it would be kindest for all involved to terminate him. She swallowed hard at that thought, blinking back tears as she continued stroking Rascal's strong neck.

"You'll be okay, darling," she whispered, hearing Skarin scurry off. "We'll find a way to help you. I'm not going to lose you. We still have so many adventures ahead of us. We're going to be riding all over the world until we're both old and grey, then you can rest in a field with lots of daisies, and get fat from all the carrots the little children bring you, aye?"

Rascal blew through his nose, pressing it further against her hand as she spoke. Rocks cut into Alaya's knees. The sun began to burn on her back, too warm against her hair and neck. It felt like Skarin had been gone for eternity. Footsteps approaching caused her to look up.

It was Skarin, trudging along determinedly and leading a frisky Cone, and a tall, light grey-skinned figure beside him, gliding along in impressive robes of purple, black, and silver. Pointed ears poked out of his long, silver hair, and a small smile graced his lips. As he got closer, Alaya was able to see his eyes, a pale blue near to white, with an odd, dangerous light in them.

The Thalrey elf hurried to her side and knelt swiftly, his robes billowing out around him. Alaya frowned. He had an odd aura, and he smelt like jasmine and... something else she couldn't name, but it made her head spin a little.

"Hello," he said, passing outstretched hands over Rascal's leg. The horse whickered lowly, observing him nervously.

"Hello," Alaya stuttered in reply. She didn't know what, but something was off about this man. At her answer he turned to study her, his odd eyes staring straight into hers as his lips twitched into a knowing smile. Alaya shrank back slightly, her instincts telling her to run. "Who are you?"

"My name is Enur. Who are you, pretty young lady?"

Alaya's cheeks flushed as her sense of danger heightened. "I'm Alaya."

"A pleasure to meet you, Miss Alaya. What are you doing out here with a hairy old dwarf? You can do much better, you know."

Her eyes widened, and Skarin protested from behind the elf. Before she could reply, though, Rascal began to stir. She quickly glanced at his leg—it was healed, with no sign that the deep, muscle-rending gash had ever been there. As she stood and moved back for the horse to get to his feet, she studied the elf with narrowed eyes.

"How did you do that?"

He simply looked at her and winked, then addressed the group as a whole.

"Please come back to my home for a little while, it will take a short time before his leg is fully healed and he should rest. I can provide you with an early lunch if that sweetens the offer any?"

Unsure if she or Skarin should accept any food from this man, Alaya cautiously agreed. For Rascal's sake, she told herself.

The delay chafed her mind. Pictures of Terra, alone and afraid, appeared before her. She gathered Rascal's reins and led him after the elf, carefully watching his injured – or, previously injured – leg. He favored the other legs slightly, but there was no sign he had ever cut himself in his frightened thrashing. Could it really be magic? Deep down she knew the answer, and it sent a shiver down her spine.

As if he had heard her thoughts, Enur shot her a smile over his shoulder as he turned into the little clearing on the edge of the road where his tower sat.

The grey building was made from some sort of quartz that shimmered in the sun. It twisted unnaturally as it reached past the treetops, not a single sharp corner to be seen, and the cone roof held a small purple flag at the top. Whoever this man was, he certainly liked purple. And himself.

"Welcome," Enur said, gesturing widely. Alaya took her eyes from the sky and studied the yard. It was a bit overgrown. Ivy crawled up the trees and over the ground – but avoided the tower – and small, unusual flowers grew in small patches that seemed to be encouraged by the man who lived in this unsettling home.

As Enur easily opened the heavy ironbound door, a high pitched, displeased voice sounded.

"I go through all that work to make you silverflower tea, and you just run off and let it go cold!"

Alaya's hair flew out behind her as she looked around, searching for the source of the voice.

"Ah, my apologies, Ninji. I had to assist this lovely young lady and her less lovely dwarven companion."

"Why you-"

Alaya unceremoniously clapped a hand over Skarin's mouth, not wanting to offend this seemingly–unstable mage. Enur turned and raised an eyebrow, but she just gave him a pleasant smile, ignoring the angry dwarf she was still silencing. She noticed something move in the corner of her eye and, looking down, met eyes with an ugly brown creature. Her face must have instinctively shown surprise and disgust, because the creature frowned, contorting his unpleasant face even further.

"What are you looking at?" he questioned angrily.

Enur swept between the two, giving Alaya a gracious, apologetic smile.

"Don't mind little Ninji there, he doesn't often take kindly to strangers."

"What... what is he?" Alaya asked quietly, hoping her question wouldn't reach the easily-offended creature's ears. It did.

"Why do people always ask that?" Ninji demanded shrilly, but went ignored.

"He's a yewt, of course!" Enur laughed, the musical sound echoing around in Alaya's head. "They're an odd breed of creatures, a species of brownie that is only found in deserts. Helpful though. Especially talented when it comes to the creation of potions," Enur lowered his voice, making a show of letting Alaya in on a secret, "those of the more... seductive kind." He smirked.

Alaya leaned back slightly, glancing around, unsure. The air that the Thalrey mage gave off certainly wasn't one of mental stability.

A sharp pain came from her right hand, and she jerked it to her side, cradling it as she looked to her left in dismay. The dwarf had bit her! Skarin glared back, before turning on Enur with a jab of his finger.

"Ye promised us food!"

Enur chuckled, nodding. "So I did! Ninji, a light lunch for us, if you please. And quickly, if you don't mind."

"'Ninji, a light lunch for us if you please,'" the yewt repeated in a high, mocking voice. "Give me some warning why don't you! Useless, skinny little kalva," he added under his breath. Alaya guessed it was an insult in another language. Enur just smiled patiently and stood aside, indicating that his guests should come in. Alaya walked back to Rascal and looped his reins over his head and secured them so he wouldn't tread on them, then stepped beyond the threshold.

The tower smelled like vanilla, and somewhere in the building tinkling music echoed down the halls and staircases. Enur led the pair into a luscious sitting room, warm cream with crimson velvet settees and chairs. Bright sunlight shone through the window, illuminating bookcase-lined walls and a marble fireplace. All throughout the room were odd trinkets – was that a dragon tooth?

Alaya entered the room ahead of the others, curious to inspect the odds and ends on the mantelpiece. There was a purple and black feather as long as her arm in the center, and she reached out a finger to see if it was as soft as it looked.

"I wouldn't do that if I were you."

Alaya jumped, stumbling backwards, bumping into Enur's chest and stepping hard on his left foot. Just as she was about to rebound forward, his hands landed softly on her waist, stopping her.

He smiled. "Careful there, Alaya."

He said her name, and it gave her the same feeling she got after placing a rich piece of dark chocolate in her mouth. Warm and relaxing.

Skarin cleared his throat. Loudly.

"Take yer hands off her, now ye've stopped her from poisoning herself," he said sternly.

"Of course, master dwarf."

Enur stepped back, giving Skarin a small bow. Alaya had never seen a movement dripping with so much disdain.

Skarin crossed his arms over his broad chest and glared.

Seconds ticked by, no one moving.

"Your *light lunch*, Master Enur," a high pitched voice announced. Ninji entered, harnessed to a full sized, ornately carved wooden lunch cart.

"Ah, thank you, Ninji."

"Thank me by getting me more of those orange mushrooms next time you go out," the brownie grumbled, unhitching himself from the cart and bustling out of the room. Alaya watched him go, then blinked disconcertedly, realizing the brownie wasn't wearing any clothes. When she looked up, mouth slightly open in dismay, Enur was looking at her, smiling in amusement as he sipped a liquid that looked like mercury.

"Um, y…your brownie, he's not… ah…" Alaya stuttered, embarrassed.

"I know," Enur replied dismissively.

"But it didn't look like he had a, um…" The girl blushed deeply, and Enur's smile widened.

"He doesn't. The poor creature was captured by some cruel dwarves many years ago, and they decided it would be amusing to relieve him of his manhood. I managed to rescue and heal him, but I can't return what they took, unfortunately."

"Oh."

Alaya decided it would be best to just take a cucumber sandwich and stop talking.

They ate in silence, Skarin glaring at the elf, Enur not taking his sparkling eyes off Alaya. It was as if he could see something that no one else had ever noticed. Alaya decided to focus on the food.

Once they had polished off the food that Ninji had provided, Skarin and Alaya stood.

"Thank you for your hospitality, but we really must be going," Alaya said, brushing her tunic top distractedly.

"Not at all," Enur replied smoothly, also standing. "Let me walk you back to your horses."

He watched as the two mounted up and prepared to leave.

"Oh, before you go."

Enur turned to Alaya, speaking as if he had almost forgotten, but Alaya had a feeling he had been waiting for just the right dramatic moment. From within his robes, the mage drew two long, curved daggers, each in their own ornate silver sheath.

"Take these. I hope they will help you save your sister." He held them up to her.

Alaya frowned. She hadn't mentioned her sister to the unsettling mage. But, with a nod from Skarin, she accepted his gift, strapping them to the saddle by her knee.

"Thank you. Farewell."

Enur bowed with a small smile on his lips.

"Until we meet again."

With that, Alaya and Skarin turned their steeds and hurried out of the clearing, away from the odd elf with the pale eyes, and rode for several silent hours. They pushed their horses to their limits, desperate to catch the slavers and make up for lost time. Only when they couldn't see the road by the waning moonlight did they stop and make camp. Both of them were sore and tired, the horses hanging their heads in weariness. Once they fell asleep, Alaya could not keep away the haunting image of Enur from behind her eyelids, he never stopped smiling.

*****

By unspoken agreement they were up with the sun, and Alaya swore Rascal was glaring at her as she saddled him and mounted up. She and Skarin were more asleep than awake for the first few hours, stopping only for a quiet breakfast when both their stomachs were growling louder than the pounding of hooves on dirt. The only sign they left behind that they had been there were warm coals covered with a spray of loose soil.

As the sun neared its zenith, Alaya slowed Rascal to a trot, not wanting to force him too much until she and her sister were making their escape. Skarin followed suit, stretching with a yawn. With the lack of anything better to do, Alaya retrieved one of the knives Enur had given her and looked it over.

The whole thing was as long as her forearm, and a decorative snake wove its way up the handle, creating a thick, sturdy guard. She didn't want to unsheathe the whole thing, but she pulled it out an inch or two and raised an eyebrow as the sun hit the razor-sharp edge. There was no doubt in her mind that there was something different about these knives. The little she knew of Enur guaranteed it.

"Look."

Skarin's gruff voice drew her out of her thoughts, and Alaya slid the knife back into the ornate sheath with a click, returning it to its twin.

The dwarf was pointing to the side of the road where a broken wagon wheel lay in the grass. The pair pulled their horses up beside it.

"I'll bet ye that belongs to the slavers. I haven't seen any other tracks that would indicate another caravan like theirs."

"That would have slowed them an hour or two," Alaya replied.

"At least," he agreed.

The sight of the broken wheel filled the girl with determination. "That means we're close."

Simultaneously spurring their horses on, the two took off. Even the horses seemed to feel the urgency, quickening their steps, nickering as if encouraging each other.

As the sun began to descend, the road twisted into a hilly area, denying Alaya the far visibility she desired as her tired eyes searched for any sign of her sister. Skarin was practically asleep on horseback, eyelids drooping heavily, although he refused to be the one to give in and ask to camp for the night.

As she was about to give in and pull off the road, Alaya noticed a large plume of smoke coming from the forest beyond the next hill. Either it was a forest fire, or…

"Skarin!" she exclaimed, pressing her legs to Rascal's sides. The dwarf jerked in surprise, shaking his head and blinking sleepily.

"Eh?"

"Look!"

As they crested the hill, her excitement grew. The large cloud of smoke originated from several distinct pillars. Not a forest fire.

"It's the slavers," Skarin confirmed. They rode along the road until they were within a half mile of the smoke, then dismounted and carefully wound their way through the forest.

"Aye, lass," Skarin spoke quietly, halting Alaya's progress through the trees. He held out a calloused hand. "Give your horse here. You're quicker and quieter than me, go ahead and see how the land lies."

Alaya nodded, adrenaline flooding her body and kicking her senses into overdrive. As she crept swiftly through the trees, she could hear every rustle, smell the pine needles beneath her feet, and taste the smoke as she neared the camp.

Locating a convenient clump of bushes, she lowered herself to her stomach and crawled forward, peering out into the clearing from between the leaves.

The slavers' brightly painted wagons were drawn into a large circle. She could see between two of the wagons that they had started a large bonfire in the center. Their crimson robes made each man into a drop of blood around the flames. They were drinking and laughing, likely looking forward to the profit they would make the next day when they made it to the city. Alaya's stomach turned, but she focused on inspecting 'the lay of the land,' as Skarin called it.

Several guards, armed with bows and long, thin, slightly curved swords, stood at various intervals around the circle. Alaya moved swiftly, darting from cover to cover, relying on the pine needles to cover her steps. As she did so, more carts and wagons came into view, and one of them stopped her heart. It was a cage, made from thick iron bars, patchy with rust. Inside the cage huddled a half-dozen people, dark shapes in the dim, flickering light. Beyond the cage was a pen in which nearly twenty horses rested or ate quietly. Alaya observed for a moment before turning back. The young adventurer had an idea.

*****

Skarin strolled into the clearing, waving to a few of the guards. "Hello boys! Have a drop of drink for a thirsty traveler?"

The guards immediately turned towards him, weapons raised. Alaya waited until he had drawn several of the guards away and crept up to the cage, picklock kit in hand. Before she had gone over her plan with Skarin, she never realized there was much more to him than she knew until he produced the kit from his saddlebags and explained in detail how to use it. Her hands shook as she inserted the tension rod (*thick stick*, she noted mentally), and pick (*skinny stick*).

The clinking of metal on metal drew the attention of the people in the cage, and they shrunk away from her. All except one.

The smallest figure crept closer, white eyes visible in the darkness.

Then, in a hushed voice, "Alaya!"

Alaya froze, tears instantly jumping from her eyes.

"Terra!" Her voice was quiet and cracked as she reached a hand through the bars, the cold metal raising goosebumps on her skin. Her sister's small hands wrapped around hers, and Alaya felt tears splash down.

"Shhh, shhh, it's okay. I'm here to rescue you, but I'm going to need your help. Everyone come close. I need you to shield me from the view of the men in the middle of the circle.

Terra nodded, and the prisoners drew around her. As she scrubbed the pick back and forth like Skarin had told her to, she spoke in a hurried, quiet voice.

"We're going to get you all out. I'm working with a dwarf named Skarin."

The pick seemed to get louder each second it moved. Alaya listened carefully for the click that would indicate the lock was disabled.

"Do any of you know where any rope or cloth is?"

One of the older women nodded, pointing to the cart next to theirs.

"Alright, once we get you all out I will need two or three of you to come with me, we're going to go tie up the guards that Skarin's distracting, gag them, and put them in here so the cage won't be empty when the others look over. The rest of you run to the tree line and hide, stay near the horses but out of sight, I don't want them spooked because of us. They're going to be our escape."

Click.

Opening the door smoothly, to avoid squeaking, Alaya ushered them all out. Three of the older girls – farmhands by the looks of it – stood by her, while the rest scurried to the tree line. Terra tried to stay, but Alaya sternly pointed her towards the bushes. Although the younger girl wanted to argue, she didn't, but instead helped an injured woman to cover.

One of the girls retrieved several coils of light rope, and the other extracted a blanket from the cart which she and the third started ripping into long strips. The four of them moved towards the small fire where Skarin was conversing enthusiastically with five guards, a hefty tankard in hand. His sharp eyes saw Alaya creeping up, and, still talking, he casually threw his beer in one man's eyes, and smashed another in the face with the ironbound container. Grabbing a coil of rope from the other girl, Alaya dashed forward and leapt onto the nearest guard's back, looping it around his neck and pulling hard, forcing him to stumble backwards, clawing at his neck. Skarin had drawn his sword and smashed the fourth guard's face in with the pommel. The farm girls rushed the last one, clawing and choking him. Alaya wasn't sure what exactly the girls had endured during the days they were in captivity, but judging by the state of the unconscious guard, they had their reasons for revenge.

Working as quickly as possible, they all bound and gagged the guards, depositing them into the cage and allowing the lock to fall back into place. Before they left, Skarin withdrew a clump of something and stuffed it into the keyhole.

"Sticky tree sap," he whispered in reply to Alaya's questioning glance.

With that, they were off to the tree line.

Alaya went into the horse pen first, frowning as she saw the red-robed raiders kept their horses saddled and bridled instead of letting them rest like their cart horses and ponies. It made it easier for her, though, so she didn't mind too much.

One by one, as instructed, the captives filed in. All of them had some experience with horses, so Alaya quietly distributed the mounts out. They ended up only one short, so Alaya gestured for Terra to come with her.

They had nearly made it.

A shout came from the circle, and Alaya's head jerked to see several slavers glaring at her, yelling to their comrades. Eyes wide, she looked at Skarin. His face was grim.

"We can't get the horses through the trees quickly enough," she said.

He grunted, staring towards the slavers. After what seemed like an eternity, long enough for the slavers to begin to gather their weapons, he spoke. "Run. All you girls. Run. I'll hold them off."

Several of the girls took off immediately. A few, Terra and the farm girls included, hesitated.

"Are ye armed?" Skarin demanded angrily.

They shook their heads, backing away.

"Run! Get out of here!" he yelled, making the horses around them shy away.

They did. Out of the corner of her eye, Alaya saw a bright blonde head duck to Terra's dark one as they disappeared into the forest. Nori had Terra. They were safe.

"I'm staying," Alaya said redundantly.

Skarin looked displeased, but they had no time to argue.

"I'll occupy them. You put damage down where you can," he ordered.

Alaya nodded, drawing her two silver knives from her belt. The hilts felt oddly warm in her hands, but she had little time to think about it. With a fierce bellow, Skarin vaulted the pen's fence and charged the slavers.

They were a dozen strong, at least. Alaya darted around the edge, heart pounding. Skarin was swinging away like a madman, yelling in his rough language. Alaya heard the name of his god, Owe. He was chanting a battle prayer. He struck one of the nomads with his elbow as he turned to attack another.

An opening.

Alaya drove the hilt of one knife into the no-mad's scarf-clad head, and he dropped like a rock. One of them turned on her, and adrenaline sharp-ened her vision. She was going to stab a man. A liv-ing, breathing person. He raised his sword, teeth gritting from behind his lips, but she was frozen. She was going to die.

An ear-shattering scream broke her out of her reverie.

Terra.

Diving to the side, she dodged the deadly blade, and her left-hand knife swept in a wide arc, slicing deeply through the slaver's thigh and coming out the other side, a banner of blood streaming from the tip.

Suddenly the knives flashed hot in her hands and seemed too big to hold. Scared and confused, Alaya dropped them, rolling away. When she looked back, two massive white cobras, with glowing red eyes had appeared where her knives lay on the ground. They were as thick as a child and near twenty feet long. The pair hissed in tandem, their massive hoods flaring, their fangs as long as the daggers were moments ago. She paled. Skarin cursed loudly and fought his way towards her, staring at the snakes.

The slavers nearly retreated in fear, but instead gathered on the far side of the giant serpents, swords outstretched. The cobras were not to be dissuaded. Hissing, they wove back and forth. The slavers whispered to each other. One, young by his face and scared as hell by the dark patch in his trousers, let out a scream and ran. That broke them. All the slavers ran, yelling and screaming in fear.

The cobras pursued with terrifying speed, catching and killing each slaver with deadly efficiency. Blood pooled in the dim firelight from the bonfire. With a rustle, a thick-muscled slaver revealed his presence next to Alaya. He raised a spear, babbling at her in a foreign language, his eyes wide. Skarin tried to pull her away from him, but he was slower than the snake. It rose behind the slaver, hood quivering as it hissed loudly. The man's face was locked in a snarl as the snake sunk its fangs into his neck. Blood sprayed over Alaya and Skarin. The man used his dying strength to fling his spear at her.

She tried to avoid it, but he was too close.

Suddenly time seemed to slow. The spear pointed straight towards the center of her stomach. Her breath shook, body going cold and fingertips tingling.

The spear veered, sliced open her side. A shallow gash, but jagged. Overcome with a burning pain, Alaya was only able to groan. Light flashed behind her. Hot blood – hers and the dead slaver's – ran down onto the ground.

Skarin knelt by Alaya's side, ripping off her tunic, leaving her in only her thin undershirt. Before she could protest, he had torn the garment into strips and was binding her wound tightly. It stung fiercely. Alaya let out a short scream.

"What are those demon spawn?" he asked, fear in his voice.

"I-I don't know! They just... oh gods." Alaya rolled over to the side, heaving by the tree as everything caught up to her, pain flooding her right side every time she breathed. Skarin rested a warm, comforting hand on her back.

"They… one second I was holding my knives, the next they were there," she said, wiping her mouth with a corner of her undershirt. Skarin was watching the snakes kill the last guards.

"Your knives, eh?"

Alaya looked to where they had fallen, now just simple knives, missing the hand guards and snakes wrapping around the hilts.

"The knives…"

"Enur, you bastard," Skarin growled.

With a gurgling screech, the last nomad died, and the cobras set their glowing eyes on the pair.

Skarin helped Alaya scramble to her feet, difficult though it was, and they backed up as the snakes approached them menacingly.

They stopped several feet away and hissed, forked tongues flickering. Then they were shrinking, transforming. A moment later they were gone, and the knives once again had their serpentine decorations.

"What... what was that?" Alaya asked, shaking slightly.

"It was that mad mage's doing," Skarin said, thinly-veiled rage in his voice. "Go get your knives. Let's get out of this cursed place."

Alaya obeyed, badly shaken by what she had seen. Terra appeared by her side, tears running down her cheeks as she hugged Alaya, careful of her wound. The older girl returned the embrace, letting herself cry for a moment, thankful to have her sister back in her arms. Nori also came into view, standing back a bit and letting the sisters reunite.

"Go get two of their horses," she said, sniffing and giving Terra a small smile. "We'll each get an extra one, so we can swap mounts and make it home in two days."

*****

Smoke. That was the first sign that they were nearly home. Not the fierce, burning, acidic smoke of destruction, but the friendlier, familiar smoke of warm homes and hot meals. Alaya slumped over Rascal's neck, her vision blurry as he plodded wearily towards the village. Her mouth was dry, waterskin hanging empty from her saddlebags. She had given the last of it to Terra when the young girl awoke, crying from dehydration. It was then Alaya realized how cruelly the girls had been treated.

Behind her, a train of exhausted horses trailed, strung together with a length of rope, happy to just put one foot in front of the other. On two of the horses, a dwarf and a young girl slept, lashed carefully to their mount to keep them from falling. Nori rode beside her, slumped over her horse's neck, conscious, but only enough to keep on riding.

The procession crested the hill, horizon glowing with the early morning light. Rascal's ears perked up, head lifting as he took in the familiar scent of home. This caused a mild stir amongst the other steeds. With a profanity-laced grumble, Skarin woke. Terra slept on, entirely drained.

As the small convoy came into view, they raised a stir in the village. Alaya heard shouts and whoops as figures materialized outside houses, gathering in small groups, hugging and waving, shouting things to Alaya that she couldn't quite hear or process through exhaustion.

A few of the younger men and women came running up the hill to meet the horses halfway. Looking down blearily, Alaya saw joyful faces on the people milling around them. Someone shoved a waterskin to her, which she took, draining sloppily as the water ran down her chin and neck. Helpful hands took hold of the horses, leading them into the village.

Someone helped Alaya off her horse, gentle arms around her waist causing her to wince as they touched her wound. She followed an older woman into the nearest house and, after seeing through the door that Terra was in her father's arms, collapsed gratefully onto the bed offered to her.

It was much later in the day when Alaya woke, her eyes crusted with sleep that had restored her body and mind. The sun was a burning beacon on the western horizon as she slowly made her way out of the house, her limbs stiff and sore, the spear gash freshly dressed and bandaged. To her surprise, the village was alive with activity. A massive bonfire, as tall as Terra before the flames, was being tended to in the middle of the square. Long tables were set out on either side, lined with benches. The rich aroma of roast boar came from one of the houses at the other end of the village. Various other dishes, hot and cold, all colors of nature, were already being arranged in a miniature mountain range down the middle of the tables. Alaya caught sight of one of her close friends balancing several bowls as big as her head in his arms, each filled with delicious, steaming soup.

"Garrett!" she called, raising an arm, instantly regretting it as her side burned, and starting towards him. He turned his head and nodded to her, finishing his precarious trip to the table. She helped him unload the bowls onto it.

"What is all this?" she asked, taking a deep breath of the light green celery and apple soup she held. A tempting dollop of fresh cream floated in the middle.

"This?" Garrett laughed, running a hand through his thick black hair. "This is all for you, Alaya!"

She gave him a sidelong glance, angled upwards as the boy stood a head taller than her.

"Well, not just you," Garrett continued. "This is for everyone. In celebration of your return. It was so odd…"

The two started walking out towards the barn, a path they often trekked together, so their feet turned there by muscle memory. Garrett continued talking.

"Very early this morning these carts arrived. A half-dozen of them, all loaded down with food. More than I've ever seen in my life, 'Laya, some of it wasn't even in season! Anyways, the head driver was one of those silent, gruff types. He just said that someone with money to spend had heard our village had been raided, and then he ordered all this food for us. He wouldn't tell us who, no matter how much pleading and threatening we did. And he wouldn't accept a single penny of payment from us."

Garrett shrugged, hands deep in his pockets. Alaya clambered stiffly up onto the rough wooden fence that surrounded the horses, giving a sweet whistle. A familiar brown head perked up, eyes bright. Rascal came trotting to her with a whinny, tossing his head, clearly in a better mood now he had rested and had some richer food in him. A soft smile on her lips, Alaya stroked one of his ears with one hand and tickled under his chin with the other, causing him to snort and nip playfully at her arm.

"That is unusual... I'm glad this anonymous donor did what he did, though," she said, stroking Rascal's velvety nose.

"Aye. Everyone will eat well tonight, and we'll have enough to not worry while we replant the fields and get a late harvest in," Garrett replied, stepping forward to run his fingers through the stallion's mane.

A loud exclamation came from behind the three, causing Rascal to canter off, kicking his heels in excitement.

"There's my girl!"

Alaya nearly fell off the fence in her scramble to run to her father's arms. Within moments, she was enveloped in his warm embrace. He rested his cheek on her head, a small smile folding into familiar wrinkles on his face.

"My brave, wonderful girl," he said lovingly, stepping back and holding her at arm's length, his grin widening. "You brought the girls back, and yourself as well. I'm so proud to call you my daughter."

Alaya smiled until her cheeks hurt, silent in the warm glow of success.

*****

Thanks to Skarin's insistence, the party was well supplied with alcohol. By the time the moon was properly in the sky, mothers had ushered the small children to bed, and there was joyful laughter. Instruments were produced, and the tables had been pushed aside. Villagers kicked and laughed as they twirled around the roaring bonfire.

Alaya, not much one for dancing, instead sat on the edge of the flickering firelight, laughing and clapping along to the music. Across the vast space, she could see Garrett doing the same, his dark eyes sparkling as he looked straight at her, his smile softening as he gave her a nod. She returned it, then retrieved her tankard of ale, taking a sip. She hadn't drunk too much, just enough to give her a warm buzz. As she went to put the cup back on the table, movement caught her eye. A slim grass snake slithered across the road, headed out hunting most likely. The sight of the reptile sent a shiver down Alaya's spine, and she could practically see the hellish cobra flash before her eyes, their unnatural white scales and eyes like orbs of blood.

She shook her head. Suddenly the music was too loud, too frantic in its pace, and the chatter around her grated. Standing quickly, she twisted her mouth as pain tightened her entire right side. She retrieved a jar of juice and an apple and headed into the darkness, quickly finding the familiar path to the horse pen.

A low whistle brought Rascal to the fence, and he greedily gobbled up the apple Alaya had brought him. She stroked his cheek as she sipped her juice, taking deep breaths to slow her pounding heart.

"Nice party."

Alaya spun to the side, breath catching as her wound flared.

Leaning on the barn wall, pale eyes and skin nearly glowing in the moonlight, was Enur. A feral air about him, he smiled.

"What are you doing here?" she asked, suddenly very aware of the distant singing, and how alone she was.

"I came to see if you'd figured it out yet, Alaya," he replied, and that odd feeling came over her again as he spoke her name. He stepped closer, his hair sparkling as if it were spun from starlight.

She didn't move. "Figure what out?" Her voice shook slightly, and her grip around the jar tightened.

"How? How did those snakes come to be? How did that spear not destroy every organ?"

He laid soft fingertips on her stomach, right where she had thought the spear should have landed.

Her eyes widened, heart dropping to her feet.

"No…" Her voice no louder than a broken whisper, but his elven ears still heard her.

"Yes. You are a Wilder like myself. You have no need for spellbooks, the magic is in your soul. It had been locked away somehow, but now… now it has come forward. I sensed it before, but it's so much stronger now."

He sounded like a man who had discovered a room made of gold, his voice low and lips curved in a smile.

"You know it's true. Even now, you can feel the currents of magic in the back of your mind, ready to be tapped and controlled. You have so much power, you just need a teacher."

That broke Alaya out of her reverie, and she jerked backwards, stepping away.

"No! I won't come with you."

Enur shrugged, inspecting his fingernails casually.

"They'll already be after you. The Circle of Magi, I mean, to ensure your magic is under lock and key for the rest of your life. That's not even the worst of it, now the magic is unleashed, well…" he blew a puff of air, raising his eyes to the sky. "Who knows what will happen. It could just lash out, if not controlled. It could destroy, hurt, even kill those around you. They'd all be at risk. Your village, your friends, your family… your sister."

His eyes locked with hers. He knew he had won. Stepping aside, he revealed her saddlebags, apparently freshly packed. The duo of silver knives rested on the top.

"Come with me and I will teach you to control your magic. You will be able to use it to protect others, to keep your father and sister safe."

Anxiety tightened Alaya's throat, but she still took the shaky step forward and retrieved the bags and knives. Enur's eyes glinted.

"I will also teach you to avoid the Magi. This is why we must leave immediately. Mages will soon be on your trail. We need to be as far from here as possible by daybreak."

"Wh…what if the mages catch us?" Alaya asked nervously.

Enur was silent for a moment. "They will tear the magic from your soul. With it will come all emotions we know as mortals. You will become an emotionless slave to the Circle of Magi. No longer will you know pain, love, hatred or any other feeling. That is why they must not catch us."

*****

"You will put them in danger if you tell them," Enur said when Alaya wanted to say good-bye to her family and friends. "The more they know, the more at risk you put them."

A feeling in her gut told her that he was right. As Alaya took one look back at her home from the top of one of the hills surrounding it, her heart broke slightly. Something told her she wouldn't be back for a long time. She turned Rascal back onto the path and caught up with Enur, who waited for her a little way ahead on his shining white horse.

I will be back, she promised herself. I will see my home again.

*****

Lying in her bed, Terra sighed and rolled over, the music outside cutting through the house's thin walls and keeping her awake. She swung her legs out of bed and padded over to a small shelf her father had made for her collection of rocks, feathers, and dried flowers. She had never thought she'd see any of them again, let alone sleep in her own bed once more. Her finger gently drifted over the papery petals of a dried violet. She shivered, cold air raising goosebumps on her bare legs.

The front door opened for a moment, causing the music to increase in volume. Terra jumped, darting back underneath the covers and pretending to be asleep. With a creak, her door opened, and a cracked eye confirmed that it was her father, come to check on her. He softly closed the door again, and Terra drew the blankets closer around her, breathing deepening as she drifted closer to sleep.

On the shelf behind her, the violet lay, color bright and petals creamy and soft, like the moment the flower bloomed.

The Teardrop Stone

By Jack Gabriel

669 AM Age of the Dracon-esti

"Hold on tight, Tana!" Heka yelled over the wind.

The ship rolled and pitched with the churning sea. Heaving hills of water bloomed white, spraying icy daggers across the deck. Two men had already fallen overboard, swallowed by the sea. Tana had known both of them. As a child, he'd seen them return from trips like this, limping back into the village, their faces salt-scarred and weathered. Now they were drowning. Their wives would wait, batting away their children's questions.

Tana's wife would wait, too. Even if he never returned.

"We need to turn back!" he shouted.

Heka laughed and gripped Tana's shoulder as another screaming pulse of water rocked the ship. Sailors bellowed as they were flung about the deck, anchored in place by ropes secured to weak and cracking wood.

Tana's elbow was hooked around the gunwale, his other hand gripping his stone pendant, tied with coarse string about his neck. He gritted his teeth as another wave punched the ship, knocking the whole thing sideways with a painful screech of bending wood.

"This is the worst of it!" Heka yelled. "We'll get through it now! Make good time! It'll be payday in no time, boys!"

The ship crested a wave, and caught the full blast of the angry wind. A great ripping tore the air, and a corner of the mainsail broke away. It slapped against the groaning masts.

Sailors wailed and pointed to a missing section of the gunwale, where Tana guessed another sailor had been tossed into the sea. He didn't see who it was.

"It'll settle." Heka's voice now wore the first note of concern. Tana closed his eyes and held on tight, wrapping his fist around a loose rigging rope.

He was at the mercy of the gods now.

There were peaceful times he should have dwelled on, but Tana could only think of how he'd seen this doom coming. Seen it and done nothing to stop it.

He had watched the storm unfold the day before as they sailed past the Dead Coast. It had come from inland, from Orek. The clouds had gathered as if smoking up from the line of trees that marked the distant shore. They hung in the sky, stalking after the ship until that morning, when the clouds had struck out over the water like a snake.

The storm was rumored to be caused by the Black Palace in Dhal-hax. The Ulstorm, it was called, a dread curse from that evil place. Attacking any who came near.

Since the ship had left Mandra, many had complained to Captain Heka that his course would cut too close to the shore. But the Captain wanted a fast trip. There was a sweet spot, Heka had promised, between the reach of the Ulstorm and the deepwater, where ancient horrors were said to swim. A narrow path of blue. Free of danger.

The sailors disagreed, and voted to take their chances with the serpents and dragon turtles. True, the tales of those vast monsters preying on merchant ships chilled the bones, but reports of their attacks were rare enough for many men to doubt their existence at all. They wanted to swing the ship out away from the Dead Coast, to avoid the Ulstorm at any cost.

But Heka was Captain. Chief of the Ship. His word was law between ports. And he wanted the fastest route to the Sea of Sarmy.

Heka had made no secret of claiming to own the quickest cargo ship in Mandra. The rich merchant from Evesburg had hired him on the weight of that bold promise, and had offered a bonus should he surpass it. To dissuade thoughts of mutiny, Heka had promised that all would have a share in the gold and bonuses when they made their final port.

Tana thought of that gold. The bright clang of the coins pouring from a velvet bag. The weight of them in his hands. And he thought of his wife,

Mona, and his child to be. What gift would he bring her from the pale and magnificent city of Evesburg?

Cracks pierced through the howling damp, and Tana opened his eyes to fresh terror.

A chaos of yelling directed his eyes up to the mainsail again. Great cracks had appeared on the once-proud mast. It was splintering apart like a twig. Slowly and inevitably, the great pole of wood leant over, dragging the limp sails down with it like an old man with a sack. Everything was caught and tangled, and the weight of the strong mast folding into the sea snapped ropes and shattered knots. Rigging whipped and flailed. Someone was flung away screaming like an arrow from a bowstring. The whole ship shuddered and bent, leaning painfully on one side. Loose and broken parts were thrown across the deck. Underwater, the sail caught the weight of the water, and dragged the whole ship sideways into a deep hollow trough.

Walls of wine-dark water loomed all around, rolling higher and higher.

The ship's deck was flooding fast.

"Heka!" Tana looked to his side.

The Captain was gone. A chunk was torn from the deck where he once stood.

The water all about was littered. A broth of broken things.

"Heka!" Tana yelled again. There were few sailors left now. All clinging, screaming prayers and sobbing, like children who don't understand the indifference of the world.

The ship began to climb up with the swell. Looming above and before the prow of the ship now, the sea began to curl over like a monstrous tongue.

A Mandran who dies at sea lives forever.

His mother's voice. A proverb told to children so they aren't afraid of the ocean.

But Tana was afraid. As the ship - a toy in the hands of the sea gods - was tipped backwards by the force of the massive wave, he was deathly afraid. Afraid he'd never tell the same lie to his own child. Tana didn't want to live forever; he was afraid to die.

He clutched his blue stone pendant, and as the water roared down upon him, Tana unfolded his arm from the gunwale and let himself fall.

The angry sea slapped his back and pulled him under. Cold seeped into every gasping pore, icy thrills searing behind his ears, against his lower back, between his legs. The water plugged up his ears. His head throbbed with the pressure.

He was under the surface. Above, the water raged in the half-light like sped-up stormclouds. Tana hung suspended. Beneath him were the infinite depths, where gods and monsters swam.

Perhaps one of those deep denizens would snatch him down into their darkness. The bodies of his fellow sailors had been bait enough to tempt them from their lairs.

Tana's lungs fought for air, but he resisted the urge to reach the surface. He let himself be taken by the pull and flow. There was no surviving this.

A blue glow surrounded him now. A great calm.

Tana knew it was his ancestors, come from the other side to collect him. He saw their shapes swimming just outside the thin reach of the light.

But the blue light was coming from his pendant, floating weightless in the water in front of him.

The swarming shapes in the fuzzy darkness were growing numerous, and a dread gripped him.

Sea scourge. Creatures come to claim the wrecked ship, to rejoice in killing its survivors. He screamed, and bubbles exploded across his face.

When they cleared, and his lungs were spent, a pale face was staring back at him. Bulbous black eyes reflected back his horrified expression as hands were placed on him from all directions. Needle teeth grinned, and a flash of light shattered all thought.

*****

"Hold on tight, Tana," his mother whispered. "If you're scared, hold on tight."

Tana squeezed his mother's rough hand as she pushed aside the curtain. Inside, the hut was warm and lit by the small fire glowing in the center. Smoke danced up through the hole in the ceiling into the pale and star-scattered sky. Hanging from the rafters were dried plants and flowers, yellow bones and rune-carved skulls, cages holding skittering lizards and fluttering birds.

The Oracle leaned in from the shadows, her face aglow with orange firelight. "Tana Laualu."

Tana watched himself - his four-year-old self - step forward and sit crosslegged across the fire from the old woman. He pushed his mother away and she stood against the wall, watching.

Tana remembered that. He remembered feeling like he had to do this alone.

He remembered the curious feeling of being judged by and talking to the Oracle. All he had known of her was as the robed and mystical person who announced things before feasts, who shook bags of bones and threw them on the ground, reading messages in them that nobody else could.

Tana was in this hut with his mother, his younger self and the Oracle. He was watching a memory. He could float around the hut as if he were a spirit, looking at every detail, exactly as he remembered it. No dream had ever been so vivid before.

It was a dream, wasn't it?

Before… there was a ship, a storm. Everything else was blank. What was happening?

"Do you know who I am, Tana?"

"Oracle," his tiny self said.

"Very good." The Oracle looked up to Tana's mother now. "You may wait outside, Sia."

Tana's heart ached as Sia - his mother - bowed slowly and ducked out of the hut. He wanted to call out to her, to embrace her. If he was four right now, she would only be alive another two years. But he made himself stay.

The Oracle watched little Tana through the flames.

Tana felt another presence in the hut. Sudden and heavy. He spun and searched the dark places. There was nobody but him, his younger self and the Oracle.

"What I tell you today may make no sense," the Oracle said. "Not today. I hardly understand it myself. But you must listen, and you must remember. Can you do that, Tana?"

The little boy, playing with his toes, heard his name. He snapped his head up and nodded at the old woman.

She reached up, and put her hand into a sack hanging above her. Her fist came out with streams of pink sand falling between her fingers. She spoke words under her breath that Tana couldn't make out, then threw the powder into the flames.

Tana remembered the acrid smoke. It had burnt his lungs.

Young Tana coughed and fanned the air with his hands. When the smoke spiralled away through the hole in the roof and he could see again, the Oracle was holding a blue stone pendant out in front of her.

She then looked at Tana. Not the young Tana of this memory, but the Tana who was watching the memory.

The Oracle looked straight at his future ghost. "Keep this with you at all times, Tana Laualu."

"Why?" the little Tana asked, reaching around the fire to take the teardrop-shaped blue stone.

The Oracle shook her head, still staring up at Tana. "The future is clouded, young one. Your purpose for keeping this stone is not known to me. It was given to me long ago. And now I give it to you. The gods have seen fit only to reveal to me that it must be you who holds it. For now. None may take it from you, but you may give it freely to whomever you wish."

She released the stone into his clutching hands, and little Tana threaded his head through the string.

*****

Smooth, wet rock dug into Tana's back. It was a dull ache, like he'd slept for far too long. He was gluggy and dazed. He tried to move his arms, his legs, but they were locked in place. His shoulder ached, and his neck burned.

He was in some kind of room. The walls were stone, but had no seams. They were dripping, and looked like rocky shorelines at low tide, where he used to find rockpools and stick his fingers into sea anemones.

A strange wavering light filled the place, and when he found the source of it, he was jolted wide awake.

High above, a hole in the wall opened up to the sea. A vertical, wobbling window of water was held in place by nothing at all. Fish swam past, and far above was the shimmering surface. He was *under* the water.

"What?" Tana croaked.

He stretched his head up and looked down at himself. He was lying flat on some kind of raised platform. His soaking clothes clung to him still. The blue pendant lay on his chest, outside his clothes. Bright pink manacles of coral restrained his wrists and ankles.

A soft splashing sounded behind him, then wet footprints on stone. He could see who or what it was.

Tana raged and pulled against the restraints. "Who are you?" he demanded.

"Calm. You are safe here."

The voice was slow and thick, like the speaker had a mouth full of rice pudding. An odd swallowing pause and a slow gulping followed each word.

"Where am I?" Tana said.

"You have survived your shipwreck." The wet slapping feet brought the speaker into view.

At his second sight of bulging black eyes, Tana gasped.

"You think yourself so pretty, to me?" the pale blue thing said.

This creature was not a sea scourge. It was male, or at least had the body of a human male. No, an elf. He was tall and angular. A mane of fur bristled and dripped around his head and shoulders, and in his webbed hand he clutched a silver trident.

"Merfoi," Tana said. A sea elf.

The merfoi showed his thin teeth and mockingly whispered, "Human."

"My crew... Captain Heka?"

"All dead."

The merfoi dismissed Tana's distress with a wave of his hand.

"Why not me?"

"You have been allowed to survive, Tana Laualu, for a very particular reason."

"How do you know my name?"

The merfoi smirked. He thumped his trident on the floor of the room. The coral shackles on Tana's arms and legs broke apart and tinkled to the ground.

"Get up."

"You trust I won't attack you?"

"You won't."

"How can you tell?"

"The weight of the ocean around you is kept at bay by the willpower of my people. They do it for your benefit only. Do you wish to anger them?"

"Good point." Tana sat on the edge of the slab, feeling the crackle in his shoulder. He'd held on to the gunwale too hard. "What's your name?" he asked.

The merfoi scowled.

"I want to know. You know my name. What do I call you?"

"Terul."

"Why am I here, Terul?"

Terul only twirled his trident. "Come."

The door to Tana's cell was an opening to the sea large enough to walk through, shimmering with water. Held magically at bay like the window. A stingray soared past as Terul approached. He aimed his trident and spoke words Tana couldn't understand.

The opening pushed itself out into the surrounding sea, creating a long hallway. A rock walkway underfoot, and a curving water arch above. The tunnel of air stretched out before Tana, writhing and dripping. At its end was another stone room.

"Come." Terul stepped out into the hallway. He didn't check to see if he was being followed, and Tana considered staying put until he heard an ominous dripping. The window was starting to leak through into the cell.

Tana stepped onto the rock walkway and quickly caught up to his merfoi jailer.

The moving water of the tunnel made his view waver and warp, but now he wasn't imprisoned in solid stone, Tana saw enough to nearly stumble in awe as he followed Terul.

All around him, huge twisted towers rose from the ocean floor, linked with bridges made of coral and stone and shell. Attached to the towers, great domes of air wobbled in place, held by great curling fingers of stone and lit with a strange orange glow that haunted the entire underwater city with a strange fiery twilight. The city climbed up towards the surface, but Tana could also see glowing coming from chasms that ran through the city like rivers, with structures built down their banks.

They stepped from the water hallway through an opening into another rock-walled room. Terul spun and shook his trident. The tunnel of water — that Tana had only moments ago stepped out of — collapsed in on itself. The water surged towards Tana, crashing up against another invisible barrier. Fish were now swimming over the rock platform he had walked across moments ago.

"Come," Terul said again.

Terul led Tana through a series of rooms and hallways, an air bubble blooming open as they approached each and violently folding back into the sea as they left.

They passed other merfoi as they walked. Some appeared as the water drained from the room. Some swam straight through whatever it was that held up the water, walked across a room, barely acknowledged Terul, then jumped through another forcefield and continued swimming.

Out in the water, the sea elves swam about the city in packs of three or four. Some were building, harnessing the power of enormous crustaceans to create their alien architecture. He recognised, too, warriors like Terul patrolling in pairs, accompanied by what Tana guessed were scouting dolphins.

"I've never…" Tana breathed.

"Of course you haven't," Terul said. "We allow no human to tell of what they've seen here."

Tana swallowed. What did that mean? Was he walking into a death sentence? Why would they save his life if they were going to take it anyway?

Terul was blocking Tana's view of the room they were coming to. A curious guttural slapping sound came from the room.

But silence dropped as Terul approached and paused in the doorway. He spoke, his voice echoing. Tana realized that the sound he'd heard was the merfoi language.

A pause followed, then a response came and Terul stepped aside, allowing Tana to move into the room.

Merfoi, their skin all patterned in different shades of blue, watched him silently. If they were shocked to see a human, they showed no sign of it on their pouting faces. Men like Terul held tridents, but there were female merfoi, too. They had the slim, tall build of elvish women, but none of their modesty: they were naked from the waist up, and

Tana did not know where to look. They held short, vicious spears and sneered at his blushing.

As he moved further into the room he saw that it was a court of some kind, with a spiky stone throne dominating a raised platform at one end. Sitting upon it was what Tana could only guess was the merfoi Queen. Her long mane draped down her body, weighed against her chest with a necklace holding a blue stone that Tana mistook for his own at first, until he saw that hers was round, not tear-shaped. On her head she wore a great crown of spiked and curling coral. She held a huge trident, brimming with such power as to glow softly in her delicate hands.

Three merfoi guards – all women – stood either side of her, their spears held tight and ready.

Tana was led to the center of the room, and Terul stood with him as he faced the throne.

Suddenly a splash sounded, and from a hall of water walked another human man. Perhaps a nord, from his pale coloring, though he had none of the bulk and power that Tana knew nords to have. This specimen was thin, ragged and desperate. In his hands he held a shaking tray. When he noticed Tana, the nord gasped and stumbled.

A grunt of anger from a nearby guard checked the poor thing's manners, and he proceeded to ignore Tana and walk in a sort of crouching climb up towards the Queen. He presented the tray to her.

The Queen picked up a thin slice of something orange, studied it, then dropped it back onto the tray. She waved her hand dismissively at the nord.

An angry grunt from one of the Queen's guards sent the nord scurrying back down the steps again. He gave a furtive look at Tana before disappearing back down the passage.

The Queen thumped her trident on the ground and all was silent. She spoke in merfoi, her mouth slapping out the words, and her thin whiskers wobbling.

"Kiralis welcomes you," Terul translated.

Tana wasn't sure if this Queen was called Kiralis, or the city.

She spoke again, thin teeth snapping, gills flapping.

"Kiralis wants to know to what purpose you were sent into the storm above the water."

So Kiralis was *her* name.

The purpose?

"We were sailing for the Sea of Sarmy," Tana said. "To trade with Evesburg."

As Terul translated, Tana watched Kiralis. Her scowl slowly morphed into a smirk, and when she spoke, she preceded it with a snicker.

"Only a human would attempt to sail through death for more gold," Terul said.

"My Captain set the course," Tana said. "I protested. I knew the dangers, but Heka insisted. He is – was – always hungry for more."

As his words were translated, the death of his Captain and shipmates hit Tana like a punch to the stomach. He felt pressure in his chest, a welling behind the eyes. He began to breathe heavily. Tried to push down the emotion. This was not the time.

He was vaguely aware of the Queen speaking, but only paid attention when Terul translated.

"If you knew better than this Captain of yours, you should have slain him and taken his place," Terul said. "Many men now float dead because you did not do this."

Tana didn't know what to say. Heka was in charge of the ship. That's what a Captain does. Tana had no right to assume the Captaincy. That would be mutiny. Punishable by drowning.

Queen Kiralis continued to speak as Tana thought, and soon Terul was speaking her words into his ear.

"Gold makes humans die for nothing. But we merfoi are no different. There is a substance we hold more precious than any life. Something so rare, but so important, that we are able to sense its presence through deep miles of water."

Queen Kiralis slowly raised one hand and pointed a long finger at Tana's chest. He looked down.

His blue stone pendant lay against his wet and torn clothes. It shimmered in the wavering light from the water-windows.

"We searched your memories," Terul said. "You were given this by a holy woman. She spoke of its importance to you."

"I remember," Tana said. The memory was still so vivid, more so for his remembrance not so long ago. But it wasn't a memory. He was *there*, in the memory. Examining it. And there was someone else there with him. Another presence. He had felt someone else there, watching his memory with him.

"We do not allow humans to return to their precious dry land," Terul said. "The risk is too great. You must remain here. Humans who we choose to save must serve us as penance for the arrogance of their race. That is your fate."

Tana felt his future closing before him. Never would he see his wife again. His child would grow up fatherless. He would never again fish for eels in the bend of the river near his village where the water pools deep, nor would he weave patterns into new sails, or hunt in the highland scrub for moa nests to plunder.

"Kiralis has no need for new servants," Terul went on. "Your life has only been spared because you possess this stone. Kiralis wishes for you to make a gift to her of this stone. In exchange, you will attain the highest status of servanthood for the remainder of your life, and serve Kiralis exclusively."

Tana reached up and fingered his stone pendant. Something wasn't right. He wasn't being told the whole truth.

He thought of the poor wretch that had shuffled through the room before. That once-a-man was the current exclusive servant of Kiralis. What must the others look like? How many of them were there, and what condition were they in?

And what about the stone?

If they had wanted it, why had they not taken it from him while he was unconscious? Why the bargaining?

"If I refuse?" Tana asked.

After a pause, Terul spoke this question to Kiralis.

The Queen's face immediately exploded in rage. She slammed her trident onto the ground and leapt from her throne. She began spitting her sentences out, writhing her hands in the air and slowly pacing down the steps towards Tana as she spoke.

Terul did his best to keep up. "Do you know what happens to a human body this far underwater? All those empty spaces in your body are crushed down to nothing. Your bones shatter inwards, your flesh, your organs, all turns to mush and slurry. You are invaded by the water. It swallows you. It digests you."

Kiralis was close to Tana's face now. Her mane bristled, and her huge black eyes reflected his own face back at him. He could see his own blue stone hanging, glowing, around his neck. A mirror image of hers.

None may take it from you, but you may give it freely.

"You can't take it from me, can you?" Tana said. "You cannot take the stone. I must choose to give it to you."

As Terul spoke, Tana considered the meaning of that essential piece of information. He had never thought about the stone, really. It was something he had gotten used to wearing, but he had never taken it off, and the twine that held it around his neck had never snapped. But what about the stone made it impossible for the merfoi to take it from him? It had to be more than their custom. There must be some reason why they couldn't physically touch it.

The answer hit him. The stone was magic.

If only he knew how to use it.

"It would seem," Terul said, "that you are smarter than Kiralis took you for. We desire the stone. It is precious to us. What do you wish for in exchange?"

*****

"Hold on!" Tana yelled to his crew.

The tethered whale breached the surface and spewed mist from its blowhole into the warm morning air. It waited, bobbing in the gentle waves.

Behind it, the whale's heavy burden broke the surface.

Tana stood on the deck of the whale-drawn carriage – a dozen wrecked and waterlogged ships fused together with merfoi magic – and watched the water sheer from the protective bubble of air that held the impossible jumble together.

The sun had only peeked over the horizon, but already the light was too bright for eyes that had been underwater for days.

"This is your home?" Terul's globular black eyes were squinting, and he was shading them with his long, webbed fingers.

Tana did not answer. He was overcome at the sight of the Mandran coastline. He saw the wharves of his village, poking into the sea. The nightlanterns still burned on the docks and shipyards. He could hear the calls of early-risers over the caw and screech of seagulls.

The rangy nord approached Tana and placed a hand on his shoulder. He spoke words Tana could not understand, but the smile in his eyes was enough. Tana looked across the mess of crumbling decks and broken masts, and saw the eyes of some fifty other men and women staring at the same coastline. They were all thin, though the shades of their skin differed greatly, all were pale and sunken of eye.

Tana wondered what would become of them. Before they had been captured by the merfoi, many of them would have considered each other enemies. Many would have considered *him* an enemy. Yet here they all were, each beaten down and dehumanized by their enslavement, and so had become equal.

Now they were free of their bondage, and had been given over to Tana's custody. Would they choose to return to their own lands? If so, would they pick up their old prejudices and hatreds, or would they be catalysts for understanding and brotherhood between their peoples? Would they stay on Mandra and create their own society?

Tana wondered if he had made the right choice.

The whale groaned and puffed more vapour into the air as it slowly dragged the pile of broken ships towards shore.

"We have upheld our part of the agreement," Terul said. The sea elf showed no emotion. He was stating a fact.

Tana closed his fist around the tear-drop shaped stone.

Kiralis had not bargained at all when Tana demanded the freedom of all human servants in the underwater city. He had thought himself bold for asking, but she had accepted immediately and began to make arrangements. Now he thought perhaps he could have asked for more.

He pulled the stone over his head and held it out to Terul.

The merfoi took the stone, bowed his thanks and threaded his head through the string.

The Oracle had never explained how she had come into the possession of the stone. And Tana would never know how important the stone was to the merfoi.

As the crumbling collection of brine-crusted, whale-drawn ships bumped up against the wharf, and his villagers began running towards the strange people that started stepping from it, Tana realized that it didn't matter. He stepped onto the wharf, and led his people home.

The Escape

By Aaron Wulf

675AM Age of the Dracon-esti

I don't remember falling asleep. When I awoke, my body was tired and numb. My eyesight failed me. I heard sounds of the morning sparrow overhead and the wind blowing across the land. Maybe I had been dreaming for the last ten years and finally awoke.

Any place is better than where I was last. Or so I thought. As my eyes began to take in the limited sunlight given to me, my heart sank into the depth of my body. Encompassing my vision was a material very familiar to me. A heavy bag covered my head. I felt the opening constricting my throat as it latched on, claiming me prisoner.

The summer heat scorched the burlap bag. Its fibers prodded my face as if they were taunting me, daring me to find a way out. I breathed tediously and tried to recollect what had just happened. Memory escaped me. Every time I thought back to previous hours, a sharp pain bit me right behind my temples.

Sweat trickled down my forehead and cheeks. I tried to lift my arm to wipe it away, but as every muscle struggled to move, I found I was incapable of any motion below my neck. By the gods, I feared I had lost my limbs. Then I discovered it was only the earth constricting me in a warm embrace. The more I focused, I could feel grains of sand dancing against my skin and seeping into open pores. I heard the familiar sound of waves. Once they soothed me to sleep, now they bellowed like a banshee.

I was buried in the ground like a vegetable, and I was somewhere near a body of water, most likely the Ritco Sea. I hoped and prayed to the gods that it was high tide. For if it wasn't, that would mean that I was already residing in my shallow grave.

Now think, concentrate, I told myself. Never had claustrophobia penetrated my thick skull until now. Even as a child, as I hid away in our attic fearing a loathsome beast destroying our home beneath my feet, I found a way to remain calm in such a tight and dangerous space. I applied all of my strength to break free from my prison and slither out of this sand trap like a serpent from his burrow. My muscles began to strain, and I tried to lift my arms. I felt the blood being pumped out of my heart and flowing into every bulging appendage I tried to force my way out with. No luck at all.

To my surprise, a shriek echoed from beyond my veil. I struggled to find from where it came. A voice called out with urgency and my heart sank into a pit of despair.

"AGH!" The voice screeched. "Curse your worthless life! I never deserved this! Unbury me now and fight me like a man. Wait, oh no it's… it can't be you! Put down that weapon and… dear Corenthen save me. No! Stop! I pray your mother burns in the- NEAAGGHHH."

The male's deep voice strained and choked. He gurgled what could have been water, but most likely blood, as I heard the unmistaken sound of ripping flesh and bone. A rush of air passed me. Then came a thud – the same noise I heard when the local hunters dropped their prey's carcass onto their cart. And then came the screams. I heard men, women, and children screaming and yelling from every direction. My head pounded with the pressure of this infuriating situation. Moments later, the calamity ceased.

I know I shouldn't have wept. I have seen death more than I've gazed at the sunlight these days. Grown men cannot cry. They must be brave, my mother used to tell me that. But I couldn't resist. Besides, if anybody was near me, they could not see my flushed red face or my sore throat forcing out revolting sobs for the life of someone I did not know. Maybe it felt ever more real to me because now I knew I could be next. I regained my composure – what little I had – and listened for any clues as to what sort of situation I was in.

The waves beating upon the shore were drowned out by the unnatural silence that only comes with death.

I dared not cry out, but despite my tightened lungs and sandpaper tongue, I yearned desperately to seek out anyone else in my vocal range. Before I could speak, I heard a woman's scream not far away to my left, and then two more men shouting reassuring promises close to my right.

They said they will all find a way out, that everything will be okay.

She yelled that she couldn't see.

A dull thud shook the ground beside my ear. Footsteps crept so dangerously close to me that my neck hair stood on end. I almost gasped. But the footsteps receded farther, farther. Three more gut-wrenching rips of flesh and bone broke the anticipation, a barrage of screams surrounded my head again. Then came silence.

This must be a disgusting game, I thought. Every time a person speaks, death answers. No one can talk, no one can help any other.

Despite how many others may have surrounded me, I felt helpless; I was alone.

I took a moment to collect my emotions. Given the fact I could do nothing but take in my surrounding of jute fibers, I attempted to peer between the overlapping strands and out into the world. Slight glimpses of light cut through the bag, but not enough to see beyond. Damn. My fingers grew sore and felt like thick roots as I tried to spread them from the fists I was making. I felt as if my body was being pulled down towards the underworld. The only thing that was real to me right at that moment were the sparrows still singing overhead, the waves of the water, and the burlap sack, along with its distinct odor.

This bag was once used for potatoes. I could smell the mustiness still lingering from the spuds. This scent took me back in time. Back to my seventh year of childhood, when I still lived with my mother.

There she was. I could see her. Stirring a pot of freshly peeled potatoes, flowing brown hair cascading over her shoulders. We had grown potatoes in our garden ever since I was an infant. Due to an enduring absence of coin, we never had much meat. We could not afford to purchase a cow after my father's death, so my mother opted for a cheap alternative: potatoes.

*****

My mother and I sat at our table for my seventh birthday dinner. She made potato cakes, my favorite. The table was almost empty. Only our plates, two wooden cups of water, and a melting candle were placed on it. My father died when I was five, and since then it had been my mother's duty to raise me. She had much farming experience, but no hunting skills. The soil of our land was fertile, but the air flowing through the village of Markrak carried with it a dense fragrance of death. Some say our village had been cursed. This was because no fruit was able to grow on our trees, and farm animals would unexplainably choke on their tongues in the middle of the night.

Yes, the air was death; no vegetation at all could be grown above ground, or very little at least. The farmers that fed our capital city Renhet lived in a village to the north, where the most delicious and fulfilling food flourished. Those farmlands were reserved for the middle class. The great city of Renhet, which lay between that village and mine, was reserved for the wealthy upper class. We were only allowed into the city walls while selling merchandise in the marketplace or paying dues to Lord Hayward.

We said our prayer to the gods and began to eat. Just as I took my first bite, my mother gasped as she dropped her potato cake. It sounded to me as if she swallowed her tongue, just like our farm animals.

"Minotaurs." Her hands shuddered as her eyes focused on our lone window.

I shot up from my chair and scampered to the front door in horrified excitement, but as I looked out, I was stricken with fright. Homes and buildings were aflame. Minotaurs tore through the village, taking some people prisoner and mercilessly slaughtering others in the streets.

I peered down the street, my mother embracing me from behind. One of the beasts had a hold of a young man's arm as he tried to defend himself. In a rage, the bestial minotaur ripped the lad's arm from his shoulder. Blood spurted gruesomely from the missing appendage. My mother quickly pulled me inside, away from the flames and the chaos.

"Hide upstairs, my son. Quick, to the loft." She led me to the ladder. "Do not leave until you hear the songs of the morning sparrow, do you understand? If our house catches fire, take the blanket you see there, soak it in water from the pot above the fire, wrap it around you and run. Find safety." Her eyes welled up with tears, and she left my sight.

I hid away as our village burned. Half of me felt guilt, the other half cowardice. The smell of smoke seeped in between cracks in the roof. The loft only had room for myself, a few crates of cloth and old keepsakes. My head had to bend downward to avoid the low ceiling, and my knees rested against my chest, otherwise they would dangle down through the opening. I had to stay still.

That's when one of the beasts burst through the door.

Its head was massive and threatening. Dark eyes looked down at the table where the candle was still flickering, and then to a dark corner where my mother hid behind a clay vase. His muscular legs strode over to the cowering woman. She had a knife in her hand. His broad chest and bulging arms tossed the vase and smashed it into the wall across the room. My mother looked sparingly into his face. Not as if pleading for her own life, but as if she was praying the monster would not find me up above. Her arm was outstretched, shaking with the weight of the knife.

Though he stood upright, this was no man. This barbarian had a head of a bull and large sprawling horns that occasionally scraped the ceiling. Its bovine face twisted in disgust at my mother as she waved her blade to ward him off.

"Don't try," the minotaur grunted. He picked her up, ignoring her as she punched his chest, and effortlessly disarmed her. She was thrown back to the floor hard, knocking the wind from her body. I wished more than anything to be bigger. I would have jumped down and pummeled the monster. I would have taken the knife and gouged out his eyes. I would not have spared his life. I would have saved my mother. But I was too small, and I was told to hide, no matter what. I wished I had never listened.

The minotaur gave a throaty chuckle, at least which is what I assumed it was, "You're a fighter. You will be sold to the mines in Argo, human. Be happy I let you live. Now get off your arse before I change my mind!" He grabbed her arm as she once again tried to fight him off.

I wanted to scream when the minotaur hauled my mother out of the door by her hair. But she trusted me to be strong willed and survive this torment. I remained in the attic, crying until the sun rose.

As the morning sparrows sang their delightful tunes, the village was in contrast. Smoke billowed in the air amongst several homes, bodies lay scattered throughout the streets of Markrak. Faint screams echoed throughout the land, and from behind homes I heard whimpers. Children swarmed the streets crying out for their lost parents. I walked to the end of the street, then to the edge of the village. I was in a trance, stumbling along blindly, not knowing where I was going. A tear trickled down my cheek, but I just ignored it. I had to be strong. I kept walking north.

By midafternoon, I had arrived in Renhet. Everything was kept clean and organized. The shops bustled with customers, and the wheels of carriages rolled over cobblestone streets. The people of Renhet were upper class. They respected that Renhet's significant punishments for criminals kept the crime rate down within the city walls. Everyone worked for their share of goods and food. Everyone had a part to play, as long as they had a home. Lord Hayward vowed to keep the dirt off the streets, even if that meant people.

Although I had resided in a neighboring village overseen by Lord Hayward, I was seen as an outsider, a dirty farm boy. I had no place here. Farming was for the poor, and I had no skills to offer these superior people. I found scrapped manuscripts and scrolls in the alleys on occasions and took a great liking to the stories they told. I found paper and charcoal and taught myself to write. My hopes were high as I thought I may be able to obtain a job, but with months of self-learning came months without bathing. It was obvious I was a street rat, and the people saw me as such.

This was a city of masters of trade, explorers, doctors, inventors, politicians, and war heroes. My home became the streets. I grew passionate about writing tales of the city. Other street rats enjoyed my stories once a week while I read to them, but this was only a hobby for the time-being. I couldn't reunite with my mother without money.

Having no way to get coin, I had to steal food on a daily basis. I didn't want to be a thief, and I only took enough to get me by until next sunrise. Maybe one day the gods would be on my side. My luck didn't last forever though. Soon enough, the city turned on me in the cruelest way possible.

"Gotcha!" announced a vendor. "You little rats been carrying off me goods for the better half of a year now. I betcha this will be the end of your theivin' ways!" He dragged my squirming body for several minutes until we had reached the center of town.

"What do you bring me this time?" inquired the city guard.

"This bastard here been stealing me goods. Caught him in the act I did. Thought you might wanna show 'im the type of living arrangements we give to these theivin' imbeciles."

"Playing prosecutor again, are you Finn?" The guard rolled his eyes. "Come on kid. This man may be crazy, but he's right, crime cannot go unpunished in the city of Renhet. Off to the prison cells with you."

We arrived at the jail gates, and I heard the guard order some men to make room in the cells.

New prisoners were filing in and the walls could not contain such an occupancy.

*****

I felt as if I had just swallowed a whale, and the weight of it was creating tremulous waves in the deepest corners of my stomach. Even twelve years after I had been subdued, and as my body was turning into a vegetable buried in the sand with a bag over my head, I still felt the weight of guilt in the bottom of my gut. I felt it pulling me deeper and deeper into the bowels of mother earth. I wasn't actually sinking, I realized, but I had other things to worry about. Water licked my bottom lip and alerted me that the tide was rising.

My jaw locked as I stretched my neck towards the top of the burlap prison. A hair-raising shudder ran up my spine, as if spiders were parading across my skin. My neck experienced a sharp pinch, my eyes darted for the southern most right corner of my vision. A scorpion had made its way up through the back of my shirt and out of my collar. Its obsidian claws and curling tail dripping with either water or poison pointed in my direction. My jaw remained locked. I was a statue. It felt as if days were passing while I tensed my muscles beyond their limit. The deadly critter began to scale my perspiring face. During this moment of torment, I was surprised to notice I was still able to sweat despite my inevitable death from dehydration – that is if the scorpion or the tide didn't eliminate me first.

The sweat trickled down my brow and burned my eyes. My forehead twitched. I couldn't control it. The scorpion attacked. My head violently flung from side to side as my lungs surprisingly released a scream like a demon from the Nether. The six-legged killer grabbed on to my cheek with one pincher as its tail tried to puncture me and inject me with its lethal venom. I know he felt threatened. He had nowhere to go, but neither did I. All life is a fight for survival, only to die a hopefully more beautiful death later on.

My head thrashed to and fro until the scorpion fell into my mouth. Amazingly the pest had miraculously missed its attempts to sting me. I had no time to celebrate, however, for I still had the live creature inside my mouth. Its legs danced frantic steps across my tongue. The claws were clenching my teeth and the back of my throat, I started to choke. I bit and chomped the scorpion before it could inject me. Everything happened in a matter of seconds. Pure panic took control and finally my teeth tore through the tough armor of my opponent, the bitter flesh burned like acid into my tongue.

The scorpion fell dead before my chin, only the bulbous stinger remained behind my teeth. I could not explain why, but as my tongue tossed the stinger from side to side it soothed me. Much like a trophy to prove I had won a victorious battle, it gave me courage for the next. I released a sigh of relief, only to remember my audible scream. I listened for any footsteps approaching me, any noise at all to warn me of the oncoming threat. To my understandable surprise, nothing came near me. Was everyone gone? Why was nobody coming for my head? I was worried. This silence was not right.
Water caressed my bottom lip as I lowered my chin back down. I was going to drown here, that's what they were waiting for. No need to sever my head or bash my skull, whoever was doing this to me wanted me to be buried alive by the sea.

Fragments of a recent memory suddenly returned. They came in quick flashes, like a lightning storm. My temples hurt much less now, though I did suffer from a nefarious headache. I remembered the words talked about while in prison, I recalled the events after I had finally felt my cell after twelve years. It all fell into place, I finally knew where I was.

*****

I knelt down in the garden next to my mother as she pulled the potatoes from the warm earth. It always relaxed me, being with her. The thought of the spuds spending most of their life tucked in, warm and safe inside the ground made me jealous. Amongst the roots lived hundreds of ants, earthworms, centipedes, slugs, and the occasional garden geckos. When it rained, the slugs and worms would wriggle their way up to the moist, flooded surface to break free from their underground home. Perhaps the ground had become too constricting for them. Maybe they grew tired of the darkness, the confined quarters, and the inability to stretch out their bodies in any direction and finally inhale that sweet taste of life.

Perhaps my mother and I were giving the potatoes a new breath of life as well as we ripped them from the soft dirt. We would place them inside a wicker basket, take them into our three-room home, and wash them inside our only water bucket. I peeled them and tossed the spuds in the pot to boil over our fire pit. At the end of their journey, they would fulfill their life's purpose as a root to nourish our appetites, just as the worms soon served their purpose to offer themselves up as a meal for the birds. Perhaps the worms were better remaining underground. Maybe breaking free from darkness will only result in death. Though it may be fulfilling for another, I was not going to let my death be in vain. I was also more than merely a worm. Out of all the grubs that give themselves to the birds, there is always one that gets away.

*****

My memory of the garden was washed away with the bitter taste of salt rushing into my mouth. My eyes clenched shut as I inhaled what seemed to be a gallon of water, forgetting my body needed air to breath. I gagged. My neck stretched up as high as I could get it until I tasted the dry air, and I spit up the contents of my throat.

I gasped for air, but the bag only seemed more suffocating than ever. I flexed my fingertips, feeling the sand around them become moist and loose. My neck twisted in a violent spasm. The water hit my face again, this time covering everything up to my forehead, I held my breath and closed my eyes in anticipation for the end. I waited for the waves to recede one last time, and I took one last breath. The ocean covered my entire head when it returned to me. Everything went quiet. The sounds of the waves transformed into the silent underbelly of a large body of water.

Time seemed to stop. All was still. Everything now seemed like nothing. If I were to die, I swear I would wake up in a cold sweat, thanking the gods it was only a dream. Was I crying again? It was impossible to tell. I just know this: I didn't want to die, not like this, not a foot or two under water. And finally, I knew I would not wake up from any dream. It was time to act and face whatever prey would feed off an earthbound worm.

The burlap bag must have floated off of my head as the tide overcame me because when I opened my eyes, all I saw was misty blue laced with crimson. I quickly shut them again as the salt began to burn them. I had to think fast. I had a limited supply of air in my lungs, I was inches under water and was still confined by the earth. My arms and legs retaliated with a vengeance. My jaw clenched as I inched my way upward, feeling the sand give away against my skin.

I remembered the earthworms in our garden surfacing after the rain. Crawling their way to the surface for a taste of fresh air, a taste of freedom. My shoulders broke free from the earth's embrace and sand cascaded down my arms. A couple more inches, my elbows broke free, then my hands as I pulled them toward the sky. I pushed myself up until I broke through the water's surface and was blinded by the mid-day sun; now I could see for the first time my surroundings. At this moment, I prayed to any god that might exist.

Buried in the sand around me, also inches under water, I could see at least seven heads. Three had no bags over their heads. Their eyes sang a silent requiem. Of those three, two of them suffered wounds that words could never describe. The remaining four heads were concealed by bags, but two no longer had bodies attached to them. The gore scattered before me had made me hack up chunks of scorpion and bile. My palms pushed down onto the ground, and the rest of my body broke free from the sand as I rose from my prison.

I hadn't looked out beyond the water at this point, I didn't care where I was and was triumphant to still be alive. I cried out joyous nonsense in celebration of my escape. Tears clouded my vision, but I scurried towards what seemed to be the shoreline.

I crawled on hands and knees away from the waves behind me. My energy was gone, and I fell flat on my face onto the warm, dry sand. Then something strange had happened.

Amidst the tormenting sounds of ocean waves and the birds calling out overhead came a calamity of screams which led to a roar of cheers and celebration. Crowds were chanting and making so much noise I felt reverberations throughout my entire body. I managed to sit up, resting all my weight on my right arm. I used my left arm to wipe away the remaining tears that had clouded my vision. To my regret, the sight which lay before me injected me with fear and pain as my assumption was proven correct. I remembered where I had been before I awoke buried in the sand. I remembered where I have been living for the past several years. As I was buried in the sand hours ago, I had denied myself the recent events of my past. The blow to the head I had suffered before they carried me away would not have helped my memory either.

I had hoped the last decade was just a dream, a nightmare. That being buried here was the climax of this epic dream, and I would wake up with my mother again in our cozy, tiny house. I imagined I would wake up to the smell of potatoes and cinnamon cooking over the fire pit again. I prayed I wouldn't wake up back inside the same jail cell I had spent nearly ten damned years in for robbing the street vendor of a single spud.

When I did finally awake, I was not in a prison cell but in the ground. I had a slight belief this was all a dream, to torture my consciousness as a result of the crimes I committed back when I was a street rat, but it was all actually happening. As I had said before, the punishment for crime was strict in Renhet. Also, when the cells overcrowded, the city couldn't just put the prisoners back onto the streets. Before me stood a massive grandstand of seats embedded into colosseum walls, forming a giant arch facing the beach. Each side of the colosseum wall met at the Ritco Sea. In those seats occupied the wealthy townspeople of Renhet. Their hatred for the wicked guided them here to watch people like myself die and suffer. They would place bets on who would survive the longest. I only knew vaguely of this event. Most prisoners refused to talk about it, knowing they could be next. An outsider like myself assumed they were crazed, which the guards always agreed upon.

A man came to speak on a high mezzanine. With his voice came the demand for attention and respect, for it was none other than Lord Hayward, ruler of Renhet. The townspeople's chaos diminished to silence as this distinguished man spoke to them all, before he turned his attention to me.

"People of this fair city, we pride ourselves on being a safe metropolis, a sin-free paradise." The ruler paused, then looked me dead in the eyes from his perch. "We cannot let any crime go unpunished. You all know this. One day a boy steals coin, the next day he murders for gold. It is all a cycle. These evil men and women were locked up before they could rid us of any of our lives. We live by this law so that we may continue to live fearless lives."

The crowd cheered in agreement.

The man continued. "This is why we take matters into our own hands here in our great city. We stop these sinners before they end the lives of our kinfolk. Unfortunately, the walls cannot contain all the evil we encounter! After nearly a decade this man and these corpses before you have served their time. But now as the younger spawn of sin moves into our prison walls, we have no room for such vermin such as this man. In hopes that they used their time of solitude wisely, and turned to the gods for repentance, let them be judged by them. This is why every year we host this gathering: The Last Execution. Ladies and Gentleman, collect your winnings, but this man must now die as well."

The crowd cheered once again. Children threw rotten fruit. Parents laughed and encouraged their younglings.

A vision of my mother blurred behind my closed eyes for just a moment. Where was she now? She was all I had. She was love. These families before me, they showed no love. Any love that was left in my heart was gone when I opened my eyes and saw in the corner of the colosseum a creature.

Now, only rage burned within my soul.

The spokesman raised his eyebrows, and with a crooked smile, he spoke. "Our honored guards, please release the filthy beast again, one last time today." He scowled at me. "Young sinner, I pray the gods receive your debt in the afterlife, for the time when you join them is soon."

Two Renhet guards held a hulking body confined by metallic chains. The creature's biceps bulged, thick hands grasped his mace, and his heavy boots kicked up dust and sand. The eyes were as red as I remember. The minotaur pulled violently on his manacles and thrust his massive head towards a guard. He roared ferociously and stomped all about, knocking over barrels and boxes. Five men flanked him and prodded him with spears and swords to reestablish control. They only angered him more. He was a prisoner as much as I was, and though he wanted to murder those who held him captive, he wouldn't hesitate to kill me as well. But that was all for the better, for I found the strength to stand as I charged toward him with no plan in my mind, only blind rage clouding my judgment.

I knew I wanted this beast dead for what his kind did to my mother, to my village. I picked up a broken blade next to a severed head and wielded it desperately. My feet pushed off the sand, my teeth clenched, this monster must die, if I didn't keel over first. I was only ten feet from the minotaur and screamed profanity which alerted a soldier to my left, who clubbed me with his hilt. The beast shouted in his native tongue and tore open his manacles with sheer force. He swung, and landed his mace on the face of one soldier. The blow bashed in all his features, leaving him dead and expressionless. Another soldier stabbed the minotaur in the thigh with his sword, but this only infuriated him more. He drew the sword out of his leg and pierced the soldier clean through the neck.

All soldiers attacked the minotaur and he deflected every blow they made. The beast bellowed in the common tongue, "My name is Rykar, once a mighty gladiator. You, foolish humans, have put a weapon in the wrong minotaur's hands!" he roared as he snapped the remaining chains.

Dual wielding the mace in his left hand and sword in his right, Rykar lay into the guards. One man thrust his sword clumsily at the minotaur, leaving himself open. Rykar quickly deflected the sword with its mace, then in a smooth motion sliced open the man's neck, leaving the guard stumbling backward clutching at his throat in a vain attempt to stop himself from drowning in his own blood. Rykar, despite the leg injury, deftly stepped out of the way of a spear thrust from another sentry, then brutally slashed the man deeply from ear to cheek bone, exposing his jaw bone and teeth. More guards in the grandstands drew their swords and charged at the beast. The audience fled in a panic.

Chaos was eminent, order was void. Rykar severed another man at his knees, leaving bloody stumps, and decapitated another. The sight before me was so grisly, I wanted to clench my eyes shut. I wished to run away from the beast, yet I still wanted to charge the monster and slay him at the same time. As I approached the bloodshed, I swallowed my vomit and crawled on my belly amongst the fight trying to find my way to the center where I could jab my serrated blade between his legs. As more men fell to their death amongst me, my consciousness returned, what little I had at that moment.

If I helped kill the beast, the soldiers would organize soon after, find me, and kill me. I may have had nothing to live for, and dying was probably in my near future, but I did not want to die on my hands and knees. I thought of my next best option.

I ran.

I simply got up and ran away from the fight without looking behind me. I expected to hear arrows whizzing past my head, but there were none. Nearly three hundred feet to the north sat the empty grandstands. On either side was the stone wall curving around into the sea. I sprinted over carcasses and scattered armory, almost tripping several times. I arrived at a massive black iron door, just to the east of the stands. It was unlocked, and I burst through. The hallway offered five doors, one of which led below ground to the holding quarters, three others were irrelevant, and the last door at the end opened to the streets of Renhet.

I stepped onto the cobblestone streets, cautious of city guards, but I had quickly assumed every armed man in the city was trying to take down the minotaur. I stopped for a moment, caught my breath, and sought out the best way to the docks. I headed west. I ran past shops selling beautiful furs and trinkets, I ran past the cobbler, from whom I once stole a simple pair of shoes to keep me warm during winter. I slipped around many corners, the sounds of the ensuing battle in the arena growing faint after time, and I stepped beyond the buildings of the city and into the docks and marketplace.

Business was bustling as if folk here had no ambition today to see the execution. The ignorant looks of each face also told me they had not yet caught word of the events that had taken place. Stands flooded the open grounds of the docks. Men and women shopped for fresh fish, juicy fruits, and green vegetables from the northern villages. I squeezed between people and prayed no one would recognize my prison attire. Then I came upon a familiar sight, as a table of potatoes and a man appeared to my left.

"Thank you, Finn," the customer complimented. "These will taste fantastic in our dodo stew later this evening."

"Ya be welcome there missy," Finn replied. I grabbed a dark hooded cloak from behind Finn's stand as I ran by the old bastard and drew it over my head to conceal my face. I quickly dodged around tables and stands until I heard no more of the old man's bartering. My feet came to a halt. Before me sat five cargo ships at the dock, all unguarded, all offering countless nooks to stow away and escape from this city forever.

My heart had leapt high into the air before it sank once more to the depths of the sea, for down on the last ship were slaves loading cargo. Five men and women were all chained by the ankles, passing boxes to one another. At the very end of the line was an aged lady. Beauty still danced on her face, but her once long brown hair was now turning gray and cut short. I still recognized my mother even after all this time.

I wanted so badly to hug her and tell her I was ok. I still could not comprehend that she was, in fact, alive and in Renhet! But the slave owners would put up a serious fight if I tried to free her, and I barely had the strength at all to go much further.

Across the marketplace, I saw raised spears and swords running through the crowds yelling. The guards had grouped together to find me. They were looking for me. I could not save my mother, but a part of my heart had returned in knowing she still lived. One day I would find her again, and we would be together. I took one last look at her. Her image embedded into my dreams from that day on, her face giving me hope to fight on another day.

I raced to a ship to my right, the furthest away from curious eyes. I boarded the wooden walkway onto the deck, eager to find cover before my location was compromised.

Around stacks of barrels, I overheard chatter coming closer. I darted the opposite way down a dark staircase into the underbelly of the ship. I stumbled over something scattered on the floor, it was too dark to see what it was, but I felt my way into a hidden corner and knelt down between what felt like shelving and wooden crates.

Figured. My newfound sanctuary was as dark and lonely as the grave I had so narrowly escaped not long ago.

"Last call for cargo," a man called out from above deck. "Last call, then we ship off to Mandra!" The boat rocked, and soon I could hear the waves crashing into the sides of the ship, almost as if they were coming from every direction.

I had no idea what lay in Mandra. I just knew that whatever adventure lay ahead would be more promising than what I'd endured. For the next five days, at least, I could stretch my arms.

Silent days and nights passed by. I fed off of turnips and apples from the crates around me. Soon I regained much of my energy. The crew remained above me, so I was still confined to this incredibly dark storage room. One day, at last, we docked. Orders were shouted from above, shoes scuffed above my head. Then the door atop the staircase opened.

"I'll be up momentarily, Vansal." A man descended the stairs. "I think I heard something down here."

Korik's Quest

By Aaron Wulf

728 AM Age of the Dracon-esti

Black robes wrapped around the mage as he held himself with one arm to keep warm from the night chill. Several men and a couple of dwarves sat before him on the moss-covered clifftop overlooking the ancient elven city of Mythalis. The men and dwarves awaited orders from their leader, but the mage was deep in meditation.

A large muscular man by the name of Strenbard was the first to stand, and he silently touched the mage on his shoulder.

"My friend, we have been patiently waiting, but our families do not have long before our town's curse overcomes them. We need action, what are you to do for us?"

The mage opened his weary eyes and blinked.

"I am still without my power, as you are all aware. However, this one last mission will recover an enchanted artifact which will restore my power to its full potential. As promised, I will free your homeland from its curse, and shower you and your families in gold so that you may never go broke again. Don't forget, I have a family as well, and I feel your pain. It won't be long now."

He sipped warm tea, as did a few others who were all anticipating the next step in their journey. Strenbard, on the other hand, was tired of the waiting game.

"I know we have a history between us, but you have changed dramatically since this journey began. You are not yourself. I know not what happened to you, so I cannot judge, but I have yet to see your newfound magic. So please, for the sake of our wives and children, have you been honest with us?"

A stout dwarf spoke up. "Strenbard! We know he would never lie to us. He is repaying his debt. We saved his life before he was Magi, did you forget? Now he has the power to save us and our homeland, and you accuse him of lying? You are truly daft."

"Our family's lives are at stake, Gunthar, and he has not proven himself worthy! We have spent five weeks traveling for a magical remedy." Strenbard waved his hands in the air. "And the curse has still not been lifted."

"You humans are always so hard pressing on those different from you!" Gunthar threw down his tea. "Remember when you underestimated me? You nearly died."

Strenbard grazed his fingers across a scar on his left cheek. "What of it."

Gunthar continued. "Or the other time when you believed that gnome stole your coin purse. He was returning it to you from a bandit, but you pierced his poor heart before he could explain."

Strenbard gritted his teeth. "History or not, he wears the black robes of evil." His stocky arm pointed to the mage.

"We all know that black does not inherently mean evil," Gunthar groaned.

"Perhaps," Strenbard combed his fingers through his hair, and gazed back down onto Mythalis. "But I don't trust a mage any more than I trust an orc."

"Silence, both of you." The mage spoke. He outstretched his arm toward Mythalis. "Have you heard the tale of Korik the Lion?"

"The orc? Bah!" Gunthar stomped in circles, mumbling to himself. "Not this tale again."

"No, I have never heard the name." Strenbard agreed with the other humans. "What is your point, mage?"

A smile crept onto the mage's shrouded face. "A beast so terrifying he couldn't possibly be capable of good, eh? Wrong! He still resides in the broken city, and is unlike any other orc you will meet. We are like one and the same, Korik and I. Underestimated, and surprisingly not like you would assume."

The humans and dwarves looked around puzzled.

"If an orc can show more compassion and integrity than the average human, you know damn well a mage can abide by any laws he sees fit. Korik did what no other orc could do, and needless to say, no one expected much from him, not even his tribe."

The mage turned to look upon the ruins of the once beautiful city. The people behind him were now curious about this Korik, and what made him such a unique orc. All humans despised orcs, as did dwarves. But a heroic tale of an orc? This one had to be good, everyone thought. The group was drained from their long journey, and soon enough, the mage's story relaxed them as they sat in silent fantasy hearing the story of Korik.

The mage itched his left shoulder, and shuddered as if recalling a horrible memory; those behind him knew the Mage trials were worse than anyone could imagine.

The mage collected his composure and began telling the story of Korik the Lion.

*****

"Mythalis used to be a grand city built together by elves and dwarves. When the sun once shined on the magnificent stonework and archways, it illuminated everything like a diamond. The faces sculpted into the stone seemed to come to life, some used to say. The radiance gave the sensation that the city walls held something much more beautiful than elves. Passersbye would stand for hours, wishing and hoping to enter into its heavenly gates.

Long ago the city was destroyed and long vacant of elves and dwarves. The upper level of the city is now home to orcs, goblins, lizardfolk, and occasional animals that wander into the mouth of Mythalis. Humans have never been inside the city and lived to tell about it.

Walls of earth and stone protruded hundreds of feet high and met with jagged rubble casting a shadow over the dark city. The ground level spread out over several miles, and each corner was occupied by one species or another. Giant torches lit the entrance way to the Kona's territory across marble floors. Anyone brave enough to enter this section was greeted with a grand arch, which was carved with elven writing and faces of leaders past.

Deep in the southwest corner of Mythalis, death was in the air. The chieftain of the Kona tribe had been on his deathbed and had no heir. So it was in the second week of his illness that he called together his best fighters, workers, and hunters to offer them a quest. Kartzar Skullsplitter was as honorable as an orc could be, for he understood it was better to be on good terms with the surrounding inhabitants of Mythalis than to be hostile; as was the other orc tribe, the Bloodfist Tribe. That's not to say they never stole from the surrounding inhabitants. He made a point to smile to their faces but stab them in the back, so to say.

Kartzar looked into the eyes of the strongest orcs in his tribe. The warmth in his own eyes showered compassion over the onlookers. He removed his blanket and attempted to sit upright to speak to those present.

He delivered to them a quest: Whoever finds and returns something of the greatest value for the tribe, shall be chieftain after his passing.

Kartzar's red eyes peered through the near darkness at the orcs before him. He picked a few boogers from his snout and inspected them for a bit as the rest of the tribe stood awkwardly awaiting his words.

"Ruthmuntz the Devourer, chosen," The Chieftain spoke very low, and often was interrupted by spurts of coughing. He continued to name off the chosen ones.

"Balthrakar Bloodspiller, you chosen. Krudkrubler the Thinker, chosen. Gnarthorb Lizardeater, chosen."

He named off several more orcs: Buuggug Fingersnapper, Vlorgnoth the Reader, Zinsbog the Cooker, Rogbut the Sharer, Yagnar the Ox, and

Karrdrognod Bonecrusher. Then he looked at the last orc standing close to his side.

The last orc was the tribe's best hunter, and he provided them all with the most bountiful of feasts. Kartzar worried though, that if this orc were to be chosen as Chieftain, no one could live up to his hunting skills. All the orcs were thinking the same thing, for Chieftains never left for a hunt. The last orc in line knew this too, but his chin was held high in confidence that he could, in fact, benefit the tribe even more with the status of Chieftain. Kartzar sighed as he worried about the future of his tribe.

"Korik the Hunter, you chosen."

Kartzar picked up a bowl of hot water and spices. Each chosen orc drank from it, as was the conduct of this ceremony. Each orc left the room with the frail Chieftain, and they all parted ways into the depths of Mythalis.

*****

Korik the Hunter stormed out of Kona territory and into the vast city. The streets had remained intact for the most part, though pillars fifty feet high lay broken on top of the now dull golden walls and archways. He had seen this beautiful elven and dwarven architecture many times on his raids against the other inhabitants. Most orcs never took notice to artistic endeavors. They simply loved to hunt, many loved to kill, some more inhumanely than others.

The hassle of armor was left behind. The orc dressed in dark green cloth and leather, covering only his torso, groin, and thighs. Korik thought that metal armor was too noisy to sneak around in, and opted for minimal protection for greater stealth. Two single-handed war axes hung by each hip. Both were fine silver, probably crafted by dwarves. Korik pulled them off an undead one time during a raid on the lower levels.

He stomped passed puddles of murky water on the stone streets, then arrived at a three-way split. His snout twitched, and he fell back into the shadows of a darkened doorway. Two lizardfolk walked past him. He thought to himself whether or not he should attack, but decided that it would give away his position, so he remained quiet and still. Then he heard swords being drawn.

"There he is!" One of the lizardfolk hissed in his native tongue.

The other unsheathed his sword and began running.

Korik's brow grew cross as he gritted his yellow teeth and stepped out of the shadows to face the enemy. To his surprise, they were running away from him and began to attack another Kona tribe member, Gnarthorb, who wielded a giant stone war hammer.

"Die!" He gargled.

Gnarthorb swung his hammer and pinned one of the lizards against a gold wall, caving his skull in. The other lizardman stuck him with his sword, but the orc lifted him by his scaly neck, and threw him effortlessly into the same wall, rendering him breathless. The orc pulled the sword back out of his flesh and licked the blade.

"Want?" He gestured to Korik, who grunted in disgust and walked toward him. "Lizard will pay. Lizard always pay. Make Chief happy."

"Make sick," Korik pushed the sword away from his face.

A metal clank echoed from the ground around the lizards. Both orcs looked at what had made the sound and saw a golden goblet with inscriptions etched into it. Gnarthorb dismissed the seemingly irrelevant object and belted out a loud battle cry as he ran off into the dim-lit city streets.

The cup lay nearly five feet away from Korik, and faintly gave him the feeling it was calling to him. His big clunky feet dragged toward the cup as his grimy hands picked it up. He inspected the insignias, rolling it back and forth between his fingers. Then he stopped and gasped. On one side was the face of a god, and around his profile was inscribed a phrase.

HERE EMBODIES THE ESSENCE OF TASAR: GOD OF THE LAND AND THE LIVING WHO INHABIT IT.

Korik understood very few written words in common speech, but this was inscribed in elvish. He had no chance at decoding it. The only word that stood out to him was *Tasar*, for it was the same in nearly every spoken language.

Many years ago, Korik was hunting above the city of Mythalis and was preparing an attack on a caravan of humans. As they lay out camp that night, he stalked them in the shadows and came across an old man who seemed to be talking to himself. He crept behind the tents to get a closer peek at this peculiar person and noticed he was speaking not to himself, but to the sky.

The man called out to the ancient deity Tasar for safety and good travels on their journey, and an object in his hands began to radiate. He shifted the object around in his hand and Korik could see it was a small metal disc with a warm face molded into it. Some form of esoteric energy released through-out the campsite that night, and left the orc feeling oddly at peace, which he had never felt or under-stood before. This strange event had resulted in him not attacking the caravan and spared many humans lives.

This night within the walls of Mythalis, as Kor-ik held the goblet, he felt the same energy pulsating through his monstrous body. It was a feeling he had long ago forgotten. An invisible force began to draw the orc out of the confined walls of the city as he walked onward, not knowing where the goblet would take him.

The streets became wider, and it was now much easier to make haste. Few torches illuminated the depths, but orcs are able to see very well in the dark, so much so that they rarely used torches. Only in infinite darkness did they have use for illumina-tion. As the earth above his head rose higher, the city walls were left behind him as a grand opening under the ground greeted him with terror. The natural walls and ground gradually sloped and spired downward into a dark abyss. This is usually where orcs and lizardfolk would stop their hunting and scavenging. Korik had been in the lower levels before, but this particular entrance always turned even the brave hunter away.

He looked behind him at the broken city and could see faint moving lights and heard the shouts of orcs and lizards as they battled one another. As far as he knew, his whole tribe was searching the upper levels of the city for an item to prove their worthiness to the chieftain. He highly doubted they would dare journey into the lower levels of Mythalis, where the undead roamed free. When an orc was confronted with two or three undead, killing them was simple enough. But when a single orc was faced with a horde of undead, and inside tight quarters, it proved much more challenging, especially when one hand had to hold a torch.

The last torch of this trail hung on the wall behind him. He backtracked to retrieve it and used its flame to study the goblet more precisely. The words seemed to glow by his touch. He murmured the few words he remembered from the old human chanting in the camp long ago. Then he headed down the path to the lower levels where the invisible force continued to lead him. Behind him, the shadows of Mythalis seemed to follow until he was out of sight.

The pathway grew narrow and damp, and then Korik found himself walking down an ancient set of stairs. The depths of Mythalis made it impossible for anyone to tell time, not that orcs had a need for time, but the journey down seemed it had taken hours.

The decline leveled out. The flickering flame revealed a giant golden doorway beyond the stairs, which smelt of rot and decaying flesh. The evil that lurked in the air made Korik's spine shiver. He grasped the handle of his axe with his right hand and held the torch outright with his left. He was standing in an elven tomb.

The room beyond the doorway was immense beyond compare, for the light from his torch and the orcish eyesight could not even see the top of the chamber as he stepped through. On either side, flying buttresses elegantly arched skyward toward second level mezzanines. The center of the chamber had what seemed to be a long and narrow pool of sorts, lacking the water.

As Korik walked across the indented path, he searched for any signs of movement in the darkness far above, anything that could be indications of the undead. Taps and scratches faintly echoed through the hall. The orc stood straight with courage, and raised his axe high in the air, taunting the evil.

Firelight began to illuminate the mezzanines above. Incoherent chatter and screams electrified the air. A cold rush of wind engulfed Korik. This was quickly followed by a wall of bodies cascading down from between the buttresses. Korik's eyes bulged, and his jaw dropped revealing his jagged fangs. The undead flooded around him in chaos as he hacked their heads clean off with his powerful swings.

Their lifeless eyes peered into his as they slashed at him with their swords and axes. The orc kept blocking the blows with his axe and torch. He then hunched down and plowed through the bodies with his broad shoulders, extending his arms and flailing them widely. Bodies fell all over following the orc's rage attack, and heads rolled. Korik looked up at the lighted mezzanine and saw that they kept coming down, filling the giant room. There were even grotesque creatures crawling down from the shadows of the seemingly endless walls, their white teeth gnashing. Korik kept plowing through the mob of undead creatures as his skin was slashed and torn. Then, an open doorway unveiled itself from the shadows. He pushed with all his might, ignoring the wounds being inflicted upon him, and ran through the door. Once inside, he slammed the door shut, and lowered a wooden beam attached to the door to brace it.

Beads of sweat raced down his green leathery skin. He tried to suppress his heavy breathing while devising a plan of escape after he claimed his goal.

The door before him was solid metal, silver by the looks of it, but it could have been another material. The wood brace and brackets had been newer additions, and lacked aging. These were fresh materials. No Orc or Lizardfolk could have done this, they would have no reason to venture down amongst the undead, and definitely no need for locks and braces.

Korik stepped back from the door as it shook and rattled, the screams and groans on the other side seemed as if they were never going to cease. He tried to ignore it, he turned around to inspect the room he had just entered.

There was a table. On it was food that orcs would never eat, and it was all rather fresh, just as the door brace. Candles and maps were scattered about. Behind the table on the far side of the room were a pile of blankets and other fabrics. Besides the latter, the rest of the room was nothing but empty bookshelves and empty crates, all rather dusty.

The goblet now hung from Korik's waistline from a strand of cloth, but its power still pulled him through the mysterious room and into a long cavernous corridor going both left and right, countless doors and passageways throughout. One passageway led out of the elven-built walkway and into a naturally made cave system. The way was concealed by fallen stonework, but Korik knew something had to be behind it. He smashed through it with his axe until a new moist air arose from the opening.

Korik's orc sight was now in better use down in the labyrinth of tunnels. The only view of life was mushrooms which illuminated a soft glow that would be almost unnoticeable to any other eye. The cave walls started to become sticky, as did the ground Korik walked on. After a few moments, spider webs occupied everything. The path widened and ended in a reservoir of sorts where five more tunnels met in the room. In the center lay a hole no more than ten feet wide, blanketed in a silky spider web.

That same old feeling told Korik to head down a passageway to his right, but noises from below disarrayed his attention. Korik's small ears could still hear faint sounds, and he swore he heard human words being spoken in pain. Shivers crawled up Korik's skin, but he shook them off. A true leader would not leave anyone without a chance to fight their way out. Whether it be friend or foe who lay beneath, he felt he must investigate.

The middle of the reservoir was concave as if something recently fell through. The dome shape of the room echoed every footstep Korik made, and he wished it would not attract any unwanted guests.

There were still enough glowing mushrooms in the chamber to see by, as it seemed there were on the lower level. He set down his torch and dropped his beastly body down into the hole.

The drop was about twelve feet down, not far for an orc. Orcs were not frightened by much, but what he saw on this level left his mouth agape. Large sacks of white silk hung from the cave ceilings. Korik cautiously slipped between them, and stopped to study one. There was a distant face beyond the silk, a man who had long ago drawn his last breath, had suffocated inside a spider's web.

The spiders that inhabited Mythalis's lower levels coated the entire circumference of these passages with their webs. The webs were so sticky that even a fallen orc would have trouble getting back up before being eaten by the eight-legged beast. Korik knew this too. He heard the words spoken again, this time much more urgent and loud. He ran past mummified carcasses toward the voice and halted right before a dark webbed tunnel.

Eight red eyes were no more than ten feet away inside the darkness, and they seemed to glare right into Korik's. The spider's legs twitched in anticipation for Korik's move. Korik put his hands on both his axes, but didn't want to attack for risk of the spider attacking the conscious man, half woven beside the spider.

"Are you going to free me, orc? Or are you just going to stand there like a statue and watch me get turned into a spool of silk?"

The man seemed rather calm for being halfway tied up in spider web. His cocky attitude proved him to be too optimistic for any deadly situation, however.

"If you're planning on killing me as well," the man continued, "I'd say, do it quick. This spider has been chasing me around the tunnels for the better part of the day, and I doubt she would like it very much if a dirty orc claimed her kill. Come on now, when will you-"

Korik's axe cut through the strand of web holding the sac to the ceiling. The man crashed down onto his chest, still confined by the web, his forehead smacking hard onto the cave floor.

"Son of a bitch!"

But Korik bravely ran up to the sack and jumped off of it, compressing the man's chest which made him wheeze, and the orc leapt onto the spider's back and began to chop at its eyes with his second axe.

The creature flailed wildly into the wall, staggering with each blow to her face. Sharp shrills rang out as the spider was being butchered, but with the last blow she reared forward, Korik flew off and fell onto his back right on the spider's web. Her fang's dripped venom, and she staggered towards Korik as he struggled to get up, but the silk proved too strong.

"Run! She's going to attack!" The human wriggled around on the ground, his forehead bleeding from the fall.

Korik searched for his axe, but couldn't find it after he got thrown off the spider. She was getting closer and her two furry fangs thirsted for fresh blood.

"Roll over," Korik commanded to the man, who had a difficult time understanding his dialect.

"Wha-what good would that do, beast? We need a real plan here; this is becoming absurd." The man continued to struggle to get out of his own entrapment.

The spider was now only a few feet away from Korik.

"Do it!" Korik shouted.

The man grunted, "Fine, let's do things the orc's way, humans always turn out fine and dandy."

He tried to roll over on his side to Korik's request, but the webbing fastened him tight to the ground as well.

"Well, I see the orc's plan didn't work, shall we try mine now?" The human taunted.

Korik had never been this fearful or this vulnerable in his life. His thoughts were jumbled, and half of his ideas were not at all convenient. He had run out of plans for escape, and he remembered the tribe, alone, without Korik the Hunter to provide them with enough food. He wished he had never come down this far.

The spider inched forward, then sprang in an angry attack. Both the man and Korik braced for an inevitable kill, but instead a giant insectivore penetrated the tunnel like a flash flood and pummeled into the spider. This giant insect moved like liquid, was flatter than a centipede, and had many legs too close together.

The spiderpede swooped in and wrapped its many legs around one of the spider's legs, and sunk its two venomous pincers in between the spider's joints. The spider hissed in pain and tried ramming the spiderpede against the wall. The spiderpede eluded her as it fluidly crawled underneath and repeated the same procedure on the spider's other leg, this time severing it in half.

The battle of the giant cave insects continued behind Korik's head. The Spiderpede's rear flailed like a pendulum above the orc's head as he desperately tried to grab hold. Finally, the rear end dropped close enough to Korik's hands as the creature continued to sever the spider's legs, and he clasped tight as it pulled him from the webbing.

"Ha!" Korik shouted as he departed from the fight. "Come." He grabbed the sack the man was in and pulled it behind him as he ran the way the spiderpede had come from, holding onto his goblet tight around his waist. "This way, I feel."

Korik was being pulled again, but this time the pull was stronger than before, and he felt that he was closer to the object he sought out for. But after running, and pulling the man, for near what seemed like a mile, no more spider webs were around them, and the sounds of the battle were long gone. Korik slowed and walked over to a rock to rest.

"Ok, so can you cut me free now?" Asked the man, rather annoyed.

Korik stared blankly into space for a moment, then looked at the man, studying him.

"What I use? No blade," Korik gestured to his bare hips where he had carried his axes before he lost them back in the tunnels.

"Well great, that's just fantastic, I'll just lay down here and die while you run and go get help," the man said.

Korik's eyes narrowed. "How you down here?" He grumbled.

"Look, I'm a cobbler by trade. I have a family at home and just want to get back to them." He sighed and rested his head finally. "We were all out in the forest, my daughters and I. Spring is a difficult time to sell shoes, you see. So we were picking tangleberries for springtime harvest, as we do every year, when my eldest daughter went missing. We searched for her until dusk, and got lost ourselves. Soon, the entire forest began to crawl, and that's when the spider attacked me and brought me down here for his food. Then you came along and rescued me, thank you. I suppose I was being a bit over-dramatic. It's just I was afraid of being eaten, and the sight of you was not less intimidating, forgive me. My name is Basoul. Are you going to take me to the surface? Are you looking for something? What are you doing down here anyway?"

"Talk too much," Korik snorted.

The whole time Basoul spent ranting, he had failed to notice that Korik had picked up a loose stone that was rather sharp.

"Let try," Korik sauntered over to Basoul and started cutting away at the silk with the jagged rock, but it just wasn't sharp enough. "Kroumflaug!" He cursed.

Basoul relaxed after his initial excitement. "Anyway, as I was saying, you should probably take me with you wherever it is you're going, I would like to think it's better to travel in pairs. We just need to find weapons. Oh! We can search the-"

Basoul's voice trailed off as Korik's attention was drawn to the goblet which had been leading him thus far. It was glowing pale red but was surprisingly cool to the touch even though heat radiated from it. This shocked the orc who unhooked the goblet and threw it to the floor in bewilderment. Basoul ceased to talk as he looked confused at the goblet, glowing like embers.

"Burns," Korik spoke thoughtfully. "No pain."

"No pain?" Basoul retaliated. "Bring that cursed cup over this way!"

But Korik was already halfway there, and placed the goblet on top of the webbed sack, which began to melt away the thread.

"That's amazing!" Basoul began to push the webbing onto the ground. "Where ever did you find that?"

Basoul's clothes were ordinary civilian clothes, ragged and worn, but his boots were brand new. They were made of dark leather with black straps and buckles from the ankle and disappeared underneath his pants. His waistline carried a dagger and many pouches, all of which looked full.

Korik stood up and stretched his massive arms. "Close."

"Wait!" Basoul ran after Korik as he stomped through the cave amidst the faintly glowing mushrooms and stalactites and stalagmites. "I can be of help to you, with whatever you are looking for, in exchange for an escape from this dismal underworld."

Korik shifted toward Basoul and put his hands on his shoulders, rather roughly too. Basoul started and bit his tongue in fear of the orc's apparent aggression. But Korik did not attack, he stared at him with pleading eyes.

"Human stay, forever, Mythalis. This, not world under. World under, eyes, wicked, black."

His aged green hands trembled; he was trying to relay something important, Basoul knew this. The orc's speech was so broken that the human could not put the puzzle pieces together. Korik's eyes were warm, sincere, but pleading, which Basoul had never experienced in an orc before.

"Come."

Basoul followed Korik's request, and followed close behind him through the tight dark quarters of the cave system deep beneath Mythalis.

*****

Korik had been following the pull of the goblet for many hours now inside the tunnels of Mythalis and only coming across mushrooms, small rock formations, and the occasional bat. Basoul trusted this orc without doubting his lead. Orcs and humans rarely ever got along. Orcs raided from human villages, and humans killed and slaughtered orcs. Korik had no need to keep Basoul alive, and Basoul knew this. He also knew Basoul had no chance at reaching the land above without his help, and he had to build his trust.

Basoul was getting hungry, so he reached inside one of his pouches and pulled out a couple slices of bread.

"Want some? I'm not too sure what orcs eat, but it's all I have other than tangleberries. I wouldn't advise the berries though, they can have a nasty effect on those who are not acquired to them." He began chomping on the stale bread, his mouth open wide and chucks of bread danced from cheek to cheek. "Honestly, it's not as bad as it looks." He held out the bread to Korik.

He casually accepted the bread and popped it into his mouth and swallowed it whole without chewing. He didn't make eye contact with Basoul at first. Basoul felt a little offended, but soon after, Korik glanced over at him.

"Thank."

His chunky palm swung around Basoul and smacked him on the back. Basoul assumed this was an attempt at a friendly human gesture, and he laughed silently to himself.

Korik too felt the awkward silence. The bread was not enough to satisfy him, and he was also getting hungry. Hungry for meat. Basoul would make an excellent meal, and any of the orcs from the Bloodfist tribe wouldn't hesitate to dig into his warm flesh. Most of the Kona tribe fed upon animals, and only fed on intellectual beings when other food was scarce. Korik wasn't near starvation, and felt the man's sympathy for his lost family.

Orcs had no real family; though they were all somewhat considered family if they were in the same tribe, they mated with whom they wished. The children were then raised by the mother only.

When Korik raided the nearby villages above ground, he seemed to be the only of his tribe to really observe the humans. As the homes illuminated with the soft glow of light in the late evening, he would peer through the windows at the families inside. Adults would prepare the children for bed, and kiss them goodnight. The man would place his hands on the woman's soft, elegant shoulders and kiss her lips. The passionate energy would sift through the walls of the house and warmed his heart.

The rest of his tribe all noticed this, but did not question the massive orc. He was named Korik the Hunter, and as the name proves, there was no better hunter in their tribe than him. He always collected the highest bounty of goats, sheep, dogs, and other animals to bring home in their corner of Mythalis.

One night several years ago, as the Kona tribe was raiding a village they frequented, all was not silent. Korik was peering into houses as he always had done, but was in a hypnotic daze. He was not aware of his surroundings this night, and human guards snuck past him without his notice. These men, in result of not being found by Korik, snuck up on other orcs and began to attack without warning. Yells and roars erupted, clanging steel and shattering glass broke the silence. Korik had failed his tribe.

That night, they lost over half of their tribe in the attack. Korik was held responsible, and was punished by ten nights of brutal beatings. the Kona now rarely ventured out of Mythalis. That event shook fear into the beasts, which was not normal for southern orcs. By order of the Chieftain, however, no orc must leave Mythalis unless absolutely necessary.

Korik tried his best to explain his story to Basoul. There were many human words that orcs did not know, or have terms for, but Basoul understood. He felt emotion for the orc. Korik then explained his tribe's chieftain was on his deathbed, and told of his mission to find a valuable object for the tribe to display his worthiness of the chieftain.

Basoul believed he understood. He understood the redemption that this could bring for him after the deaths in the village. Basoul bit his tongue in shame when he almost brought up his wife and children. His hand rested on one of his waistline pouches.

"Here," Korik whispered.

The cave walls opened up into a massive cathedral-like room. Elves had built the structure, with tall, slender pillars lining the far walls, and carved stone blocks set into the floor. A circular formation of stone lay in the center, and inside of that was fresh dirt and a tree, no more than twelve feet in height. The tree was very alive and emitted light. The tree itself was not bright, but the air around it somehow was. There were no light sources anywhere on the walls or ceiling.

"Magic," Basoul gasped. "Never before have I seen such beauty in a place so void of joy. What do you make of this, Korik?"

Inside the circle with the tree was a stone with a flat top and indented center. On the side was the inscription:

The goblet of life will overflow with the wonders of this world, and all will return to the call of Tasar.

Basoul read the script to Korik, who closed his eyes for a few moments, and with a deep sigh of release, he delicately placed the goblet on the stone. Basoul fidgeted with excitement.

"What happens now? What does this mean?"

"Not end, look."

Korik pointed beyond the tree. The room curved to the right, and something around the corner also emitted a soft glow, this time of flame. Shadows danced on the walls, inviting them in. Basoul gestured a shrug to Korik who did not haste to proceed. He rounded the corner, and as he stopped dead in his tracks, a look of joyous horror plastered his face. His eyes dripped harmonious tears of love and fear, and he fell to his knees. Basoul cautiously passed the tree, unsure whether or not to go further, and was confused by Korik's conflicting reactions.

"Are you quite sure that you're an orc? I mean, I've seen my fair share of orcs in my day, and none have behaved such as yourself. You haven't been eating too many tangleberries, have you? Are you burning something? I smell fire. No, wait, brimstone. Why is it getting darker? Why are you looking at me like that?"

All light faded. If it was possible for a shadow to be cast in a dark room, then a new moon at midnight would never find its way to a waxing crescent again. The air grew thick and swelled Korik's and Basoul's lungs with what felt like shards of glass. The growl began low as it rumbled across the floor, shaking up loose stone and tempting the leaves to fall from the tree. Then the sound rose from the depths of the underworld, as it seemed, and now sounded like a thousand hornets returning home. If hornets had fiery red eyes, they were gradually getting closer to the duo. The ground boomed with each step, knocking the goblet off the stone, and was accompanied with the slow drip of some kind of liquid, and it sounded heavy as each drop plunged into stone.

Basoul held an amateur battle stance and unsheathed his dagger. He felt disoriented, the only sense of direction he had was when he stared up into the flying red dots. As the darkness crept closer, Basoul felt hot air flow down onto his trembling body. He could sense a gigantic mass before him, it was not only darkness, but something much worse.

"Korik, I could really use some help right about now. Where are you?"

Korik moved as one with the darkness. He could see what the man could not, though not much more. Surrounded by the black, the goblet called to him still. He saw it to the right of Basoul, glowing brightly as the long forgotten stars, but it seemed, only to him. He moved so that he stayed out of sight from the red. He crouched as he circled the tree, Basoul still blindly held his dagger, hoping it would do him well. Korik put the tree directly between himself and the eyes, and was now close enough to whisper to Basoul.

"Coal no hide in black. Coal is black. Coal burn. Light kills black."

Basoul swallowed his courage. His throat closed in that it was hard to breathe. His teeth bit one another, his eyes swelled, and he dropped the dagger from his tense forearm. The blade clinked as it resonated like the birth of sound in a land void of life. The large mass roared so loud the room shook, but this time the energy remained constant, and shook even Basoul and Korik off their feet.

"Run!" Korik shouted above the ear-piercing cacophony. He caught his footing and stretched out for the goblet, and regained ownership of it once more. He planted his foot firmly on the raised stone around the tree, and outstretched the goblet toward the red eyes. The eyes fumed when they redirected their attention to Korik, and the goblet exploded with light as the room could once more be seen again, as well as the monstrosity of horror that towered above them both.

"Tasar help us," Basoul choked, still on his hands and knees.

It stood a whole foot taller than Korik. Underneath the black plate mail armor, it had no skin, only solid stone. Its head was covered by a double horned helm, and only his eyes shown through which had the stare of a demon. Its body was like a walking mountain, and his rage was that of an avalanche. In both its hands, it clutched a giant iron spiked mace, which the sight of it doomed any weak man to tears in fearful fantasy of it bashing into his flesh with pounding unimaginable pain.

"Stone golem."

Long ago, when Mythalis thrived, an elven mage had animated the golem to guard the many treasures, both rich in value and magic. For centuries the stone monster obeyed the commands of its master, and for centuries the treasure had remained untouched by greedy hands. Now, the master was long dead, and no living being could reverse the commands given to the stone golem. The only force that survived now was the hateful eagerness to kill any threat that sought out the elven treasure.

"Basoul! Move!" Korik yelled, but all Basoul could hear was a deafening silence penetrating his mind. He was frozen in horror, and the golem lifted his mace and viciously swung it down at Basoul's cowering body. Time froze for Basoul, his life flashed before his eyes. There were no pictures of his dear wife, and lovely children; he only saw hatred, fear, lust, greed, and death.

The mace reverberated when it hit the goblet Korik held valiantly in his hand. The force enraged the golem. The branches on the tree shook, leaves fell to the ground, but Korik stood unshaken. The golem roared and attacked Korik with a blow to his side. Korik whipped across the room like a child's doll from the unexpected blow and cracked a pillar with his impact. The goblet whirled away.

When an orc is in battle, they feel no pain, only adrenaline. His mouth curled and eyes clenched when he stood up. He closed his fists and ran to the golem who was now interested in Basoul. Korik jumped onto his back and slammed his fists into the sides of his helm. He continued his attack as the golem tossed his arm back to grab Korik. The monster peeled the orc off his back and slammed him into the ground with a stone-shattering crack.

The golem swung his mace at Korik. Korik ducked under the iron weapon but was not ready for the second swing, as it crushed into his ribs, breaking bone. Within the rage, Korik did not feel the pain in his side, although he knew he had broken something. He sought to destroy this monster before it could harm Basoul. The two continued to duel Korik swiftly dodged the mace many times, but could not counter the attack. He knew this could not go on. He had to develop a new plan of attack.

The golem seemed to have forgotten all about Basoul. He was laying too still to bring attention to himself. The golem just wanted Korik dead. But Korik was much more enduring than the golem had anticipated, if the monster was capable of mentally anticipating anything at all, which was unlikely. Because after he had passed Basoul, he was hit in the helm with a tiny object only small enough to coin a puny *tink*.

The monster stopped in confusion and turned to face Basoul. He was standing, with a slingshot in one hand, and a bunch of berries in the other. His pouches were open and much emptier than they had been earlier. When the berry made impact, it smashed against the armor and created a bit of smoke which had a stench that could kill a troll.

"Can you handle my berries?"

Korik's face looked like he had just seen a jester toss flowers at an enraged dragon about to engulf him in flames. Basoul didn't miss a beat. He kept shooting little blue berries at the monster who now walked towards him, unfazed. When he was close enough, Basoul started shooting the berries inside the helm where his eyes were, hoping to impact his face. Four, five, six fell inside as light smoke erupted from the openings in his helm. Basoul laughed in amusement.

Basoul appeared to be an idiot. To think his poisonous berries could alter a golem's state of mind, how juvenile to think such a thing. This was Korik's first impressions of the human, until he saw Basoul give a slight nod toward the glowing goblet on the ground. Then the orc remembered the spider webs. How the power of the gods had flown through him and into the goblet. The pull was drawing Korik back to the cup.

He grabbed his ribs as the pain began to resonate into his nerves, but ran back to the goblet of

Tasar. With the glowing cup raised high, he roared with victory as the stone giant turned to face him. The mace began to rise into the air, but it was too late. Korik the Hunter was already charging and penetrated the armor with his artifact.

"Tasar," Korik spoke to an unseen being. "Help Korik set fire. Make dark light. Break evil."

The power of the goblet tensed the golem's entire body as the orc pushed with all his might. The more he pushed, the goblet melted into the monster's armor and into stone.

"MAKE. THIS. GOOD."

Korik dripped with sweat and his muscles began to ache.

"BREAK. THE. EVIL. AT. HAND."

Basoul couldn't believe he had heard the most complex sentence this orc had ever spoken.

With one last effort to push the goblet into the monster, it was engulfed by an explosion of light and vanished into the golem's chest. The chest plate crashed onto the ground, and Korik and Basoul stopped for a moment and stared at the monster's chest. Embedded inside was the circular base of the cup. The golem stopped moving. Only for a moment.

Both Korik and Basoul stood right before the statue in amazement at the magic at work.

"Incredible," Basoul stammered.

But Korik knew this wasn't over yet, a feeling of uneasiness drew him back a couple steps. The golem's eyes still glowed red, and the amber aura of the goblet was still slowly expanding across the stone chest.

The stone golem broke from his stance and attacked. The mace fell and ripped into Basoul's left shoulder and tore his arm from his shoulder. His arm fell to the ground, the weight of it hit like steel. Korik had never heard shrieks like the ones he heard this night. The man cried out in agony, holding his shoulder, writhing in pain. Blood and gore seeped from the open wound on both his shoulder and dismembered limb. Korik's glare narrowed on the golem, and he charged at him in full blown rage. Then Korik heard a voice:

Come, follower of Tasar. You have done well on this night. The evil you have been dealt is now detached from this world, but only for the time. Come and claim your right as Chieftain.

It was a baritone voice coming from every direction, but no one seemed to hear it but Korik. He looked at the goblet. Its fury danced through the entire being of the stone golem. The ground rumbled, the earth shook, and an explosion of light came from the goblet which forced Korik back in the air and onto the ground.

Then silence fell.

Particles of light skipped in the air, and Korik felt peace within himself. Metal armor and fragments of a former stone body lay scattered on the ground. No goblet was found.

Basoul's cries had erupted again. Korik ran past the tree and grabbed a torch that had blown out during the explosion, and used the end to cauterize the bleeding stub on Basoul's left shoulder.

"Wait here," he told Basoul, who lay still, but seemed barely conscious. Korik looked at him with kind eyes. He held out his hand but stopped inches from his hair. He then jerked his hand back and turned away from him.

Korik made his way to the end of the room where the wall curved right towards a glistening glow. Embedded in the rock of the earth was a double door crafted from pure gold. It stood about eight feet high and was one of the most beautiful things Korik had ever seen. The faces of the doors had golden branches twisting all about with silver serpents with diamond eyes.

Each door mirrored the other. The outsides were occupied by the trunk of the tree, and as the branches slithered their way to the top, they met together and rested underneath a magnificent golden sun.

Korik hesitantly placed his palms on the doors and parted the sun. The room opened up before him with glistening silver and gold artifacts rising up the walls. The floor seemed as fine as dirt, and the ceiling rose a good thirty feet high. A stone statue of Tasar was in the back of the room sitting upon a golden throne.

Korik felt peace all around him. The room seemed untouched for many hundreds of years, and there was not even dust that had fallen; all was unnaturally clean.

The statue began to glow, and its features animated before Korik's eyes. The statue stood up! It was another stone golem, yet this one wore a friendly face. He grumbled and stretched his arms as the sound of stone cracked and snapped. His voice was low and godly.

"You are no elf kind. What draws you here into the Hall of the Forefathers? Never have I seen another being other than an elf in this room."

"I seek," Korik paused, still in magnificent awe. "Tasar?"

The golem looked down at Korik's body, all bruised and broken.

"I am afraid not. Before my body died many years ago, I had been a cleric of Tasar. Now I serve him in the afterlife. His power still lives in this room. My name was Falthrough in my past life, my dear Korik. Tasar looks down upon you with loving eyes."

Korik pondered at how Falthrough knew his name.

"Don't know why here," Korik stammered.

Falthrough stretched out his arms. "Tasar has been guiding you in your life. He has been protecting you while you serve your tribe. You are not like the other Kona, but that is exactly what they need in a Chieftain. You will not understand now, but for the first time in decades, humans will begin to enter the forgotten city of Mythalis. Many will enter for selfish reasons, and they will fail; few will come for the good of Draston, and you must serve them well, my dear Korik. Tasar grants you his blessing and wisdom. Take this and return to your tribe. They await you." He reached around his neck and took off an amulet of radiant white gold. The medallion hung heavy, and in the center sat an emerald stone.

Korik grasped it, and his hand dropped, surprised by its weight. Energy surged through his body, and he began to cry uncontrollably.

"There are few good hearts in this age who can withstand the love of our gods. You, my dear Korik, have the opportunity to be the first cleric of orckind in Draston, but Tasar wishes you prove to him you have the power of good within you. Lead your tribe and grow your numbers. Harm no one but those who seek harm upon you. Take nothing that is not yours by right. Help a companion in need. And if you continue this path, Tasar will continue to work through you."

Falthrough sat back in his chair, and his face grew expressionless once more.

Korik then remembered Basoul and returned to his aid. The golden double doors magically closed behind him. Basoul was unconscious, so Korik heaved him on his shoulders and ran.

*****

Above ground, Korik placed Basoul on the dirt right outside the city. Korik fumbled with the amulet and clenched his eyes shut.

"Help. Tasar, help."

Nothing happened for several minutes. Korik had wrapped up the stump where Basoul's arm had once been before exiting Mythalis. Korik asked for

Tasar's help once again, and this time, he heard a voice drift softly across his pointy ears.

Just once. Just once. The voice repeated. *Now go, prove your worthiness.*

Korik sat for hours with Basoul until his breathing returned to normal. He looked underneath the bandages and saw the wound had completely closed up! Korik's chest shivered. Then voices were heard around the tall rocks and hills. People were coming this way! Korik knew Basoul would be safe, or at least kept alive above ground. He left him to be found, and took the amulet back down into Mythalis to return to his tribe.

After Korik had descended, three figures walked around large boulders and gasped at the sight of a man lying on the ground.

"Strenbard! Get your arse over here. Looks like we found more trouble." A dwarf grumbled.

A human walked behind him. Strenbard corrected the dwarf. "You mean we found him before trouble did. When will you ever be positive, Gunthar?"

Gunthar sighed and dropped a bag he was carrying. "Fine, but we need to get out of here before trouble finds us all, this is no place to be at this time of night."

"This is no place to be at all." A second human stated as he crossed his arms.

The two humans and dwarf lifted Basoul onto Strenbard's back, and they walked away into the darkness."

*****

"What in the name of the gods are you telling us!" Strenbard shot up and towered over the mage.

The mage's eyes kept looking over the clifftop at Mythalis.

"What I saw down there that night, made me aware of an ancient power I always thought was only in children's tales." He stood up and turned to those staring at him. "Imagine where I can lead you with that power! I've seen the treasures and their magical properties. We can all go there and take as much as we can!

The mage dropped his robes and revealed a stump where his arm should be. Basoul looked at them all dubiously, waiting for a response. One of the humans stood up along with Strenbard.

"You have been promising us great power, fantastic treasures and freedom from our lands. Never had you actually showed us any such magic; it's always another excuse. Now tell us, are you truly a mage?"

Basoul stammered in embarrassment, "Y-yes of course. I am, damn you. I have told you, my power was drained by dark magic, and only an enchanted artifact can restore that which was taken!" He grew red in the face and glowered at the unconvinced looks.

Strenbard's face turned red. "We have put our trust in you that you will lead us to great riches, and here you sit diverting your time telling us child's tales! Mark my words, if you are a simple mortal man such as we are, then we have no use for you and you should be thrown from this cliff top. Now," he paused for a moment. Strenbard stroked his chin. "Jump."

"What?" Basoul trembled.

"I said, jump," Strenbard held steady. "If you are of magic, then prove it to us; otherwise, we will have no need for you."

Many men got up with anger in their eyes, the promise of freedom now breaking. They wanted Basoul's head for leading them so far from their village to die. Their woman and children now waiting at home for news of a new homeland and new wealth. Now the men felt that future slipping away.

If this man was not capable of the feats he had claimed, they would surely see him murdered.

"Fine, you have said nothing, which is more than enough." Strenbard grasped Basoul's wrist so hard he felt his hand pulse faster. "Men, throw him over and see if he flies."

"No!" Basoul sobbed. "Please! You're making a mistake! Stop!"

But Basoul's cries for help would not save him. Four men hoisted him up. Gunthar turned away with his hand over his brow. As the men neared the edge, Basoul looked down to his death, but had one last idea. He screamed loud enough for the gods to hear him.

"I know a mage! One so powerful, yet so wicked, she can still give you your freedom!"

The men looked questionably at Strenbard, who nodded to them to set him down.

"You better explain yourself."

"Yes, I know a mage, but only I can show you where she is."

"You mean to tell us you bloody lied to us?" A man spat.

Y-well no, I mean, yes," Basoul slumped in sorrow. "I have no wife, no children, and no family. I am not a mage."

Murmurs moved through the crowd, most of which were "I told you so's," or "this bastard is gonna pay." The men were desperate, they needed salvation for themselves and their families. Gunthar faced his friend, maybe enemy now, but spoke in hopes to reason with him.

"Lad, why go to all this trouble? Telling us story after story, and only to sell yourself out at the end. We dwarves know that no man has ever gone into Mythalis and lived to tell the tale-"

"But that was true!" Basoul interrupted. "Korik is real, I can sh-"

"They'll be no need for showing. We are all desperate."

The dwarf spoke in odd compassion, the likes of which Strenbard has never seen in his comrade. Every human still held hate in their face, but Gunthar remained calm.

"What did you lie about?"

Basoul wheezed between coughs. His tears were flowing like a child. His shame hung over his head. "Everything."

Everyone was quiet, all but Basoul.

"Everything but the story of Korik, that much is true. I wanted to make a name for myself but had no skills other than scheming others. I sought out the wealthy in many cities throughout Draston. I've seen many great things and learned much. I was soon hired as a mercenary spy for the militia. I had worked with humans, goblins, elves, dwarves, you name it. I had all the gold I wanted, but one night as I slept in an inn, a group of orcs struck. Nasty beasts they were too. They set fire to my building, I ran, and everything I had was lost. I wanted re- venge, so I began to spy on them. It took several months to find a way to get inside for more than a few hours without being killed, but I was skilled. They did not have much, but one orc, in particular, caught my attention. So I became entranced by him; he wasn't like the rest. And then I followed him! That is where I found a great treasure! It had a room of pure gold. Millions of jewels and diamonds lined the walls. It can all be ours. I know the way, I can show you!"

The men still glared at him, annoyed with his antics. Basoul's eye's darted back and forth. He then hung his head again after his excitement wore down. He sighed.

"Okay. I wanted to take a group with me to retrieve the gold, and–" He paused for a very long time. "And, make off with the lot of it while you rested."

A strange thing happened. No yelling or curs- ing broke the silence. All men pondered their own desires and dreams. Much of them would do the same in his situation.

Gunthar walked to Basoul's side. His dirty hand rested on his back as trying to calm the man down.

"I may not know much about magic, mages, or orcs even. But I have seen many treasures from when the Daignar lived down there." He gestured down towards Mythalis. "Gold has only one power that I have seen; the power for humans to have power over other humans, and that doesn't even need magic. Besides, even if you make it in, you will never return again. It's a death trap, lad. Only by the kindness of that orc did you get set free. My kind was long ago defeated and chased out of Mythalis. Believe me, I would want nothing more but to return home and kill every one of those bloody orcs, but it's useless. Besides, it's been many years since we found you wounded at the entrance of Mythalis. Owe only knows what evil lurks down there in this day and age, or even if Korik still lives."

"The dwarf is right," Strenbard admitted. "If you still want to live, you better begin talking about this mage you know. Our homelands can only survive if the curse is lifted. For that, we need a powerful magician, as well and the funds to build our home back to the great place it once had been. You take us to your mage friend, and we'll spare your life, as long as we never have to see your ugly amputated wretched self again."

Basoul turned red but held his fury. "This one will not go easy. You will need to use brute force with her, and be ever so careful when convincing her to help. She has an attitude you do not want to tempt with. But, we may have a chance; she owes me a favor."

"Well?" Strenbard was impatient. "What is this woman's name?"

Basoul pondered on this decision. He knew that she would not help these men. She was better than that. He also had no previous relation to her, and in turn, she did not owe him a favor. But Basoul was a man of quick wit and devious lies. He wanted to remain alive, and improve when necessary.

He recalled hearing of the magic-user in songs and stories throughout the cities he had visited. He decided to tell one more lie, for the sake of his own worthless life. His lips parted, and out flowed the haunting namesake of an elf mysterious as an illusion.

"Morrigan. She was last seen in the town of Barnett."

Strenbard sighed. "Good. That's all we needed to hear from you."

*****

Far below the cliff the men occupied, a lone silhouette stood arms crossed on the outskirts of the old city. His bulking head looked up at the rioting group. It seemed the men were arguing again, but this time getting violent. One more time, the silhouette saw the group raise a man up into the air, but this time, he saw the body fall. Korik held his breath as the man he once saved plummeted to the jagged rocks far below. His big green hands clasped the golden amulet around his neck. He knew Basoul had brought this fate upon himself. He also knew it wasn't long until humans came to Mythalis. The Chieftain Cleric said his final goodbyes to his old acquaintance, and returned to his corner of Mythalis, as Korik the Lion.

Woven Destiny

By Joel Norden

732 AM Age of the Dracon-esti

Thorvald Caelson, High King of the Daernor, drank deeply from his horn. Mead overflowed the brim and trickled down his beard. Thorvald belched and wiped the honey-alcohol from his face with the sleeve of his fur coat. The large nord looked down at the city that lay in the valley below his army's camp. Heliga looked cozy from the hilltop. Smoke rolled out of the many chimneys, painting trails that snaked into the cloudy evening sky. Thorvald could even see the Life Tree from his perch, its leaves eternally green, as it would remain the rest of the winter.

The nord force had been camped outside of Heliga for two days now. Thorvald knew better than to move his troops into the city. There they would grow weak, chasing women and starting fights with the townspeople out of boredom. The only reason they were here was the fact that his scouts had reported an enemy force two days march from Heliga. To Thorvald's disappointment, their rival clan – the Vina – had not yet advanced on Heliga. He would be glad to finally end this civil war. He just needed the Vina to make one wrong move, and he would crush them.

Thorvald sighed as he turned to glance over the small camp from the large throne. He leaned in closer to a blazing campfire, enjoying its warmth. Snow fell with intensity, quickly building up on his long brown hair and braided beard. Around the fire with Thorvald sat his men, their hands also out to catch the warmth of the flames. Many more men stood behind the ones sitting closest to the blaze. A scout was bringing word, and they packed close together to hear.

The scout was a young man, not even twenty-five if Thorvald had to guess. His shaved head proudly held high, he made his way through the crowd of soldiers to Thorvald.

The scout dropped to one knee as he reached the king. "My king, it is as we thought. The wendigo have taken Osaellgar Tower. They've slaughtered everyone and now head south for Frostreaver Pass through the mountains. They will reach Heliga within a week depending on the snowfall." The lad's breath formed into a mist as it entered the cold air of the Ice Plains.

Mutters ran through the men around the king but were quickly silenced as Thorvald raised a hand.

"How many?"

"Five thousand strong, my Lord. They march under the White Völva's banner, the black flag with a white dragon insignia."

Thorvald sat quietly for a moment in thought. He had heard much of this White Völva. Her raids increased with intensity over the last year or two. But instead of standing together and protecting their lands from this outsider, his people had been busy fighting their kinsfolk.

Thorvald shook off his irritation and spoke. "Yes, I am familiar with their banner. Thank you, Bjorn, you have done well. Get yourself some stew and mead. Warm your young bones by the fire."

Bjorn nodded gratefully and moved near the flames with Thorvald's warriors.

Thorvald turned to Ongull Gillanson, his most valued captain.

"We must speak with Greloo."

Ongull nodded, his brown eyes glaring at the men who stood gawking around them. The long scar that ran from forehead to jawline made him look all the fiercer. Ongull would have reminded Thorvald of an enraged black bear, if his black hair had not greyed long ago. Ongull strode off without any questions.

The captain went himself, so as not to offend Greloo by sending an errand boy.

Greloo was Thorvald's court völva, the highest ranking of all the crones in the Ice Plains. Every king or jarl had a völva as an adviser, to give him advice on the hold they ran. Most völva specialized in magic, herbalism, and midwifery. Some could even perform surgery, which gave these woman an important place in nord society. Thorvald trusted Greloo over all other völva, for she had been the first to lay hands on him as he exited his mother's womb, kicking and screaming, covered in blood. Thorvald would follow Greloo to the Grey if given the choice. Ten minutes or so had passed in silence, but the warriors knew better than to question why Thorvald did not jump to action. He always spoke to Greloo, hoping for some advantage that he had overlooked. Thorvald cocked his head, hearing cursing and shouting as Ongull returned. The large nord was shoving men out of his and Greloo's way.

"Move you fools!" the large man growled angrily.

Thorvald chuckled as he took another deep drink from his horn. Ongull was as brave and loyal as a man could be. But he definitely was not a person you wanted to anger if you were below his rank. Thorvald had seen Ongull break a lieutenant's nose once for asking a question after Ongull had given him an order. He was calmer now – a trait gained by age – but still had that no nonsense attitude. Following Ongull out of the crowd was an old woman. Thinning gray hair clung to her face as she leaned heavily on an oaken staff. Her left eye glanced around at the crowd, glimmering with knowing and intelligence. The other eye was blank, clouded, clearly blind.

Greloo inclined her head as she approached Thorvald. "My King," was all she said, watching Thorvald with her undamaged eye.

"Thank you for coming, wise one. The situation is dire. Five thousand wendigo march for Frostreaver pass, carrying the banner of the White Völva. I want your insight before I make a decision."

The old crone cackled as she drew a small bag from her tattered brown robes. She spoke words of magic over the pouch, and the contents started to glow through the cloth. Greloo hobbled to Thorvald and handed him the small bag.

"Follow," she said.

Thorvald followed Greloo through the crowd of men until they reached his tent.

The tent was large, of standard nordic make. Two guards pulled open the flaps, allowing Greloo and Thorvald entrance. The inside was simple. Only mere necessities garnished the king's tent. In the corner sat an oaken table with a map of the Ice Plains sprawled crossed it. Small items lay on it representing the nordic clans, the White Völva's armies, and small clans of Arctic ogres. In the center of the tent blazed a fire, smoke wafting through a large hole in the ceiling.

"Cast it into the fire, Thorvald. Look within the flames," the old völva cooed.

Thorvald nodded, taking the pouch from Greloo. He poured the contents into his hand, and a glowing sand-like substance filled his palm. Thorvald eyed it dubiously, looking to Greloo. "What is it?"

Greloo glared at Thorvald, "Into the fire!" she hissed fiercely.

Thorvald trusted her but remained cautious as he began to pour. He let the sand sift through his hands into the fire.

Greloo quickly dropped down to her hands and knees and stared into the fire.

Thorvald joined her more slowly.

The pair stared intently.

There it was.

The flames swirled. Images appeared blurry at first, but soon clarified in the fiery background. The images were not the only magic at hand. The inferno seemed to sweep him inside. Thorvald felt as though he was falling into the depths of the Nether.

Wendigo stormed over Heliga's walls. What vicious beasts they were. Deer in humanoid form, with grasping hands instead of hooves, gnashing their sharp teeth with carnivorous intent. They poured over the walls, slaying nordic warriors in scores. Some stopped to collect scalps of fallen soldiers. Cervidae faces twisted in rage, the wendigo scattered through Heliga. They slaughtered children, putting their heads on spears and parading through the streets in a grisly display of victory. The wendigo beat and raped women before hanging them from the Life Tree of Heliga, mocking the gods' gift of life. The treacherous creatures laughed as they did so. The flames burned brighter. Thorvald seemed to bathe in it.

This is a dream, he thought fervently. It must be!

The flickering flames surrounded him.

The scene changed.

Tall towers of dwarven make pierced the clouds with their sturdy, pointed tops. It was Skykeep. Thorvald recognized it instantly. The vision quickly swept through the air around him and now he could see into the highest tower. His tower. A völva wearing white robes stood there on the balcony. Turning, the witch stared at Thorvald from behind a metal mask. Those eyes were colder than ice. It was her, the White Völva. The invader from the north.

Below, ice covered the city and battlements. An eternal ice, one which Thorvald knew there was no melting. Large blue-skinned giants loped through the streets. Frost giants. Impossible! They had been destroyed hundreds of years ago by his great-grandfathers.

Looking back to the slender woman at the edge of the tower balcony, Thorvald realized a wolf sat next to her, staring at him with its unblinking yellow eyes. Thorvald's lip curled in disgust. Wolves had been hated by nords since the beginning, when the god Xanzth waved his hands and created the frost giants and wolves.

The fire scorched Thorvald so much he was reeling. He tried to scream in anger. The scavengers from deep within the Nether would have neither him nor his people!

The blaze changed to a greenish color. The scene changed.

A nord army marched out of the northern side of Frostreaver pass, led by Thorvald.

It felt so real, Thorvald had completely forgotten it was a vision.

The wendigo army reached the base of the hill that led up to Frostreaver pass.

Perfect timing, Thorvald thought, turning to shout orders.

Flames flickered.

Thorvald almost vomited. Surprised at how believable the magic scene had been, the smell, sights...

Thorvald's thoughts were cut off as the image changed again.

A face of a young grey elf, a male, with silver hair and a strange gaze. For some reason, the elf seemed essential. The young elf wept, thrusting forward his two manacled hands. The elf's mouth moved, trying to speak to him, but Thorvald couldn't hear. Before the nord could reply, the flames roared up.

A nord lay dead at Thorvald's feet. Blood stained Thorvald's sword. An army cheered around him. Joy surged through him, even though the crown upon his head was covered in blood. It dribbled down his face and into his mouth, yet Thorvald roared in laughter for his unknown victory. He knew not why he was laughing, but couldn't stop. Thorvald felt like his head would explode. This was madness, none of this made sense.

A scream broke him from the fire's enchantment. Thorvald inhaled winter into his lungs. The air burned. He quickly wiped sweat from his brow. As if he had broke a fever, it took him a moment to realize where he was. The sight of Ongull's fierce face at his side brought him back to reality.

"My king, are you well?" Ongull said gruffly.

Thorvald nodded, dazed. His gaze fell to Greloo, who lay on her back staring at him, groaning as blood trickled from the corner of her mouth.

"She screamed, and I rushed in, found both of you like this..." Ongull muttered to Thorvald, his voice somehow still sounding harsh.

Greloo coughed roughly, spewing blood on the ground. "You..." Greloo had to pause to spit more blood from her mouth. "You must take your men to Frostreaver pass… It is woven in your destiny. The gods will it to be so."

"I will take my two hundred men north to the pass. As long as one of us stands, I swear none of those creatures will ever get through the pass." Thorvald spoke proudly, though still confused and more than a little shaken from the vision. The thought of what the wendigo had done to Heliga made him shudder.

He looked at the old crone with concern. "Will you be well, Greloo?"

Greloo reached up a hand to Ongull, and the large man helped Greloo to her feet, where she stood feebly.

"The vision has drained my old bones," Greloo whispered between shallow breaths. "If you do not create time for Heliga to be reinforced, all of the Ice Plains will be taken by this invading völva. Holding Frostreaver pass for three days is vital."

Thorvald grinned. "It will be an honor for me and my men to sacrifice ourselves for this beautiful region. We shall fight until the last man to give Heliga the time it needs."

Greloo smiled. The few teeth the old woman had were covered in blood. "Glowt awaits you and your men in Valhöll, with mead and women aplenty!"

Thorvald gave a small bow to Greloo, then turned and left the tent to address his men. Ongull followed his king closely.

As Thorvald exited the tent, he saw determination on the gaunt faces of his men. Winter had not been easy for them in this war-torn land. This news would give the men hope for the afterlife. It was better to die in battle than to die from cold, disease, or other unworthy ways to pass into the next plane. Thorvald knew his men felt the same. All nord warriors shared this belief. The gods had woven each man's fate from birth. No sense in worrying about death. With the pleasures that came with entering Valhöll, what kind of nord would fear death?

Thorvald drew his sword from his scabbard and raised it high. "Who's ready to bloody their sword, axe, spear and shield with invaders' blood!"

Thorvald paused as the crowd of nords erupted in cheers. Large grins split their faces as they raised their drinks in celebration.

"We march for Frostreaver Pass! The wendigo outnumber us by many. It will be a glorious end for us, one we will celebrate in Valhöll!"

Ongull stepped forward when Thorvald was done. "Greloo has said Glowt awaits us, mead and big-racked woman for all. But if you don't move your arses, I will be waiting in Valhöll, already showing your wenches a good time with my sea dragon. Move it, you bunch of bastards! Tonight we march to meet the scavengers!" Ongull's speech was fierce, but the men cheered again while rushing to get ready.

Thorvald sent a messenger down the rocky cliffside to Heliga to warn Falki Otterson of the oncoming wendigo army. He did the same to the Daernor clan's capital, Skykeep, which lay farther south. Thorvald hoped Skykeep could reinforce Heliga before the wendigo overtook them at Frostreaver Pass, or worse. If the rivaling nord clans – the Vina, Falkrie and Svenor – heard of the weakness of Heliga, they would certainly make a move. Thorvald prayed it didn't come to that. With this new intruder, the nord nation needed to throw the civil war to the side and stand as one.

The army of two hundred Daernor set out for Frostreaver Pass. They marched north, making good time despite the darkness that closed in with the coming of night. Guided by the moonlight, they walked over the snow-covered ground without much hindrance.

Several hours into the march, Thorvald glanced around at the men walking behind him. The snow fell fiercely from the sky, swirling amongst the warriors. The wind quickly caused the snow to drift. Most of the men laughed, some saying it was a gift from the god Zarth. They claimed Zarth knew the snowfall wouldn't slow the nordic warriors or dampen their spirits, but it would slow down the puny wendigo.

Thorvald shook his head. They will all be dead at the end of this, he thought sullenly. Though he and his men did not fear death, the king was no fool. Dead men did not protect the innocent. Thorvald tried to avoid sending his men into certain death if at all possible. This time made sense though. The fate of the Ice Plains lay in their hands. This was something that had to be done.

The company marched hard for two days, seldom taking breaks to eat and drink. Thorvald's legs burned, as did his warriors'. No one complained, knowing time was of the essence. The sooner they reached the pass, the more time for setting up defenses.

Travel grew strenuous, with long stretching hills and nothing but snow and ice as far as the eye could see. Not a single pine tree littered the white canvas. The backdrop of the mountains in the distance seemed almost unreal. So close, yet so far away. The scenery reminded Thorvald of an oil painting.

On the second night, the nord company came upon a sheer cliff of ice stretching hundreds of feet into the air.

Ongull stood next to Thorvald and cursed loudly. "This should be the pass! We must have gone too far east or west."

"Not hard to do in this weather. Send scouts east and west along this wall. Tell them to search for a blue light emanating from the frost runes."

Ongull bowed his head then turned to shout orders. Thorvald stood for a while, thankful for the wall of ice acting as a barrier against the northern winds. Ice still swept off the top and caused a cyclone of snow. Thorvald chuckled as it swirled around him. He'd have it no other way. Harsh environment, dangerous enemies and even deadlier predators, this was life on the Plains. The atmosphere made anyone appreciate the small moments of life, for the next day they could be dead.

Two hours passed before the scouts finally returned. They had found Frostreaver Pass to the east. Again, Ongull shouted orders and the nords continued to press on along the gigantic cliff wall. It didn't take long until they reached the south side of Frostreaver Pass.

Thorvald quickly identified the pass by the glowing blue light of the frost runes through the heavy snow. He quickened his pace, pausing only to eye the giant ice obelisks. Runes covered the mighty pillars and were engraved as if they were stone or iron. Blue light emanated vividly from the runes, lighting up the night around them. In legends, it was said the frost giants tunneled the pass straight through the mountain. They placed these magic hieroglyphs that kept the pass free of their enemies. Frost giants were long gone, but the runes and their magic remained active to remind all who traveled through Frostreaver Pass of that ancient race.

Thorvald pushed his men on without break through the pass. The king of the Daernor knew they had to hasten, for there would only be a day or two to ready fortifications to defend against the assault, if that.

The ground was solid, frost covered stone. The walls were a thick, impenetrable wall of ice. It was so sleek that Thorvald marveled how flawlessly it had been cut. Torchlights on the icy walls flickered and danced, making the ice look as if blue magic shimmered underneath it.

Thorvald paused again, this time to speculate. He shook his head in wonderment. Had frost giants really been that towering? The ceiling of the cavern was almost thirty feet high, and massive icicles hung down.

Travel through the cave was quiet, if not rather eerie. No one spoke, but every cough or stumble echoed through the cavern. The journey was smooth at least, the only worry was slipping on the slick stone. After an uncertain amount of time had passed, the two hundred warriors emerged from the north side of Frostreaver Pass.

Thorvald called Ongull to the front of the ranks. "Have the men set up camp on the inside of the pass to catch a few hours of sleep. Then we will cut wood from the forest down in the valley below. We'll build a palisade in front of the pass. Anything we can do to slow them down."

"As you command." Ongull gave a little bow, but then looked at Thorvald seriously. "Between you and I, Thorvald. I have a gut feeling that we will survive this fight. I don't know why, perhaps I feel Glowt smiling down upon us. I've fought wendigo before in battles on the coast of Fragmar and crafty bastards they are! But I doubt they expect to fight their way through the Pass. Hell, I doubt they sent scouts ahead."

"I hope your gut is right, Ongull. I look forward to Valhöll, but I hope to end the civil war before I leave this world. But that is a matter for another time. Ongull, speaking of scouts, send a few out and see if they can find any sign of the wendigo."

Ongull chuckled. "Of course, my king!" The stout grey-haired captain set off whistling and shouting orders.

Thorvald smiled, it wasn't often that he saw Ongull like this. In fact, it was only on the eve of battle. The more the odds favored the other side, the more mirthful Ongull's mood.

Fires were built, and many quickly fell asleep. Thorvald was one of the few to stay awake. He sat by the blaze staring into its depths, images of the vision that he had seen in the flames flashing through his head. What did it all mean? Greloo, as usual, never explained much. She had just told him what he needed to know. Hold the wendigo off for three days once they reached the pass. Thorvald sighed. He knew he'd regret not sleeping.

Thorvald grabbed a blanket and walked out of the pass. The wind and snow had both died down, leaving the air crisp and cold. Thorvald leaned up against a boulder, staring into the dark sky, only illuminated by the stars. Captivated by the beauty of his surroundings, he slipped into a slumber, gazing into the vault of the Empyrean.

The sun wasn't yet over the mountains when Ongull started shouting orders. Men ran around getting ready for a long day. Thorvald took a bowl of steaming stew Ongull brought him.

You need to eat, my king," Ongull pressed.

Thorvald nodded and assured him that he had planned on eating.

As soon as Thorvald was done, he joined a group of warriors who were starting down the hill.

The nord army worked hard, cutting down timber and hauling the logs up the large hill. They sharpened the end of the wood they used for the palisade walls. Then dug pits on the other side of the walls as best they could. The ground on the hill was hard and frozen, making work difficult.

As the morning and afternoon disappeared, the guards were posted along the finished palisade wall. They watched for any movement in the valley below, any sign that the wendigo had arrived earlier than expected. Inside the pass, the nords started a roaring fire. Several hunters returned with large deer, rabbits, and squirrels.

On the afternoon of the fifth day, a loud banging echoed through the valley below. Ongull had already shouted orders before the guards could blow several sharp notes on their war horns.

The wendigo battle drums grew louder and louder until the army could be seen moving through the forest-covered valley below.

Thorvald imagined their twisted deer-like faces as he watched from behind the barricade above. He had battled with the wendigo some five years past in Fragmar, near Ogena. It had been the first invasion from the north as the orc tribes expanded and pushed the wendigo tribes south out of their original territory. The battle had been glorious. Many wendigo had been slain by Thorvald's sword. The king prayed to Brimlad that this fight would be victorious as well.

The wendigo army advanced out of the wood line and halted. Thorvald could see their commanders running up and down the lines shouting orders. The sun glared off their antlers, and their faces were twisted with hatred. Many wore paint smeared across their deer-like faces in an attempt to be intimidating. Thorvald chuckled as the lead wendigo waved his sword. The entire army surged forward, climbing the hill.

Let's give these deer-humpers a taste of nordic steel," Ongull laughed.

The whole nord army broke into hearty laughter.

Someone in the ranks shouted another insult: "The deer-men are heading south for greener grass to graze!"

The wendigo army faltered a bit at the site of two hundred battle-ready nords laughing and jeering. That didn't last long. Wendigo commanders screamed in their crude language and raised their whips. The army quickly proceeded.

Ongull moved his way to the front of the barricade, spear in hand. "You know the drill, ready your spears! Don't throw until I give the order. Hold!"

The wendigo were some forty yards away, rumbling up the hill. Some wendigo arrows flew out at the nord army.

Thirty yards away.

Twenty.

"Now!" Ongull screamed. Spears flew into the advancing creatures, impaling those not quick enough with their shields. In turn, the wendigo chucked spears, taking out several nords.

The wendigo clashed upon the barricade as waves against mighty cliffs. Many of the deer creatures attempted to hack the barricade apart, but to no avail. Nord spears stabbed over the top rhythmically, spilling the blood of any wendigo in reach. The men roared with bloodlust as many of the deer-men tried climbing to the top of the wall. They were quickly sliced down before they could even lift their axes.

A barrage of creatures rushed forward, smashing into the barricade. They attached grappling hooks before the nordic spears could pierce their flesh. Before any of the nords could react, the ropes tightened. The barricade creaked. Wood snapped and splintered into kindling.

The sun was dipping down behind the mountains to the west when the wendigo finally broke through the barrier. The two armies clashed, with the Daernor army widening its lines of defense.

Thorvald swept his sword through the invaders, leaving a trail of bleeding, dismembered wendigo. It seemed never-ending. He would slash one invader down, just to have it replaced by another. Sweat beaded on his brow, despite the freezing night air. His blood boiled with battle rage, his muscles tightened.

Finally, a horn blast sounded in the forested ravine. The wendigo all turned and fled down the hill. The nords pursued halfway down, hacking the deer-men as they retreated. Thorvald and Ongull both shouted orders to halt the charge down the mountainside. This could quickly turn into a massacre if they were caught out in the open by fresh troops. The slope below Frostreaver Pass was littered with carcasses, nord as well as wendigo. The snow was stained with blood and guts. Body parts lay strewn from their previous owners.

Thorvald and the remainder of his troops scoured the battlefield for living men, and to send any wounded wendigo to the Nether, where their souls would be devoured by Wesif, god of disease and decay.

Thorvald's chest swelled with pride, looking around at his fallen men. They had battled hard. They knew what had been at stake. Glowt, the god of courage, would meet them at the gates of Valhöll. Thorvald closed his eyes and wished them well on their journey.

Ongull limped over to Thorvald. He didn't say much for a while, he just stared out over the battlefield.

"Well, we gave those bastards a taste of our steel," Ongull spoke finally. "Maybe it will make them think twice about invading the Plains." He flashed a grin at Thorvald.

"They will not have an easy fight ahead of them. Even with the clans being at war, women and children will stand and fight for this land if need be." Thorvald looked out past the battlefield. Hill after hill of snowy pine trees. And in the background more mountains. Far out in the trees, hundreds of fires burned, marking the wendigo camp.

"It's always been a battle for us. First, the gods tested us by sending the snow and ice. Our forefathers didn't falter. Then the gods of dark sent ogres, wendigo and frost giants. The frost giants were defeated and banished from our world. The ogre race in the north is shattered, they now roam in small bands. Used to be hordes. The wendigo were pushed further north, all because of us. Hell, not even the once mighty empire of Tenthrolen could take the plains!" Ongull stated proudly.

Thorvald nodded in agreement. "It will be so again if I have anything to say about it. The wendigo will have the same fate as the damned frost giants. What are our losses, Ongull?"

"We lost twenty men. Thirty or more wounded, most too proud to admit it, my king."

"Like yourself?" Thorvald grinned heartily.

"What, this?" Ongull said, pointing to a cut on his leg. Where a wendigo weapon had gone right through his armor. "This is just a flesh wound. A big white-furred bastard got me. But if we are talking about looking rough, you seem pretty shoddy yourself, my king." Ongull chuckled, pointing to a small gash on Thorvald's arm.

"I will be fine," Thorvald grinned, shrugging off the wound. "How many wendigo dead?"

"Around two hundred. That barricade really slowed them down."

"Well, only three thousand, eight hundred more to send to the Nether. Hopefully, we can hold this pass for a day or two more."

Ongull didn't say anything. He looked out over the battlefield.

"Let's go help the wounded back up to the pass and rebuild the barricade. They will come again at dawn," Thorvald spoke softly, then headed up the slope.

Both men quickly went to work. Ongull gave orders and helped the wounded up to their makeshift camp. After the remaining warriors swept the battlefield and collected any weapons they deemed useful, they fixed up the barricade and reinforced it the best they could.

Night came quick. A full moon shone, lighting up the night. They doubled the watch, just in case the wendigo decided to attack during the eventide. Thorvald doubted they would though, for the wendigo had marched a long way, and their commanders would let them recuperate.

Thorvald sat around a large fire with Ongull and some other warriors eating venison stew and munching on some old bread. Sipping from his horn, Thorvald leaned in as one of the warriors told a tale of a kralle that he had defeated. He was not drinking this night, for he would need to be fresh for tomorrow's battle. Honey water was all Thorvald would have tonight.

"There I was in the mountains, trudging through the snow, dark as the damned Nether." The warrior waved his hands while telling the story as if it would add to the intensity.

"Suddenly, I heard a roar. The kralle came at me in a flash, smelling my blood. Hungry, he was! I feinted with my sword. It growled and jumped back. He was a good two heads taller than I, slender and covered in white fur. Long black horns like those of a mountain goat sprawled from his forehead! He stared at me with red glowing eyes, hatred lit up in that glare. It was like looking Wesif in the eye, but I didn't waver. Finally, the beast leapt at me. Somehow knocked the sword out of my hands. We wrestled for a moment, then the beast threw me against a tree."

The warrior paused to take a long drink of honey water before contiueing. "Then before I could pull out my dagger, the kralle gave me this,"he beckoned to his missing eye.

"I stabbed him quickly a few times. Then, as he retreated, I rolled to my sword. He clutched his wound, which was the creature's mistake, not paying attention to the nord in front of him, sword in hand!" The man chuckled. "The beast lost his head, he did."

"What did you do about your eye?" Ongull asked.

"Patched myself up and on my way I went. I was just thankful it wasn't the other way around. Could have been the beast carrying my head back to his lair. Glowt had an eye on me that night."

"Indeed, he did," Thorvald said, standing. "I'm going to catch some sleep before morning. I suggest you men do the same, so you're fresh for battle."

The men all nodded and started setting up spots around the fire.

Thorvald lay for a long while before sleep swept over him.

Morning came fast. Thorvald was up before the sun came over the mountains. He paced the barricade, waited for the horns.

They came soon enough. Horns sounded, and the wendigo advanced out of the tree line just like before. They marched with much better organization, Thorvald noted. The wendigo commanders had better control over their formations. This time, the wendigo came two hundred at a time. Fifty or so halted some fifty yards from the barricade, all of them gripped bows in their twisted hands. The archers made a weird bleating sound, almost like sheep. Thorvald imagined they were laughing.

The wendigo charged the barricade, some with swords and spears, others with grappling hooks. The wendigo bowmen loosed a flight of arrows at the nords.

"Shields!" Ongull yelled. Arrows fell all around them, many stuck into wooden shields. A few who weren't quick enough to raise their shields were stuck like pin cushions. The Daernor clan answered with a volley of spears at the creatures who rushed the wall, impaling many of the cervinae creatures.

The first wendigo assault smashed into the palisade, many hooking up their grappling hooks and retreating. Thorvald rushed forward, slicing the head from a wendigo trying to climb the barrier and hurriedly slicing a rope from a grappling hook that its comrade had hooked up.

Ongull was shouting. "Cut the goddamned lines! Now! Or we lose the barricade!"

The men rushed to cut the grapple hooks free just as the wendigo started to heave.

Behind the melee squad of wendigo, archers kept firing mechanically into the nords, felling many. Two hundred more wendigo charged up the hill to aid their fellows who were thinning out quickly. Thorvald frowned. They were sitting ducks here, they had two choices…

The second wave slammed against the palisade, their grappling hooks grabbed hold even as nord spears met their flesh. Many wendigo climbed over the wall, only to end with a sword or spear buried in their gullets before they landed.

One of the wendigo fell in front of Thorvald. It slashed wildly with its rusty blade, bloodying any nords around it. After it had created space for itself in the melee, it met Thorvald's eyes.

The creature confidently swung its, sword, but Thorvald ducked under the blow. The sword whistled over his head. Seeing his chance, he jabbed his sword forward, impaling the wendigo's throat. He met the creature's eyes as the soul left its body. Blood gurgled in the beast's mangled throat, red film bubbling on its lips. Such intensity in that gaze filled with contempt. Thorvald didn't break its stare. This wendigo would know who sent it to Wesif.

Thorvald let the body slump to the ground as the light within its eyes disappeared. Looking behind him, there were roughly twenty men. Most had large axes or greatswords, their faces were painted red, and a crazed look glazed their eye. Raising his sword, Thorvald rallied a war cry. The men behind him took it up as well, surging forward with their king.

Thorvald jumped over the palisade into the wendigo, swinging his sword in a wide circle, cleaving through armor, flesh, and bone. Behind him cried howls of berserkers as they jumped into the fray. They hacked through the wendigo warriors like they were straw dummies. Many wendigo began to flee as the nords formed a wedge formation at the outer base of the palisade; it was an axe machine of certain death.

"To the archers!" Thorvald shouted as he picked up a spear off the ground. Over the heads of his comrades, he thrust the spear, catching a wendigo with its mouth open. The spear cleanly pierced the back of the beast's head.

By the time the archers realized the tactic, it was too late. The berserkers were upon them like madmen. Arrows aimed at the berserkers seemed to do nothing. One man on Thorvald's left caught an arrow in the throat. The man still managed to reach the archers and kill two with his axe, before he died gurgling in his own blood. The berserkers slammed into the retreating archers, Thorvald at the lead, slashing through the beasts.

As they finished off the archers, Thorvald looked up to realize that a good five hundred more wendigo soldiers marched up the hill at them. The berserkers breathed heavily, eyeing the army with glee. Thorvald looked back to the wall and realized Ongull had led the rest of the army to the right.

"Ready yourselves, my warriors! Glowt, give us strength in this moment in need, for we will meet you in Valhöll soon! Hit their left flank!" Thorvald yelled as loud as he could, rushing forward at the left side of the five hundred warriors. His blood rushed through his veins in the excitement of battle and the chance to finally see Valhöll.

Slashing the spear points away from him, Thorvald bashed his way through the wendigo ranks. His muscles bulged as his sword sliced through foe after foe. He paved a way into the creatures, but he stopped short to stare.

Through the melee, a figure stood in a white robe, an ornamental mask covering their face. Then it was gone. It had been a human, of this Thorvald was sure. Thorvald rubbed his eyes and suddenly he was face to face with a massive wendigo commander. Gigantic antlers that rivaled those of the majestic elk, and scars covered its body, it gave what Thorvald imagined as a toothy grin as it advanced.

The giant creature swung his sword, and Thorvald met it with his blade. Again and again, the creature slashed. Thorvald ducked, dodged, and parried. Finally, one of the wendigo's blows flung the sword out of Thorvald's hand. He had to quickly duck to avoid a killing blow, causing the beast to lose its balance for a second.

That was all Thorvald needed. He slammed his body into the wendigo's, not giving him room to swing his sword again. The wendigo tried to push him away, but Thorvald had a firm grip on the captain's giant antlers. They struggled briefly, grappling. Thorvald quickly yanked his dagger free from its scabbard and plunged it into the creature's stomach multiple times until it slumped to the ground.

Grabbing the head by the antlers, Thorvald hacked at the commander's neck. He twisted its neck, then followed a loud crunch as the bone broke and the wendigo's head came free from its body.

"Your leader will make a nice mount in my longhouse, you grass grazers!" Thorvald roared, holding the head high. Thorvald's men raised a hearty cheer and started swinging their weapons with even more vigor.

Ongull's men met the few remaining berserkers that Thorvald led in the middle. That was it for the wendigo. They were outflanked and with their leader dead, they fled. Thorvald thanked Glowt as he watched the rest of wendigo army disappear behind the cover of the forest. The death of their leader must have caused confusion. If they had advanced the rest of the wendigo army, this battle would be over.

"Back to the palisade!" Thorvald trotted up the hill. His muscles ached, but he pushed on, his men right behind him. Whatever reason the enemy's failure to execute a killing blow was, he would take advantage of their folly.

As they reached the palisade, Thorvald looked over his shoulder. Still no sight of the wendigo army. Perplexed, he climbed atop the palisade and eyed the pine forest. No sign of the wendigo. A few of the men cheered, but the most seasoned warriors knew something was wrong. It was in the air, an uneasiness that hovered with the stench of death.

Night slipped in, and the feeling did not ease up. Only twenty men or so remained from the two hundred that marched to Frostreaver Pass. All of them, tired and injured, sat quietly around the fires. They knew they'd need every ounce of energy soon enough.

They posted five men at the barricade and rotated all through the night so everyone got some sleep. Thorvald thanked Glowt that the night passed uneventfully.

Mid-morning hit before the sound of war drums sounded from the forest below. All the nords rushed to the wall and eyed the woods. From the pine forest, the remaining wendigo army emerged but stopped at the base of the hill. Behind them was movement. Humanoid figures emerged from the tree line, by the thousands. Tall reptilian creatures, with scales of white and large fangs protruding from their mouths. At the lead was a figure in a white robe and ornamental mask, leaning lightly on a staff.

There was no movement among the reptilian men for a while as they filed into ranks behind the wendigo. The white-robed völva walked to the front of both armies. There were hand movements and then a loud boom echoed through the valley below the hill, ringing all the way to the pass.

"Surrender your weapons. We don't wish to kill any more of your people. Drop your weapons and you will be granted mercy." A woman's voice rang out, echoing through the valley, but sounding as if it was right next to the barricade. Magic. The remaining nords of the Daernor clan looked at each other for a moment, then burst into hearty laughter.

When the laughter died down, Thorvald wiped tears from his eyes while still chuckling, "With all due respect, völva, we will die with honor battling you."

The völva didn't answer right away, but when she did, she spoke slowly. "So, you will all die pointless deaths? We will crush you. I offered life, and you refuse?"

"As long as one of us stands, you and your army will not pass. Did you not see what I did to your commander? Your head will be the next that I hold victoriously in my grasp, witch!" Thorvald shouted back, his men cheering and raising their weapons high.

"So be it."

Chanting sounded all around them. The spidery words of magic. Thorvald eyed the White Völva. Suddenly, a man-sized ball of fire flew from her fingertips towards the nords.

"Get back!" Thorvald shouted.

Too late. Men dove everywhere as the ball of fire struck the center of the barricade. It exploded, flinging warriors and burning wood chunks everywhere. Thorvald rolled in the snow, making sure his clothes and beard were not on fire, then searched helplessly for his sword. The world seemed to move slowly, and he felt a dull ringing in his head. Around him, nords struggled to their feet, most with bad burns or splinters of wood stuck in their flesh.

Thorvald looked up as someone offered him a hand. Ongull. Black smudges covered his face, and his beard and hair were all but burnt off.

"Shall we meet them, one last charge for the Ice Plains?" Ongull's voice was hoarse.

"For Glowt and Valhöll, my friend." Thorvald clasped Ongull's hand and stood up. His body ached everywhere but he did his best to shake it off. He glanced around at the gathered men, all of them injured in some way.

Thorvald watched as the wendigo army advanced forward, while the white lizardmen army held back with the White Völva. Thorvald guessed they were to swing in if the wendigo needed back up. Fifteen men stood around him. All wounded, but each man had a smile on his face. They would be feasting in Valhöll soon. The Valkyrie of Glowt would lead their souls to the gates. A place to feast, fight, and make love.

"Let us end this. We have held the pass for long enough." Thorvald looked to each warrior, a grin upon his face. "The next time I see you will be at the gates!"

Picking up a random axe, he started striding through the blackened debris. Ongull, sword in hand, trotted next to Thorvald, and their men followed suit. Down the hill they marched. To certain death. They had only advanced several paces when a crisp, long horn blast stopped Thorvald and his men in their tracks. The marching wendigo halted as well. Thorvald whirled around and looked into Frostreaver Pass. There it was again. A nord horn. All eyes were on the opening of the Pass.

Out of the Frostreaver marched nords, but Thorvald and his men did not cheer. For at the lead were several nords holding clan banners. The Vina, Falkrie, and Svenor. Daernor rivals for over two hundred years. Now Thorvald and his men were trapped between two enemies. Hundreds and hundreds of nords marched out of the Pass. At the lead was a large nord with brown mohawk and a braided beard. Tattoos covered the sides of his shaven head. He approached Thorvald's men alone, slipping his battle-axe in his belt and slinging his shield on his back.

"I take it you're Thorvald of the Daernor?" The man spoke, and it was clearly stated in the man's eyes that he considered Thorvald no king.

"Thorvald Caelson, high king! Respect him while you are in his presence, or my axe will take your head from your body!" Ongull spat, stepping forward. But Thorvald's hand on his shoulder stopped him.

The man nodded. "The problem is, I am Eirik Aslinson of the Vina. And they also call me high king." Eirik gave a toothy grin. "But I'm not here to argue about who is or isn't king. You have fought bravely here, Thorvald. You should be a paragon for this act of valor." Eirik walked forward, hand outstretched.

Thorvald stared at the man. Looking behind Eirik, his eyes widened. Men still marched out of Frostreaver pass, but he saw two more banners now: the Skjord and the Daernor.

Eirik turned and saw what Thorvald was staring at.

"As I told your messenger, the man leading the Daernor to you now – Bjorn, I believe his name is – unity is required to ensure that this witch does not take our homeland. When she is gone, we can go back to our petty civil war. So I ask for an alliance until then." Eirik walked to Thorvald, his hand still outstretched.

Thorvald clasped Eirik's arm. "You are a wise and honorable man, Eirik. Not what I expected."

Eirik smiled and raised his battle axe. The army of united nords advanced down the hill.

"Let us celebrate this unity with some bloodshed of our enemy, shall we?" Eirik stalked away, quickly yelling orders to his men.

Bjorn reached the wounded nords with a sullen look on his face. He bowed low. "My king." He did not look up from the ground.

"Why do you act ashamed? You have somehow created a unity none have known for two hundred years."

"The Vina captured me on the way to warn the southern cities. I told them the situation, praying to Glowt that Eirik was no fool. I betrayed the locations of the army, the penalty for that is death my king."

"Yes, yes it is." Thorvald eyed the young man for a second. "Bjorn, you had what was right for the Plains on your mind. I pray to all the gods that you die a warrior down there today. For if you survive, you will be banished."

Bjorn looked up at his king. Joy danced in his eyes. "Thank you, my king!" The chance to die a warrior was not often given for a war crime.

Thorvald and the wounded nords laughed and raised their weapons in unison as the horns rang through the valley. Thousands of nords charged down the hill, each howling with glory and bloodlust. Praying that the valkyrie that met them was beautiful and the halls of Valhöll full of crisp ale. Thorvald smiled at the sight of fear in the eyes of the wendigo, as the rumbling united nord nation charged down the hill, ready to lay waste.

Glowt smiled down upon them this day.

The Moral Dilemma

By Aaron Wulf

732 AM Age of the Dracon-esti

"Evil acts often arise out of good people. Some of you may see something you do not understand, and will therefore feel threatened. You will think it is evil. And so, without the proper knowledge, many people in this land will destroy something beautiful in the name of good."

The cleric stopped speaking for a moment to look about the tiny tavern. Only three had been listening to his speech. As always, everybody else was drinking and socializing.

The cleric's long gray hair and sapphire eyes hinted at his wisdom, seducing the attention of a growing audience, now five people. Shadows danced behind the rafters, cast by the light of a small fire in the center of the room.

"Old man!"

The voice echoed across the floor. At the counter sat a soldier holding a tankard of ale. His features were chiseled, his presence demanding. He was captain of the army. He stood and walked toward the cleric, silencing everyone in the room.

"Do you know where you are, old man?" the captain asked, frustrated.

"I am in the land of my people," the cleric replied. "All men and women are equal in this world, though the world may not accept this. I aim to bring peace to Draston. To do this, one must translate the chaos within society into beauty."

"Damn your teachings. They're not welcome here. I know you speak of the so-called One God." The young captain ground his bearded jaw.

"Did I ever say that?" the cleric asked, stroking his own beard.

"Our village remains small for a purpose. Five years ago we all lived to the west in the city of Xerxas. There were those of us who felt betrayed by King Vavrinec, forgotten about, and put down because of clashing views and beliefs. We did not wish for a civil war. Our group was only two hundred strong. They had the rest of the city on their side, their minds brainwashed by the king. They wanted us to kneel to their new ways and abandon our gods of old for this new One God he so believed in. Such an act was sacrilegious, and we could not stand for it! But neither could he stand for our reverence for the gods of old. We opted to leave in the middle of the night, with the promise of threat eminent. We only wanted freedom. They wanted order. After this I learned that there will never be peace. There will always be the threat of violence and death. So here we built the village of Barton, where we are free to follow our beliefs and our ways. Anyone who wishes to push their opposing beliefs is not welcome here. I am sworn to defend our land for our people."

A door to one of the back rooms swung open and out stepped an even larger man with an even more demanding presence. He was dressed in skins, furs, and metal plates. His dark beard was thick, and scars carved the right half of his face. The left half was covered by an iron plate. It was forever a part of his distorted face, and yet there was never anger behind his mask. He emanated peace, and people honored and respected him. He was their chief, and brother of their former king.

Chief Bareph spoke to his captain, "Valholm, is this the way you talk to our guests?"

"This man brings foreign beliefs to our village, my chief, the same beliefs King Vavrinec spoke of," Valholm replied.

"I overheard some of what he said. I did not hear him speak of any gods, only morals. It is words he brings, not violence," Bareph said.

"It was words that drove us out of Xerxas! Words that developed into the actions of your mad brother!" Valholm reached for the hilt of his blade.

"By the gods, you're drunk," Bareph stated. "You are to marry my daughter in two weeks, and you stand here making people look like damned savages!"

The cleric stood up and began to excuse himself. He turned to Valholm. "Pardon my intrusion, I seem to have wasted your time."

"Never show your filth here again, you rat!" Valholm shouted.

"Valholm! You must sober up and rest. You're creating a frenzy," Bareph demanded.

"Elody mustn't see her future husband in this manner, thank the gods she is not here. Get yourself together!"

The whole room was standing up, watching the two large men argue as the cleric escaped out the tavern door. A girl walked up to the men and stopped them both mid-sentence.

Not much older than eighteen, Pereta was considered one of the wisest women in the village. Though she could be arrogant, the folk would come to her for advice. She had worked in the library of Xerxas in her childhood and spent most of her time reading books on philosophy, politics, and war.

Pereta put a hand on her father's shoulder as he scratched at where his beard met his faceplate.

Brushing her vibrantly blonde hair away from her caramel eyes, she spoke in the calmest but most direct matter possible. "Father, Valholm, both of you are causing the most inexorable uproar since the last werewolf sighting. Be civil. Elody would be abashed if she were here. You both know how concordant she always is."

Pereta's eyes wandered the room. Where could her sister be at this hour? It was nearly dusk.

She turned her attention back to Bareph. "Valholm is right though, you know," Pereta confessed. "If our village is to thrive, we must omit any possible threat to our ways, no matter how subtle it may be."

Bareph sighed. "You younglings take matters too seriously. You are too afraid and too literal. It will be you eventually tears our people apart if you don't give others a chance. To be naive is a mistake I will not make. You, my dear daughter and future son-in-law, were both young when the dissension at Xerxas began. We tried to settle things for years until blood was first shed. That is when things turned evil."

Valholm and Pereta looked down solemnly as they were scolded.

Screams from outside broke the silence.

Everyone in the tavern filed out into the dirt streets under the darkening sky. The land was vast and open, with only a few trees on the grassy fields. Despite the openness, the village was relatively hidden in a deep, wide valley. The buildings were few – about eight in total – as the majority of the population lived in huts and tents about a half mile south. Their lack of lumber put a hold on expanding their village.

At the end street stood Elody, the most beautiful young lady in the region of Kraos. Her hazelnut hair danced all the way down to her waist, and her chocolate eyes hypnotized any man who spoke to her. Being the daughter of the Chief and fiancée of the captain, everybody made sure to respect her, though her genuinely kind heart was enough to soften the most horrid of people.

Elody's job was to gather herbs, berries, and grain from the fields surrounding the village. She would often disappear at irregular hours of the day to search for these things, and with an enthusiasm that dumbfounded many of her people. At times she would return after finding very little, but would remain the happiest of people.

This particular evening, she had returned with only half a basket of blackberries, tangleberries, and raspberries. She skipped eagerly up to the crowd, ignoring their puzzled faces, and kissed Bareph on his scarred cheek.

"Good evening father." She stepped on her tip toes and rollicked to Valholm, embracing him in a strong hug. "Good evening my love. Why is everyone so silent?"

"We heard a scream." Valholm scanned the surrounding buildings.

Pereta put her hand on her hip. "How did you not hear it?"

"I suppose I was lost in my own little world. Is everybody alright?" Elody asked.

"That's what we're trying to find out." Bareph unsheathed a knife and walked around Elody, followed by Valholm.

"Bareth!" An old woman raced around from the back of the tavern. "I seen one of the wolf-beasts approaching our village! Attack! Guards!"

Valholm sighed. "Zu-Zu, did you actually see something again? Perhaps it was that dragon you saw last full moon."

The crowd roared in laughter. Some returned to their nightly activities.

Valholm continued to mock her. "Or maybe it was the werebear! Or what if it *was* a werewolf? The fact of the matter is, you old crone, whatever it was you saw, you were the only one who saw it! Just like every time before. Go back home, you drunkard."

Elody rolled her eyes, apologized to Zu-Zu, and guided her fiancé away from the tavern toward the bakery.

"Dear, it seems you have had too much to drink tonight. Why don't we all go inside and forget this whole night happened."

"Don't tell me how to handle my business."

Valholm looked solemnly at Elody's innocent eyes and slunk his shoulders. She was the only one who could get to him. Her voice soothed his soul, like sweet music in a field of lilacs on a starry night.

"One day, we will have a house built on top of that hill over there," Valholm promised. "We will have children, and every spring when the tulips bloom, I will look into your radiant face and be so thankful another year has passed that I have been able to be with you. I love you Elody."

"Our love is forever." Elody kissed Valholm and walked back towards her father and sister.

Her elegant hair flowing in the wind, she skipped to the melody of romance playing her heart strings. She smiled every day. Even in the darkest of times there was always something to be joyous about. But as she approached her family and friends, her heart sank and fear burned from within.

Torches approached their village. Steel blades were unsheathed, and unknown men yelled and cursed. Screaming villagers were shoved into the dirt, harassed and beaten.

"Fire!" yelled a civilian. "At the stables!"

An army of about a hundred men marched through the dirty streets. They were dressed in non-conforming uniforms and armor – a mercenary army. The man who brought up the lead wore a hooded cloak and a dark silver mask with two eye slits, a rise where his nose should be, and sculpted lips. He held up a crossbow in a metal gauntlet. An arrow pierced a soldier holding a torch, exiting the other side of his head with a red mist.

"There will be no setting fire unless we cannot find the beast!" the lead man yelled at the mercenaries.

Bareph called out. "Hold your weapons! What is the meaning of this intrusion?"

After freeing the horses, several villagers gathered water buckets to put out the burning stables.

"Forgive our aggressive arrival," the masked man hissed. "My name is Spallthrone. We are on a quest by the order of King Vavrinec."

"Whatever it is you are looking for, I can assure that you will not find it here." Bareph tried glaring through the mysterious mask.

"What we are looking for is not your concern. Just know we work for the safety of the people. Allow us to search every building and home for signs pertaining to our assignment, and we will be out of your hair. If you intend to get in our way, however, we will use lethal force."

"I demand a better explanation than that! The man who hired you is my own blood, you will also answer to me," Bareph ordered.

Spallthrone looked around the small, poor village. The villagers wore ragged clothes. The buildings were few, and there was nothing spectacular to look at. Even Bareph's face was dirty, his hair unwashed.

Elody, though beautiful, was also dirty. Spallthrone walked up to her and raised his right-hand level with the ground. Bareph stepped forward and without hesitation put his knife to the man's throat.

"My lady." Spallthrone clasped her hand in his.

The young girl turned her head in disgust, but tried to remain upright and proper.

Spallthrone let go of her hand and turned back to Bareph, who lowered his knife.

"So!" Spallthrone's voice screeched. "You are royalty?"

"I am."

"Fine. Good, good. Then you will understand my curiosity as to why you and your people live away from Xerxas in such poor living conditions. Don't answer that. I don't care. The point is, I respect people with wealth. You, sir, though you may be royal, don't appear to have any money worthy of my time."

"From a leader to a leader, I wish to know what it is you seek." Bareph maintained a stone cold expression.

"I am no leader. I just give these men orders, and I get paid the most."

"Spallthrone!" Bareph shouted in annoyance. "Do you wish for this to be civil or do you want the blood of you and your men shed throughout these fields? My patience is growing thinner by the second and if you don't tell me then the last thing you will ever seek will be salvation from the gods after I slice open your throat with my blade! Now, your next words better not be the last you ever speak."

The mercenary leader was still. The army behind him stood motionless as they waited for his command. Elody and Pereta looked at each other.

Spallthrone spoke. "We seek a wolf."

Pereta raised an eyebrow. "A wolf? You disturb our tranquility over a wolf?" She marched toward him with purpose but was caught on her arm by her father.

"Calm down, Pereta." Bareph turned to Spallthrone. "What do you mean you are looking for a wolf?"

"The wolf I seek is not only animal but human as well. I have discovered that it can control whether or not to be in its beast form. Tonight is a full moon. If it had no control over itself, your village would most certainly be in chaos right now."

Elody turned red in fear and left the crowd to find Valholm who had retired to his hut to sleep off the drink. The sounds of men bellowing back and forth faded into the ambiance of insects buzzing in the fields, toads croaking to one another, and Valholm's snoring.

Elody ran past fallen washboards, barrels of fruit, and day-old meat until she came to one of the biggest huts in the back corner of the housing perimeter. Valholm's stone and dried straw hut was half the size of the tavern – considerably bigger than the surrounding huts.

"Val!" Elody burst through the door and scared Valholm so bad he screamed and rolled onto the floor.

Elody stumbled in a frenzy to help him. "Get up, you oaf, we need you right now. I feel a battle is about to break out in the village! I'm scared, Val, I don't want to die."

"Calm down. What is the prob- Hey! Stop pouring water on me! I feel fine, get off."

She backed away and set the half-empty pitcher on a side table. "I'm sorry, I'm just scared. I need you."

"Be afraid for your people, my love. To be afraid of your own death is selfish."

Elody turned red in shame. Valholm sighed and he leaned close to embrace her.

"Forgive me," Valholm exhaled. "I do love you. Wait here while I go to the village, I don't want to see you hurt. Will you be okay?"

"Yes, just please be sure to get Pereta to safety if things get out of hand."

"I will. Now tell me what this whole ordeal is about?"

"There is an army that wants me dead."

*****

Bareph clashed his sword with Spallthrone's. The mercenary army spread throughout the village and rummaged the buildings, slaughtering any civilians who got in their way. Bareph's army scattered to collect their armor and weapons and began to fight back, but to no avail. The attacking army was better trained, and their morals did not stop them from stabbing innocents. Screams and cries were all around.

Pereta had a double-bladed sword in hand to fight off the soldiers, but she felt an enemy blade bite into her shoulder and yanked back out.

She cried out for her sister, but she was nowhere among the chaos. She screamed for her dad.

Valholm jumped from the crowd and met her attacker with the tip of his blade, piercing his heart and leaving him lifeless.

"Get to your homes!" he yelled. "If you hear them coming closer, then we have failed, and you are to head south until you reach the next town." He turned to Pereta. "Elody is in my hut, find her."

Pereta ran off as Valholm continued to fight off the soldiers.

Bloodshed has a way of turning the innocent and fearful into a ravaging force, especially when the blood of one's kin is being spilled.

The words the cleric spoke earlier played through Bareph's head as he battled Spallthrone. They struck each other's steel and pushed away from one another.

"I promise you, we know nothing of a werewolf in these parts." Bareph pleaded to Spallthrone as the people surrounding him fell. "Stop now and I will consider sparing your life."

"You're a damned liar. We saw the beast sprinting through the fields and into your village," Spallthrone hacked.

The two men met swords once again.

"I'm warning you!" Bareph pressed hard against his opponent.

Spallthrone laughed. "You believe you have power over me? Fool. Here I am, strike me down."

He stepped away and held his arms out to his side, then dropped his blade. Bareph cocked his head and stared in confusion. He hated this man who had brought war upon his people, now about a quarter of which were laying on the ground drowning in their own blood. Bareph lifted his blade and brought it down upon the menace, but something was wrong. His blade filtered through the man as if it was cutting through mist.

Not a scratch was made. Frustration got the better of the old warrior. With each swing he made, Spallthrone was not harmed.

"Is this some sort of magic?" Bareph asked. "Fight me like a man instead of hiding behind black magic."

Spallthrone sneered. "It's hard for me to fight like a man when I am only half a man. I must say, the demon half gets the better of me sometimes."

Spallthrone rammed his sword into the awestruck Bareph's gut.

Pereta and Elody, watching from the dark corners between buildings, screamed and ran out into the street. The battle paused in their presence.

Valholm ran up to the girls and tried to push them back.

"Pereta! I told you to keep her safe!" Valholm gripped them tight. "This is no place for you. Elody, these men are trying to kill you!"

The mercenary army began to murmur amongst themselves, unsure about whether to attack or wait for orders. Spallthrone seemed especially intrigued, and wiped the blood off of his sword. Bareph knelt on the ground, grabbing his wound. For the first time he looked hopelessly up at his two girls.

"You are the one we search for?" Spallthrone looked at Elody. "You are the beast we have been contracted to hunt down?"

"Get back unless you want a blade in your chest," Valholm threatened.

"No. Wait, let me explain myself," Elody pleaded.

"Yes, let the beast explain itself," said Spallthrone.

Valholm stepped up to the masked man. "If you didn't hear me, I will repeat myself only once!"

"Val!" Elody ran up to her fiancé. "There is something you must know, no matter how much you may hate me."

"What are you talking about? I could never hate you," Valholm smiled.

"This shit is making me so bubbly inside," Spallthrone spat sarcastically. Raising his sword, Spallthrone smashed Valholm's face with his pommel and turned the blade to Elody.

The battle erupted into chaos once more. Blades dug into flesh and blood flew. Elody watched as if time were standing still as her family and friends were slaughtered. She knew these men were looking for her, a beast, for whatever reason. And she knew she could stop the battle if she just gave these men what they wanted.

But what if we defeat this army? Elody thought to herself as the blade of Spallthrone weighed heavy above her, suspended in time. My family would disown me, my village would be frightened of me and cast me away as a threat. What of my future husband? My dreams would be erased. But if I run, there will be no more village to return to. We would have to rebuild all over. What must I do?

The blade was now a foot away from her face, and her eyes raged. Her arms began to bulge as fur grew rapidly on her skin. The beautiful face everyone knew so well now grew a snout and fangs. Paws appeared where her hands had been, and claws as sharp as steel met Spallthrone's blade and effortlessly knocked it from his hands.

The battle stopped once again as all gasped at this horrifying spectacle. On all fours, the werewolf stood five feet tall. Bareph could believe neither his eyes nor the fear he now felt for his daughter.

Elody gnashed her teeth and charged at Spallthrone, who then turned to his demon side, rendering him nonphysical. She jumped right through him and charged at the enemy soldiers. Not only did they run, but so did her own people. Fear rose from their screams as they ran and some villagers even tried to strike the girl they all so loved.

The wolf pounced on the enemy. She clawed at their backs, her sharp teeth tore flesh from bone, draining them of their blood, but not altogether from their life. She was still in control and did not wish to kill anyone, no matter how evil they may seem. Her own people did not appear to see that, however. Instead, they saw a ruthless monster, a savage killer.

The army tried fighting back the werewolf, but they were too weak and began to scatter. Soon they were all running off in fear of the beast. Spallthrone shouted at them, calling them cowards and bastards, but even his threats would not change their minds. They were weak, and he was strong. He could overtake this beast.

As he moved around in his demon form, he trailed a faint blue mist about him. Elody charged at him but once again fell through the hazy body. The mist disappeared, and he struck her with his blade. She yelped and scampered away to recover briefly, then with a roar she charged again. The mist appeared, and she ran through his body. He returned with another blow to her face, then once again became ethereal. Elody whimpered in pain.

Bareph grew worried. He knew this beast could be a threat, but he fought with his own thoughts, and soon tears rolled for his daughter. He couldn't lose her, no matter what she was. He tried to get up, lifted himself to stand, but fell back down from the pain. Bareph continued to crawl as blood came trickling out of his wound onto the ground. Then a hand touched him. It was Samthra, the village nurse. She had suffered hurt as well, but came to the aid of her chief.

"Sir, before you do anything stupid I would advise you to let me seal this wound," she panted. "We don't want you bleeding out."

Bareph looked upon his daughter, the werewolf, as she tried to fight back. She was able to strike Spallthrone a few times, but without much force behind the blow. She was taking too much damage. He knew her mind was somewhat clouded in this rage. She rarely took beast form, but when she did, she would run alone in the wilderness. She loved being at one with the animals, and feeling her true strength and inner being. She never harmed another while in beast form. And now, amidst the blood and gore, she began to fade out.

Spallthrone readied his sword for one final blow.

In her weakness, Elody started to transform back into a human. Her wounds were open on her once flawless skin. She sat on the ground, curled up in defeat as Spallthrone swung his sword towards her.

Blood sprinkled through the air and rained upon Elody's face.

Pereta screamed profanity as her sword cut through Spallthrone's stomach. He arched his head and wailed like a banshee in the night, then evapo-

rated into blue mist and floated away, still screaming. He was wounded, but not defeated.

Pereta dropped her blade. She ran to her crying and shivering sister and embraced her. Pereta
took off her outer layers of clothing and put them
over Elody, then tried standing her up. The village
was quiet once again, this time with fear and wonder.

"Leave her be for now," Pereta spoke to all
listening. "We will talk about what has happened
after she heals."

The sisters stumbled past faces plagued by
terror and worry, and entered the tavern. The light
was dim from the still-burning fire. They walked to
the back and into a small room where they found
Samthra finishing the bandage on Bareph.

"Oh, hello girls," he stuttered. "Pardon my
nerves. You understand. But what I saw you do today, Elody, was very brave. Honestly, you saved
us."

All four smiled and took in the silence. It was
soothing, and Elody felt she really did have at least
three people on her side. But as she lay back in the
bed, and Samthra applied medicine to each wound,
she couldn't stop thinking of Val. After the battle
had ended, she looked for him, to see if he had love
in his eyes or fear, but he was nowhere in sight.

The night grew late. Elody and her father had been fixed up. Samthra left for the evening, and Pereta found a pile of blankets to sleep on the floor. Elody was the last to fall asleep, haunted with the fear she may never know her dreams being a wife with children and having that house on the hill. Her eyelids shut and she drifted off to sleep, not knowing what she would have to face the following day.

*****

The sunshine beat down upon the village as people cleaned up the streets. It was almost late afternoon when Elody awoke. Her father and sister were gone, but a mysterious old man sat in the corner who almost gave her a heart attack.

"Please be calm, Elody," the old man said. "I am a friend of Bareph's."

"Are you a mage?" Elody observed his robes.

"I am a cleric. I heard what occurred here last night. I offered you and your father the miracle of healing. You should find your wounds all better now."

She looked at her arms and abdomen to find only scars.

"That's amazing!" She laughed. "Thank you so much!"

"It's my pleasure. Now, I am afraid I must be off. I just had to see that you pulled through. Your real test is to face your people. Unfortunately, all is not so calm outside. I wish you luck, my lady, you did a brave deed last night."

"Thank you again." She hesitantly looked toward the window. Then once she looked back, the cleric was gone.

Elody got dressed and headed outside to face her village. As she opened the door, she heard her father and sister yelling at the other villagers. People debated, cursed, and yelled. When she stepped out, she was greeted with screams and few smiles.

"She's the beast!" one woman cried out. "We are not safe with her!"

"She is our Chief's daughter!" Another called out. "We've all known her since she was little!"

"We cannot risk the safety of our people with this probable danger. She must go!" a man yelled.

Bareph bellowed out. "If she is to go, then I am to go with her. To banish my daughter is to banish me!"

"You bastards are sick!" Pereta cursed. "She saved you all! We should make you leave!"

Those in fear of Elody numbered much greater than those who supported her. She was left speechless. She searched the crowd for Valholm and spotted him in the back, speaking with an elderly couple.

"Val!"

She ran through the crowd, which quickly parted for her. She embraced the tall man, waiting to feel his warm comforting arms around her, but he never held her back. She stepped back in confusion and looked up upon her husband-to-be.

"Valholm?" She nervously giggled. "What's wrong? Why won't you hold me?"

He never lowered his head. Instead, he stared blankly into space.

"You never mentioned this to me," he mumbled. "Three years we have been together, and we trusted each other."

"My love-"

"No. Take your hand off of me. It is my duty to protect my people, and you scare them. A beast is something uncontrollable, made with magic, black magic. No good ever comes from evil, Elody. You must leave our village."

"Val, look at me." Tears flowed from her eyes. "Look at me! We are to have a family! A home together on the hill! We are to be married!"

Her tiny hands beat his chest, begging him to look at her, but he never did. She sunk down and cried. Pereta and Bareph took each side of her and helped her stand. Bareph glared at Valholm, but spoke not a word. They walked away, and Elody looked back one last time at Valholm. He never looked at her, but she saw a faint tear trickle down his cheek. This made her sob even more, but Pereta took her face with her hand and spoke faint words. The words comforted Elody a little, and Bareph turned to the crowd to speak.

"It seems we are at a crossroads. I for one will not leave my dear Elody, but I know we are no longer welcome here. It is no use to fight you. No more bloodshed is needed. Your arrogance will be the death of you all one day. We are to move on, find a new home. Those who are still with us, and who will follow my daughters and me, are welcome to come with us. Those who wish to stay will surely be judged by the gods."

Bareph was a much-respected man. In the back of his mind, he hoped his people would still have faith in him. But after last night's events, and the speeches Valholm gave while he and Elody slept, he knew it was a hopeless fight.

Samthra stepped forward. She stood straight and proud. "I will walk anywhere with you, my Chief."

"And I," A man began to walk towards Bareph and his daughters.

"And us." This time, a family of four joined them.

Several more people joined them and made a group of about twenty-five. The other villagers stood silent, and Valholm quietly made his exit into the neighboring blacksmith shop.

"Fine. So be it," Bareph muttered to himself.

He turned and walked towards the wagons that were arranged and came up to his two daughters, one of whom was still sobbing.

"Father, what will happen now? Where will we go?"

"Don't worry my sweet, I have made arrangements with a cleric to set us up with temporary living conditions. He has a friend in Renhet who will give us shelter. Soon, we shall have us a new village and begin again."

"Are you afraid of me, father?" Elody asked.

"You've always been a beast in the morning," Pereta tried to joke.

"No," Bareph answered.

"How can you not be?" questioned Elody.

"Because, in that which is good there can never be evil."

Murder in Kitanan

By Joel Norden

733 AM Age of the Dracon-esti

"We should stay the night. Let this storm pass. After all, we have plenty of time to reach the Grass-lands," Kendra shouted over the pouring rain and howling winds.

Arianna nodded in agreement. Her long brown hair clung to her face as rain pelted her. The horses neighed nervously as lightning flashed and thunder rolled.

The wood elf sisters sat on their horses upon the large hill, overlooking a small town sprawled below. On the opposite side of the valley was a giant castle nestled into the base of the mountains, a good distance south of the town. The castle looked sinister in the storm.

Arianna spurred her horse forward, not wanting to spend any more time than necessary in the pouring rain. Kendra almost laughed. Arianna reminded her of the witches from old tales, terrified of melting from any contact with water. It was foolishness of course, but she kept her thoughts to herself as her sister would not find them amusing. Arianna was a mage, not a witch.

From what Kendra knew, the five orders of magi were founded over six hundred years ago. Arianna was of the order of blue robes. What separated the blue robes from other orders was their known prowess in battle and their use of powerful combat magic. All weapons – except staffs– were prohibited by the other orders, but twin scimitars hung from Arianna's belt. Kendra had seen her sister use her arcane arts many times in a fight. More than once it had been enough to turn the tides in their favor.

Kendra wiped her wet, wavy hair away from her face. The pair made their way down the muddy road at a slow pace, so as not to injure their horses on the descent. It had been a long southbound trip from Isatarist. Her legs, back, and hips ached from the long ride. They had stopped every night for a few hours to rest, and then would hit the trail again. This night they hadn't been able to find shelter, so they decided to ride through the storm.

The sisters were compelled to see if the rumors were true of dark forces brewing in the Grasslands. Their group of friends – who dubbed themselves the Band – had split up to investigate the rumors and to explore Draston. They had done this every year for the past decade.

Kendra studied the town as best she could in the stormy darkness. It was a small town, almost abandoned by the lack of light and movement. She ignored the uncanny feeling, sure it was just the rain, nothing more.

The sisters quickly rode into the town after the ground leveled out. No one was out in the storm. Rain pitter-pattered against roofs. No lights shone from the any of the uninviting wooden homes.

Kendra shivered. She could feel eyes watching her from inside the houses.

In front of a large building, the duo brought their horses to a halt and hastily dismounted. A creaky sign swung in the storm: *Inn of Kitanan*. Kendra snorted at the originality. Grabbing the reins of her cherry bay destrier, Uri, Kendra led the horse around the side of the stable. Arianna followed closely, leading her black stallion.

Kendra was proud of the name she had selected for her horse. She had named the destrier after the first woman to ever become a Silver Knight of Kraos: Uri Vallnor. Of course, Arianna had refused to name her horse when Kendra had asked her.

They quickly stabled their horses and paused a moment to enjoy the dryness of the building.

Arianna looked at Kendra from deep within her blue robes. "I wish to be gone from this place as soon as possible."

Kendra nodded. "Is there something wrong, Ari?"

"Something isn't right about this town. I… I just sense it. Maybe it's just the weather, I don't know."

"I don't doubt you. I'm sure it's the weather though. I felt the same way at the sight of that castle."

Arianna nodded hesitantly. "Let us get a room, sister. I wish to be out of these wet clothes."

The tavern was empty as they entered except for two men who talked quietly in a corner. The Inn of Kitanan wasn't a very cozy place. The tables were thin and rickety. Cheap paintings hung crooked on the wall, many with holes in the canvas. Candles were few, creating a very dim atmosphere.

The two men stared at the sisters as they entered the establishment. Kendra's sharp elven hearing caught one of the men mutter something about knife-ears. She knew Arianna had heard it too, for her sister bristled, but said nothing. The other man told him to shut the hell up, muttering something about the Lord of Kitanan.

It wasn't long until the innkeeper bustled out of the kitchen to welcome the new customers. The innkeeper was a fat man with pudgy cheeks, squinty pig-like eyes, and a grease-slathered apron that seemed to never have been washed. At the sight of the sisters the man was instantly nervous, the inviting smile leaving his face.

"Can I help you ladies?" he asked, eyes shifting from Arianna's blue robes to Kendra's silver armor and long sword.

"Yes. One room and a warm meal for each of us," Arianna said promptly.

"Ehhh, I'm afraid we are all booked up, ma'am." The man shifted his hefty weight from foot to foot.

"Are you sure? I've heard that lying to a mage is a very foolish thing to do." Arianna's hazel eyes stared icily through the fat man.

"Uhhhh, let me check again, ma'am… err… Mrs. mage." The man almost fell over himself re-entering the kitchen.

It wasn't long before the man returned with a shameful look on his face. "I made some arrangements to fit you ladies in. No one should be out in this weather… You'd catch your death."

"Heh, imagine that." Kendra dropped a coin purse on the counter.

"Free of charge…" the innkeeper mumbled.

"Nonsense. We are not thugs. We will pay the fee everyone else pays. But we would rather not be turned away because of our race," Kendra said coldly.

The man's eyes widened. "I promise, no I swear, it was not that! I had a full-"

"Enough. We need our rest," Arianna interrupted.

The innkeeper hurriedly led the sisters upstairs to their room and rushed away.

The room was simple. A small bed, a table with one chair and a small oil lamp.

Kendra and Arianna dropped their stuff in the corner and changed into dry clothing. It wasn't long before the innkeeper knocked on the door, two large bowls of beef stew in hand. Kendra sat at the small wooden table and ate heartily. Arianna only ate a few spoonfuls, then set it to the side.

Arianna picked up a book with an icy blue binding. On the cover, arcane runes were inscribed in the spidery language of magic. She studied her spell book in silence. Every night Arianna re-learned spells she had used before, or committed new spells to memory. Arianna had told Kendra many times to never open the book, for those who didn't know magic would lose their minds. Kendra wasn't sure if that was true, but she had never had the urge to test it.

When Kendra finished eating, she sharpened her sword with a whetstone and oiled it in fluid motions. She watched the reflection of candlelight flicker along the clean blade. She had been trained to clean her blade and armor every night. A Silver Knight's sword and armor was their life.

Kendra's only dream had been to be a knight, but sadly that would never happen. At first the Silver Knights had turned her away, saying no elf — let alone a woman elf – would pass the grueling test for knighthood. Finally, after much persuasion, they had allowed Kendra to train with them. They were eager to watch her fail.

Despite being told that, as an elf, she could never be a part of the ranks, Kendra had never worked so hard to accomplish something, and passed the training. The sergeant-at-arms himself had given her a warrior's handshake and told her he wished he could add her to the ranks.

Kendra laid her bedroll out on the floor and attempted to sleep, but thoughts of a certain half-elf flittered through her mind instead. How she missed Ganith. And as much as she hated to admit it, she missed that beard. It made him look ruggedly handsome – as facial hair was non-existent in elven society, for elves couldn't grow beards. Ganith was quick with a joke, but far from immature. He was the leader of the Band.

The Band had all gone their own way that past summer, seeking news of the growing darkness in Draston. Kendra and Arianna had volunteered to travel south. Kendra had never been further south than Kraos, so this trip excited her. Kendra wasn't sure what Arianna's motives were for volunteering to explore the rumors of The Wicked Eye's evil in the south. She had asked, but Arianna had only replied that some great and powerful spellbooks lie in the south.

Kendra lay on her bedroll and turned to Arianna. "Do you miss Therin, Ari?"

Therin was another one of the Band. A gray elf they had grown up with.

Arianna looked annoyed at Kendra for interrupting her studying. She didn't say anything at first, and Kendra was sure her sister would skirt around the question, as Therin had been her lover.

To Kendra's surprise, Arianna answered. "Perhaps. Though, I shouldn't."

"I think it would be unnatural if you didn't, Arianna. We were all childhood friends after all. We've all been through a lot."

Arianna smiled gently. "Yes, indeed we have. Now sleep sister, we should be out of this town early."

Kendra nodded and rolled to her side. It had been a long time since she had seen Arianna smile like that. A smile also crossed Kendra's face as she slipped into slumber.

*****

Kendra and Arianna were up before the cock's crow, packing up their items and readying the horses. Kendra mounted Uri and exited the stable. She soaked up the early morning sun creeping over the hills as she waited for Arianna to mount up and join her.

A large board posted on the side of the inn caught her eye. Kendra urged Uri closer to the board. Many posts and wanted signs hung there. But what caught her eye were the *Missing Children* notices. Seven had gone missing in the last week. Kendra offered a silent prayer to the goddess Marthna for the children's safekeeping.

Arianna brought her black stallion up next to Kendra. "What is it, sister?"

"Seven children have gone missing in the last week." Kendra frowned, troubled by the thought.

"That is truly sad… We must be on our way, if we'd like to be in the Grasslands in a timely manner. Already we have a few weeks ride through the mountains of Rhoben."

Kendra nodded as Arianna spurred her horse forward at a slow pace. Kendra stared at the board for a few moments longer and then followed her sister.

Kendra knew she was right. After they figured out if the rumors were true or not, they could return to their friends in Isatarist.

They continued riding through town. Kitanan was in a poor shape. The streets had once been cobblestone, but the stones had sunk. Only corners and broken stone jutted out of the muddy earth. Many of the buildings were boarded up or had broken windows. Several beggars lined the streets, sitting in the muck, clothes torn and ragged. Rats ran in packs down the sides of houses, scampering into holes to escape the sunlight.

"I once heard this town was beautiful. A city of refugees that fled the War of Nine Years to build a city of peace," Kendra spoke quietly.

Arianna looked at her sister with a grim expression. "Yes, and if they don't clean it up the black plague will be upon them. Just like the cities of Southern Glandstone many years ago."

"I remember that. We lived in Eva at the time. Thankfully it didn't make it to the northern shores of the Sea of Sarmy. We didn't have to worry about it much." Kendra shook her head at the memory of the fear when the rumors reached their small village.

As the sisters reached the southern outskirts of Kitanan, a sobbing woman approached them.

"Please help us! If you have any compassion in your souls, help us!" The woman was a plump lady, with rosy red cheeks that matched her hair.

Kendra guessed she was near thirty by the lines under her eyes and the few gray streaks that ran through her hair.

"What is wrong, miss?" Kendra asked. She ignored the glare Arianna gave her.

"My husband and child of nine years have gone missing. Six other children have gone missing in the past week! Please, please help us!" The woman fell to her knees and clutched Kendra's foot in the stirrup.

"We will help you," Kendra said soothingly.

"Sister. Do you think this is wise? We should leave this town." Arianna had an icy tone, upset at her sister for making decisions without her counsel.

"I don't care if it's wise. It's the proper and moral thing to do." She looked down at the sobbing woman. "What is your name, miss? And please stop crying, we will try to help as best as we can."

"My name is Nora. Thank you so much for helping. It means the world to me… to us." Nora smiled, tears streamed down her cheeks. Kendra smiled back. It felt great to give this woman hope. In this dark world, all you could do was hope and pray to the gods that the storm passed without causing any more havoc.

Kendra helped Nora climb on the back of her horse. Arianna watched, her face an unreadable mask.

"Show us to your home, Nora, and we can talk about your husband and child."

Nora's small hut lay southwest of Kitanan, several miles out of town, surrounded by rolling green pastures. The eastern fields turned into hills, which turned into mountains. The pasture that led south eventually transformed into forests and then again turned into mountains.

A small open-sided stable was next to the hut. Farther out in the field south of the hut lay a large barn, much bigger than the hut.

Kendra talked to Nora for a while. Nora explained that her husband and son had gone to find a missing sheep in the pasture at night. They had counted several times and one was missing, which happens sometimes, Nora explained. Wolves and bears would pick one off, or the foolish sheep would just wander too far and forget how to get back to the herd.

Nora brought the sisters to the sheep barn and left them there to start their search.

"You know you could go south without me," Kendra snapped when they were alone.

Arianna looked at her sister coolly. "What happened or happens in this village doesn't concern us, sister. Thousands die and go missing throughout Draston every day." Arianna raised a hand before Kendra could angrily retort. "No, before you go on and on about how honorable and noble it is, I'd just rather not die playing town guard. I will, however, help you, sister. I know you are as stubborn as a mule and won't be persuaded on this matter. Whatever we do, we do together, like we always have."

"Thank you," Kendra replied, quite peevishly.

Arianna nodded. "She was telling the truth, in case you were curious. You so blindly believe people sometimes. I cast a spell of truth on Nora back in Kitanan."

Kendra shook her head. She hadn't even noticed Arianna casting a spell. Arianna wasn't wrong, though. Sometimes Kendra was so willing to help, she would take no caution.

"Let's find these two," was all Kendra said.

"Agreed. Then we can leave this damned city."

The sisters wandered the pastures for a while searching for footprints. What they found instead was blood and wool on a low-hanging branch where the pasture met the forest. The branch blew in the wind as the sisters eyed it.

Kendra quickly found a small blood trail. A drop of blood on a leaf. Six feet away was another drop.

"I wish this blood was a little closer together," Kendra mumbled.

Arianna nodded. "I may not be a ranger, but we could be tracking this animal for some time."

Arianna had been right. They followed the trail of blood for a long time, taking them deep into the forest. Occasionally they would lose the trail and would be forced to backtrack to find it again.

Arianna stopped dead in her tracks, hissing for silence. "Do you hear that? There! Sister…"

Arianna and Kendra froze. Some twenty yards away a man sobbed, leaning over something. Kendra's sword was out in a flash, Arianna was right behind her, scimitar out and ready. They rushed over to the man. He was around the same age as Nora, his short black beard peppered with gray. He wore a ragged tunic splattered with dirt and blood. He sat, knees in the dirt, hands helplessly at his side.

He looked crazed at the two women.

The man matched the description Nora had given of her husband.

"By all the gods of good…" Kendra swore.

Laying in front of the man was a boy, close to the age of ten. The boy's skin was pale. His throat had been cut ruthlessly and there were several stab wounds to his stomach.

Kendra pushed the man to the ground with one hand, sword in the other. He fell over helplessly. Weeping, the man did nothing as Kendra searched him.

"He's got no weapon on him. Nothing on him, really."

Arianna nodded as she stood from where the boy lay. "He's been dead for several hours." Arianna looked at the bearded man. "Did you do this?"

The man just stared dumbly at her. Kendra aimed a swift kick at him, hitting the man in the stomach. "Answer her, Wesif take you!"

The man groaned and made unintelligible sounds. He held up bloody hands in front of himself, begging Kendra not to kick him again.

"Wonderful. He's a damned mute," Arianna muttered, looking to her sister. "Kendra, I gave you handcuffs when we left Isatarist, do you still have them? Good. Put them on him."

Kendra nodded, pushing the man's face down in the dirt and cuffing his hands. Arianna wrapped the child up in the man's cloak.

The walk back to Nora's hut was slow. Several times the man fell and refused to get back up. Kendra's kicks soon changed his mind.

As they arrived at the hut, Nora came running out the door sobbing. She fell to the ground at the site of the cloak-wrapped body that Kendra carried.

Nora screamed incoherently at the man, a mixture of grief and rage. She attempted to hit him. He didn't meet her furious gaze. Kendra hurriedly pulled Nora off the man.

"How could you let this happen, Brom? Why? Tell me damn you!" She collapsed helplessly into the dirt.

Kendra kneeled next to her. "I'm sorry for your loss, Nora. We aren't sure who did this. There was no murder weapon that we could find and no other tracks."

"They were alone," Arianna added.

"No…no…you think Brom did this?" Nora looked sadly at the man who stared blankly at the dirt.

"We will leave that up to the authorities," Arianna spoke quietly.

They took the man and left for Kitanan, leaving Nora to grieve the loss of her son.

Kendra looked at the man stumbling behind their horses. His eyes were dull and staring emptily. Kendra still couldn't wrap her head around it. Who would do something like that? And if it was Brom… to do that to his own child? Disgusting.

As they re-entered the south side of Kitanan, a small group of guards approached them. Wearing rag-tag armor, most of which was rusted, they looked more like militia or bandits than a city guard. They each held a different weapon: spear, club, rusty long sword, and short-sword.

Arianna and Kendra explained the situation and the murder scene when the guards asked why the man was handcuffed and roped to Arianna's horse.

"So you're saying there wasn't a murder weapon nearby, mage?" the guard with a spear asked.

"We searched the crime scene well. But we were a bit rushed as we wished to bring this man in as soon as possible," Arianna replied.

"Aye, well third Councilman Otiker will wish to speak with you ladies, I'm sure. He is in charge of crime in the city."

Arianna nodded. "Take us to him."

The group of guards led the way through the streets, and freed Brom from Arianna's horse as they dragged him along. The man with the spear had sent one of the other guards up ahead to let Councilman Otiker know of their arrival.

The councilman's office building wasn't anything special, but it was better kept than any of the other buildings that Kendra had seen in Kitanan. Two more guards stood in front of the office, and they quickly bid the other guards enter.

They entered into a small room. Not much was in the room except a desk and an assistant of the Councilman. She quickly sent Arianna, Kendra, and the lead guard through a door leading into Otiker's study. The rest of the guards stood outside with the prisoner.

The third Councilman of Kitanan was a chubby man, his cheeks flushed. He sipped a glass of whisky as he looked over several papers that were spread out over his desk. Otiker looked up as they entered and gestured them to sit. "I'm Otiker Varoan, third Councilman of Kitanan, as you most likely know already."

"I am Arianna Gathon. This is my sister, Kendra. Did your guardsman tell you of the murder?" Arianna asked.

"Yes he did. A vile thing. Pox on the man who did it! Simon, put the man in a cell, then grab your men and check the murder scene. If he is guilty, he hangs tomorrow morning. Search for a murder weapon and bodies. We still have six children missing."

"As you wish, my lord." Simon was on his feet and headed for the door.

"Thank all the gods in the vast Empyrean that you ladies came through town. Here is some coin, stay the night at the inn. In the morning, hopefully you can see the bastard hang. Our town thanks you." Otiker tossed a coin purse to Kendra, who caught it deftly.

"What about the other six children missing?" Kendra asked.

"Dead, most likely," Otiker said sadly. "But we will continue to search for them. I will send word to Corvos in hopes he can help using his magic."

"A magic-user lives in town? Does he belong to the Circle?" Arianna asked curiously.

Otiker eyed her blue robes. "Look, Arianna, I want no trouble here. Corvos is a good man and has protected this city well. It is none of my business if he is part of the Circle of Magi or not."

"I do not wish to start any trouble. I just wish to speak to him. Where can I find him?"

Otiker sighed and set down his glass of whisky. The man looked tired. "He is up in Lord Ingram's castle, but none are allowed to enter the castle grounds, so you will have to wait until tomorrow morning. I'm sure Corvos will be here for the hanging. He is fierce about protecting Kitanan."

"No guests are allowed in the castle? Or no one at all?" Kendra pried.

"No one. This was the deal Corvos struck with Lord Ingram. No one disturbs him or his family, and he lets Kitanan be built here. So it has been for a hundreds of years. Lord Ingram took Corvos as an adviser, and that's how we communicate."

The sisters said nothing but looked at each other. "Thank you, Otiker. We must be off, we'll see you in the morning," Arianna said finally.

"Thank you again!"

They rode slowly through town. It was evening before Kendra and Arianna finally returned to the Inn of Kitanan. They stabled their horses and entered the inn. Kendra couldn't believe how fast the day had gone. She still felt numb inside, and couldn't shake the memory of the dead child. Kendra sighed as they entered. Many looked up from their drinks, curiosity or suspicion on their faces, and then continued laughing and shouting. Smells of fresh bread and beef stew filled the inn. Kendra was in no mood to be around people.

The sisters made their way through the crowd to sit at the bar. The bartender turned around, surprised to see them. "I figured you ladies would have put Kitanan far behind you! I heard about the child killer… I pray the bastard hangs."

"You have already heard, innkeeper?" Kendra asked.

The innkeeper chuckled. "Please, call me Leon. The first person to know what happens in a town is either the bard or the innkeeper. A few drinks and people love to spill out their lives. Sad news it is though." Leon shook his head and cleaned some glasses with a dirty rag. "We've never had any issues here in Kitanan. No bandits wander the lands near us, nor do any goblins or wolves. The Lord of Kitanan and Corvos makes sure the town militia patrols the pastures and woodlands around the city to ensure the town's safety. I apologize, ladies! My mouth is running instead of offering you drink and food," the innkeeper said apologetically.

"I'll take some stew and some ale. Not the cheap, watered down stock either," Kendra said.

"Wine and bread please," Arianna said. When the innkeeper went back to the kitchen, she looked at Kendra. "Maybe this Corvos knows something about the other six children?"

"Maybe." Kendra looked dubious. "You don't think it was Nora's husband who killed the children?"

"I'm not sure what to think anymore, sister. Perhaps it was Brom or perhaps not. If it was him, the bodies would never be discovered since he is a mute. Either way, I'm curious about this Corvos. As well as Lord Ingram."

"Yes, it is a shady thing, a magic-user and a lord wanting privacy," Kendra chuckled at her own sarcasm.

Arianna stared at her sister. Kendra shook her head and sighed. Leon returned with their food and drink.

"So who is this Corvos?" Arianna asked as he handed her bread and wine.

"Ehh, well Corvos has been here since Kitanan was founded. Kind of a long story, honestly."

"We have all night," Kendra said between mouthfuls of stew.

"Hmmm, okay. Well, it all started with the… Ehh, it was either the nord invasion of 307 or it was the border war between Glandstone and Cobracorpen a hundred or so years after that. I've heard both, but I must apologize, for I am no historian." The innkeeper grabbed a mug and filled it with beer from the large barrel that was tapped behind him. Taking a big chug, he leaned on the bar closer to Kendra and Arianna, foam on his upper lip.

"I do think it was the border war between Glandstone and Cobracorpen. Refugees fled south in droves. One particular group was led by an elf named Corvos.

"The refugees traveled south for a long time, many dying from sickness and lack of food. But soon enough, they came to this very valley at the foot of the mountains. Lord Ingram's castle was already here. Old Corvos rode up and entered the castle. He came back the next day, saying the Lord offered his protection in exchange for light taxes and for no one, absolutely no one, to come to the castle except Corvos. So the people – tired and hungry – founded Kitanan."

"So no one except Corvos has ever been there?" Kendra asked incredulously.

"Yep, the Lord has kept his word too. No one has ever attacked us. The lands around here are safe."

"So how do you explain the missing children?" Arianna asked.

"Ehh, not sure. I personally believed the children had run away. They were always older than nine and sometimes went missing with a parent. This is the first murder in my forty-three years in this town." The innkeeper shrugged. Suddenly, shouts rang from the kitchen. "Damn it, another grease fire."

With that, the fat man bustled into the back room. The sisters decided to retire for the night and ascended the creaky stairs to their room.

Arianna was quick to fall asleep, but Kendra lay there like she had every night since leaving Isatarist.

She should have stayed with Ganith. Then again, her sister needed her. Even if Arianna would never in a thousand years admit it. After all, finding out if the rumors in the south were accurate or not was important. If the Wicked Eye actually had taken the Grasslands, war could be on the horizon for all the northern kingdoms.

*****

Kendra jerked out of a peaceful sleep. She struggled to put together what was going on, her head cloudy. She opened her mouth to speak but a hand was firmly over her lips. Arianna was nothing but a form standing over her. As Kendra's vision slowly adapted, she could see Arianna raise a finger to her lips as she removed the hand.

With elven grace Kendra was up in an instant. Not even the floorboards creaked. She quickly grabbed her sword, but didn't remove it from the scabbard to avoid making any noise.

In a crouched position Kendra looked questionably at her sister. What was it? Why had her sister woken her? Then she heard a floorboard groan outside their room, followed by angry whispers. Kendra nodded to Arianna.

The door creaked open. Kendra braced herself. Arianna was muttering a spell behind her.

The door abruptly burst open. Three men entered the room. Kendra appeared from the shadows. Her sword was out of the scabbard and in an instant she was upon the unsuspecting men.

Her hilt caught the first in the throat. He fell wheezing and clutching at his wound. The man behind him took a sloppy swing with his club. Kendra quickly sidestepped.

That sidestep saved her from getting caught in her sister's spell.

Webs flew from Arianna's fingers and draped over the other two figures. With a few more spidery words of magic they flew against the back wall of the room. There they hung, suspended and reeling in shock.

Kendra, ignoring how close she had been to being captured in her sister's spell, checked the man on the floor.

"He's still alive, though struggling to breathe. I may have crushed his windpipe."

Arianna shook her head. "Give him a few moments, he will be all right."

The two men hanging from webs started shouting and wriggling to get free.

Arianna looked at them, annoyed. "If you'd like to live, you will both shut up."

The two men instantly stopped to stare at her wide-eyed. Arianna drew her scimitar from its sheath. "So, which one of you wants to tell me who you are and why you're here?"

The two men hung their heads and said nothing.

"Ah, I see. Let me make it simple for you. I do not enjoy being attacked in the middle of the night. I swear to all the gods available, if you don't start talking I will castrate both of you. One at a time. Starting with you." Arianna stuck the scimitar's tip into the wall below one man's crotch. His eyes widened. He stuttered and looked to the other man.

"Don't look at him! Answer me!"

Kendra knew her sister would never do such an act to someone, but Arianna's tone made her wary.

"Uh, damn it, woman! No, No! Hold on! I'm Otto. To my left is Rolan. And Vol is sucking air on the ground." Otto looked at the sisters nervously. "What are you gonna do to us?"

"Good. Now who sent you, Otto?" Arianna purposely ignoring the last question.

Otto looked to Rolan, who shrugged and looked at the floor nervously. "Corvos told us that Lord Ingram said you would do harm to our families if you remained in Kitanan, because you're a—" Otto immediately cut off and looked to the floor, avoiding Arianna's hazel eyes.

"A what?"

"A witch."

"I'm a mage. I resent and hunt witches," Arianna glared.

"Just what Corvos said, I swear! I never even thought the word! We only attacked out of fear for our families, we hoped to scare you and force you to leave Kitanan."

Kendra looked at her sister. "It seems we need to pay this Corvos a visit."

"I couldn't agree more, sister."

"What will happen to us?" Rolan asked, talking for the first time.

"Well since you just tried to kill us, you're lucky I don't turn you all into frogs. After you get yourselves down, go to your families and tell them how gracious magi are." Smiling sweetly, Arianna turned and started grabbing her items.

Kendra gathered her belongings too and they left their room.

The innkeeper was standing outside in the hallway in his pajamas, eyes wide in fright. The candle in his hand shook. Kendra wondered how long the man had been standing there. He said nothing, and neither did the sisters. Arianna walked by him, nose in the air. Kendra gave him a little nod.

The inn was dark. The candles had been extinguished, and all the customers had either left or gone to bed. In the stables, Kendra hurriedly readied Uri, then mounted the cherry bay. Arianna did the same with her unnamed black stallion.

They rode slowly through Kitanan. The horses neighed nervously in the nighttime lull. The night was cold. Summer was ending, and autumn was coming. Kendra wished she was around the campfire with Ganith right now like she would have been in Isatarist. It was perfect weather for a campfire. But no, she was riding to find out why some magic-user wanted them killed.

They left Kitanan and rode south at a canter. Lord Ingram's castle slowly grew larger as the elven sisters rode up the winding trail. Kendra shivered.

Something about this castle frightened her. Fog formed around it, and only the towers that pierced through were visible.

It took longer than Kendra anticipated, but soon they reached the front gates of the castle. Oddly, the drawbridge remained open. Two guards stood at their post, halberds in hand. Arianna and Kendra dismounted and led their horses to the gate.

Kendra opened her mouth to talk to the guards, but stopped as Arianna raised a hand.

Arianna looked around at the walls, then shook her head. "Something isn't right. I sense great magic," she hissed, looking to her sister.

Kendra let her hand drop to her sword's pommel. Tingles ran down her neck and back. Was there a twinge of fear in Arianna's eyes? Kendra shook her head. Whatever it was, she did not have a good feeling about this.

Arianna moved forward, saying nothing to the guards. They did not so much as even glance at her. Kendra followed through the gate, leading her horse.

"What the…" Kendra stopped.

Children ran about the courtyard. People stood in conversation. Guards walked by, patrolling the walls. People went about their business as if it was midday.

"It seems people here are early risers," Kendra muttered, letting her hand slide from her sword and brushing it through her curly locks.

"Why are there people *here* in the castle?" Arianna still looked around, clearly not letting her guard down.

Kendra hadn't even thought about that. "Perhaps they're the family of the Lord that the innkeeper was talking about?"

"Perhaps." Arianna looked her sister in the eyes. "I don't buy it. Magic hangs heavily in the air. Not arcane. Sorcery, or maybe something darker."

Kendra looked at the guards at the gate. A horrifying thought occurred to her of being trapped in the courtyard. All her senses screamed *ambush*! Each step was a mental battle, a fight against her training. But Arianna walked forward without falter. Kendra would not leave her sister's side. Arianna's judgment was sound.

They walked into the center of the courtyard, then stopped again. Arianna muttered spidery words of magic and waved her hands in the air. Not one person looked her way as she cast her spell. Kendra found this odd. The whole place was irregular. As Arianna finished, all the figures moving in the courtyard glowed a dull yellow. Kendra knew what happened before Arianna even looked at her. She had cast a magic sensing spell. Kendra had seen her sister cast that spell on items before to see if they were magical.

"They are illusions," Arianna breathed.

Before Kendra could ask one of the million questions on her mind, the illusions disappeared. There was nothing to prove they had been there in the first place. At a small, single wooden door far to the right stood a figure. Its eyes stared through them blankly. It made Kendra shiver. If it had been Corvos who had placed those illusions there, he now knew they were in his castle. Kendra realized the figure before them was the only remaining illusion. It glowed a dull yellow.

"Ari…"

"I see it."

"You trespass. Leave now, unless you want things to get bloody," the voice chuckled heartily. The illusion's mouth never moved. The words came from thin air.

Arianna walked up to the single door, completely ignoring the last illusion. She grabbed the large iron handle and pulled. Kendra quickly entered as the door swung open, sword at the ready.

Nothing but a long, sloping hall leading down lay before them. Many unlit lanterns hung from the walls on either side. Magical energy lit the darkness.

The duo slowly headed down the hallway.

As the sisters walked downward the air became dank and cold. Kendra could see her breath more and more clearly the farther down she went. Several minutes passed as they crept down the hall. It felt like an eternity. Kendra swore she could hear her own heartbeat.

At the end of the hall was a door.

"Think Corvos is down here?" Kendra whispered to break the silence and calm her nerves.

"We'll find out, sister." Arianna never took her eyes off the door. Her hand fell to her scimitar at her belt.

Kendra gritted her teeth. She was more irritated than scared. She walked past her sister, who followed closely, then turned the knob slowly.

"Oh please, come in!" a joyous voice called from the other side. The same voice that had been near the illusion. Kendra looked at Arianna, who nodded the unspoken command. It was now or never.

Kendra opened the door wide and stepped in, her long sword at the ready. Her jaw dropped as her eyes finally fell on the figure in the room.

Never had she seen anything so horrifying. Neither in battles nor torture chambers. The room was large and circular. The floor was grooved and tilted slightly towards the center of the room. In the heart of the floor was a large basin and on the ceiling above that basin was a large mirror.

The basin was filled to the brim with blood.

Around the edge of the chamber lay small figures, face down and hands bound behind their back. Blood flowed from their slit throats, down the grooves and into the basin.

Kendra turned away, unable to look at the small bodies. Arianna stared coldly into the man's eyes that stood before them.

The man was an elf, maybe a little older than Kendra. She was sure the man was a Cobracorpen elf. His muscular physique almost making him look half human. The man was bald, and his pointed ears looked much larger than they actually were. The bright blue silk tunic he wore was splattered with blood. The elf's blue eyes stared back into Arianna's. Two magic-users squaring up each other's power.

To Kendra's surprise, his gaze turned to her. She saw madness in his eyes.

"I apologize for the mess. I was in a bit of a rush to get this little task moving. And what do you know? Done right on time! I am Corvos, and you are?"

"In the name of the Circle of Magi, protectors of magic, you are under arrest. You will be tried before the heads of each order for sorcery and blood magic," Arianna stated coldly, walking forward and ignoring the introduction. Her eyes never left the Cobracorpen elf.

"So typical." The elf shook his head in disappointment. "You don't even want to hear the story behind all this?"

"Do not utter a word of magic or wave your hands. If you do, I shall strike you down, blood mage."

"By the gods, you will pay for the death of these innocent children." Kendra gestured with her longsword to the poor figures on the floor.

Corvos ignored both of the sisters, continuing an imaginary conversation. "You see, when we first arrived here, I was a mere sorcerer. Lord Ingram took me as his apprentice, and my power grew!" Corvos paused as if recalling a pleasant memory.

"Soon I discovered my master was a blood mage. To my horror I tried to escape. You see I was young and foolish, much like you." He gestured to Arianna. "Lord Ingram caught me. Yes, yes. He made me see the power in this beautiful form of magic. Soon I excelled in this style. But he was a foolish man, playing it safe. Lord Ingram only used the blood of animals, a much weaker source. He wasn't a gambling man, so to speak."

"Enough! I will gut you and leave you to die!" Kendra shouted and stepped forward.

"Hold on now, my brave warrior! We will have plenty of time to spill each other's blood after story time." Corvos gave her a twisted smile.

Arianna walked to his left. Kendra circled to the right. Corvos watched both, chuckling. "So," Corvos continued, "I got sick of his weakness. Ended his life two weeks ago. Plans were going well until you showed up. These idiots would have fallen for my framing of the shepherd."

"It was sloppy. No murder weapon left at the scene. Though we would have believed it, had we not been attacked in our sleep by your men." Arianna drew her scimitar.

"Yes, the fools were supposed to attack you the night before. They were too frightened, apparently. I hope you killed them. As for the murder wea… no, it matters not. Kitanan will burn after we are done here. Or perhaps I will continue to harvest blood from their loved ones. Just as the farmer chooses what cattle to slaughter and saves the best stock for breeding. Either way, soon all will know my name. Their knees will become weak before me, and they will bow to me as a god or fall beneath my power!"

The blood flowing down the grates in the floor and the blood from the overflowing basin rose above the ground. Like bloody raindrops, hovering, frozen in midair.

At the sight of the droplets floating around her, Arianna spat words of magic and lightning appeared in her hands. She still wasn't fast enough. More and more blood filled the air, swirling about Corvos. It pelted Arianna, causing her spell to be disrupted before she could throw the bolt at the blood mage.

Corvos stood with arms raised high. The blood swirled faster and faster. It pelted Arianna like hail. She attempted to wipe it off her face, but strangely the blood that struck her reformed and joined back into the bloodspout that swirled about the chamber.

"Witness my power, you fools!" Corvos laughed wildly.

Arianna and Kendra were both flung back against the wall of the room as an explosion took place in the center of the chamber. Kendra's head smacked hard against the wall, and she fell onto one of the children that lay face down.

The blood that floated about the room now shot towards the mirror, shattering the glass. Pieces of mirror exploded across the chamber. The blood took its place within the frame, spiraling where the glass had once been.

*****

Arianna stood, fury upon her face. Her sister lay crumpled on the ground. Anger bubbled up in Arianna. If she lost Kendra here… Arianna shook her head. She needed to concentrate, or all was lost.

Arianna was too late, she realized. Before her, the portal swirled, beckoning her to enter. Arianna ignored its call.

"Kendra, Get up, my sister! I need you!" Arianna shouted, trying to keep her voice composed.

Kendra groaned but didn't move.

Arianna cursed vilely.

Corvos laughed shakily. "I've done it! I've really done it. A portal to the Nether!" The elf stumbled forward weakly. Corvos seemed to have aged a few hundred years since he cast his spell. Many wrinkles covered his once smooth face.

Arianna had no idea how this blood mage had opened the gate to the Nether, if that's even where it led to.

In the Age of Empires and Age of Destiny, many mages had created permeant gates to different planes of existence. But they had done so with the help of ten or twenty other wizards. Clerics were invited to oversee the project, in case any demons entered Harthx through one of the gates. Arianna was sure a permanent gate hadn't been created ever since the Circle of Magi was founded, for they had banned gate creation.

"Close it, you fool! Before something comes through!" Arianna raged.

"I will conquer the demons' wills, like the magic-users of old," Corvos said, stepping back to look into the swirling depths, as if hoping something would come through.

"You know not what you do. Whatever comes through that could destroy all of Draston. Maybe all of Harthx! Close the gate now!" Arianna wanted to use her own magic to close it, but she knew it would weaken her, leaving her helpless to this maniac. She would take her chances with a demon.

"Bah, you underestimate my power—"

Corvos was cut off as a figure stepped through the swirling depths of the Nether portal.

Arianna cursed even louder. But to her surprise, she recognized what stepped through the portal. It looked much like a human, though it lacked any orifices. It was nude but without genitalia. Its body was smooth and hairless. It reminded Arianna much of a blank page.

A mimic.

Corvos chanted spidery words and drew his dagger from its sheath. He ruthlessly slit his own palm open, leaving a wicked gash. A mixture of pain and exultation crossed his features. He closed his eyes, using his own blood as magical energy.

Kendra groaned, finally reaching for her sword which lay next to her.

"Sister, a little help please!" Arianna shouted over Corvos' chanting.

Kendra raised her head, looking at the portal and the creature. Blood matted her brown curls. "What… What in the Nether is that?"

"A mimic, sister! Do not meet its gaze!"

The mimic turned slowly, advancing on Corvos. Horror dawned on Corvos' face as his magic failed to control the demon. "No! No, you are not me! Obey me, fiend!"

The mimic's body changed in a flash. A flawless image of Corvos.

The mimic reached a hand for the elven blood mage. Arianna knew if the mimic touched its victim's skin its own pale skin would merge with it, becoming one. Arianna waved her hands. Magic burned in her veins. She poured everything into the spell: her anger, frustration, everything.

A ball of flame struck the mimic on the shoulder, searing its flesh. The mimic stumbled to its knees, writhing in silent pain. Corvos' image was gone. The blank humanoid's skin was blackening. Corvos frantically scrambled away from the demon.

Kendra stumbled to her feet, bracing herself against a stone wall, attempting to blink the stars from her vision.

Arianna looked to the mimic and then back to the portal. There was but one choice. She chanted a spell to close the portal. Even though it would drain her, it was a risk she was willing to take.

The mimic didn't look at her as she began casting the spell. It kept advancing on Corvos.

Arianna breathed a sigh of relief as the portal stopped spinning. It now looked like a dark amber mirror.

It still called to her even though it was closed. *Enter me, you have the power to defeat them, you have the power to become a god.*

She ignored the call of the demons from the other side. Arianna knew she only had a few spells left before she was too weak to even walk. Running over to Kendra, she placed her hands on her sister's head and chanted a healing spell. She looked to Corvos as he cast a spell.

Large silver spikes sprang from the ground, shattering the stone floor. Chunks of debris flew everywhere. The spikes pierced through the mimic, yet it trudged forward, impaling itself deeper.

Corvos seized the moment to escape, but was too slow. He tried to dart past the sisters for the door. Kendra, now healed, swung her blade and hit Corvos in the back of the head with its flat edge. It wasn't a strong enough blow to knock him unconscious, but caused him to stumble to the ground.

The elven man struggled to his feet, but Kendra was on him. She dropped her blade and attacked him viciously on the ground. Choking him and slamming him against the floor.

Arianna turned to the mimic. It was freeing itself from the stakes and starting towards her.

"Kendra, do not kill him. Those shackles I gave you, do you have them? Yes, those! Put them on him." Arianna took a breath and dived into the magic, pulling out all she had left. *"Ishaan, Valtra ist var Corbani!"* she shouted.

The mimic's walk slowed, ice formed on its hands and spread rapidly across its body. The ice spread until not an inch of unfrozen flesh remained.

Arianna shivered. The mimic had taken her form before it froze. She stared into her own hazel eyes.

Arianna swung her scimitar. The blow was weak, but her aim was true. The magical scimitar sliced through the mimic's head neatly, sending it flying through the air. The head hit the ground and burst into thousands of pieces. The body quickly followed.

The mimic was dead. To be sure, Arianna cast her last spell. Flames shot from her fingertips as her magical chanting struck home. The chunks of the mimic's flesh burned and bubbled.

There would be no regenerating. What was left of the mimic was burnt into nothing. Arianna was happy that she had studied demonology in the Tower of Red Robes. Many said it was a waste of time. Demons in Draston were rare. This had been the first she had ever encountered, and Arianna prayed it would be her last.

Kendra had successfully manacled the still struggling and cursing Corvos. She panted heavily on the ground.

"Are you okay, sister?" Arianna asked.

Kendra nodded.

Arianna bent down to Corvos. "So what do you think about my magical manacles? It cuts you off from magic. Keeps you from casting anything.

Soon as they are removed, you will regain your abilities. Though, I would get used to the lack of magic if I were you. When we reach the tower, they will sever your tie with Liola the goddess of magic. Magic will be non-existent in your soul. You will be a thoughtless derelict, forced to do the chores of responsible magi."

"Will they hang him?" Kendra asked. "He deserves to hang, Ari, if not worse. Perhaps blood eagle as the nords do. Seems fitting to me."

"They will cut him off from magic. A mage doesn't survive long after that. They tend to lose the will to live. Many die a few years later. But… I may have a better idea."

"Shall we turn him over to Kitanan? He will surely hang."

"No, please! I beg you, have mercy on me!" Corvos blubbered.

Kendra kicked him cruelly. "Shut up, you piece of garbage! I have half a notion to kill you right here. Honor be damned. What you did to these children is disgusting. I pray Hithal takes your soul and tortures you for eternity."

"We give him to Kitanan. Let them decide what to do with him."

The sisters wrapped each of the six children up in linen found in the castle's upstairs rooms.

Hooking up a shoddy wagon they discovered in the courtyard to their horses, they took Corvos and the bodies down to the village.

By mid-morning Corvos was drawn and quartered. The mayor was so thankful for what the sisters had done that he gifted them Corvos' castle, which to Kendra's disappointment Arianna gladly accepted. Kendra, like the townspeople, wanted nothing to do with it after what had been done there. The darkness that had fallen over Kitanan had dispersed. Tomorrow was a new day, and the sun shone brightly.

*****

Arianna finally reached the top of the west tower of her castle. The stairs had spiraled for what had seemed like an eternity.

Kendra was downstairs inspecting the armory. Soon they would leave Kitanan and continue on their journey to the Grasslands. But there was time now for a little exploring of the castle.

Cautiously Arianna pushed open the large double doors that lay before her and entered the large room.

This was what she had been searching for all afternoon while her sister had been sleeping.

Shelves lined the walls, filled with books and spell components. In the center of the room lay a large sprawling oak desk of dwarven design. At the other side of the chamber was a balcony, over which the sun shined brightly. Walking up to the shelves in wonder, Arianna inhaled the air. But her breath caught in her throat. She pulled a book from the shelf in shock.

The Power Within by Necrolis Varunal.

Necrolis had been the most powerful sorcerer to walk Harthx. He had grown greedy with power and turned to necromancy, soul and blood magic. It had been said that all of his books had been piled up and burned by the Circle of Magi.

This was indeed a jewel.

The book was cold to the touch. Smiling, Arianna opened the cover.

All About
the Adventure

By Aaron Wulf
&
Anna Warkentin

733 AM Age of the Dracon-esti

Galin hadn't bathed in over a week. He couldn't account for half the stains on his battered chainmail and leather armor. His feet ached from walking so many miles every day, his coin purse was depressingly flat, and he hadn't talked to another human in days. As he approached The Lucky Miller's

Inn in the town of Wellsford, he wondered if his voice would even work.

Thankfully it did. He was able to turn over nearly half of his coppers for a tankard of beer and a plate of meat and cheese. With food in his belly and weight off his feet, the rugged man was able to turn his mind to other matters.

Mainly, why was that man standing on a table, wildly gesticulating?

"'Twas a dragon, I swear to you!" the man declared, rousing a spattering of laughter from the small crowd surrounding him.

"Dragons have been extinct for over two centuries, ya daft twit!" someone responded, waving a tankard.

"It was!" The man nearly stomped his foot in frustration. "I saw it from a distance, but it had great wings, scales over its entire body, and that ferocious-looking head."

Sensing an opportunity to fill his purse again, Galin slipped forward and caught the man by the arm before he stormed out of the tavern.

"Eh? By the gods! You're quite a sight, stranger."

Galin grimaced. "Thank you, I am aware. My apologies, I have just returned from a long trip. But I think you and I can help each other, sir."

A knowing glint entered the man's eye. "How so?"

"I am a monster hunter," Galin replied, gesturing to the rusty bloodstains on his armor. "You are a man with a monster problem, are you not?"

"Aye, dragon problem," the man nodded.

"Not likely," Galin rubbed his brow in thought. "But for a decent price I can track down this monster and rid you of it for good."

A knowing smile grew across the man's lips. "'How much d'ya want when you kill whatever's been terrorizing my sheep?"

After bartering back and forth, the two agreed on a price, with Galin promising to bring back proof of the creature's demise.

After all, he thought, exiting the tavern into the afternoon sunlight, it's likely just a cockatrice or a giant skink. The man smelled of ale and was probably over-exaggerating. Whatever it was would be easier to take down than half the hell spawn he'd dealt with. An easy job, to be sure.

Looking around the busy streets, he noticed women pulling children away to the other side of the road, men glaring at him heavily.

"Why…? Oh…"

A quick survey of his appearance and odor gave him the answer quickly, and he made a beeline for the bathhouse.

It was nearly evening by the time the monster hunter was scrubbed clean. In his only outfit without suspicious stains, Galin stepped out onto the cobblestone street. Orange light reflected off every window and turned the fountain in the town square to liquid fire. A pleasant melody floated through the square, hanging in the warm summer air like a cloud. Galin felt his rough, browned face crack a smile as he ran a large hand through hair still damp from his bath. As a high singing voice joined the melody, his stride quickened. On the other side of the fountain were performers, and Galin's smile became a full grin.

"Still enchanting people out of their coin with that voice, Milo?" he asked after the singing finished, strong arms crossed over his chest.

The bard spun around. Long, coppery hair fanned out around him. His thin face split into a huge smile when he saw the monster hunter.

"Galin!" Milo's high, melodic voice bounced around the square. With a few quick strides that sent his orange robes flapping, his arms were around Galin.

If Galin were smaller, he would have been lifted off his feet, but the brawny man just grinned down at his friend.

"I didn't know you were here!" Milo continued, stepping back a little. "You're looking well, my old friend."

"As are you." In comparison to Milo, Galin's voice was rumbly and deep. "What brings you to Wellsford?"

"Why, the dragon of course! The news is all over town, have you really not heard? I am going to see it slain, and I will write a magnificent ballad about it that shall be repeated across all the land. I shall become famous and live in luxury with wine and women aplenty!"

Galin rolled his eyes. Dear Milo was a good friend, but incredibly gullible.

"There is no dragon, Milo. They've been dead for centuries."

"But, but… just hear me out here." The bard leaned in as if sharing a secret. "What if… they're back?"

Galin chuckled. "I almost hope so. I'd make a hell of a lot more money."

"Milo?"

A new voice cut in, lower than the bard's but sweet and feminine. Milo turned, revealing a young woman in a simple blue dress. Her brown hair, nearly the same color as Galin's, curled softly around her face, framing a pair of bright, ice blue eyes. She held a small violin in one hand and a tin tray in another.

"We have enough money for rooms tonight, if you want to go get something to eat."

She looked up, seeming only now to notice Galin. "Oh! Forgive me, sir. I did not see you there." She gave him a quick curtsy, shifting a fold of her dress to reveal a longsword at her side.

Galin raised an eyebrow. The hilt was well oiled, and the sheath new. It seemed a piece of decoration. She caught him staring at her and she looked back through thick, dark lashes, prompting him to blush and look away. He missed the pink that tinged her cheeks.

"Oh, Albree, allow me to introduce my friend, Galin. Galin, this is my assistant, Albree of Evesburg. She's saved this valuable throat quite a few times, both in time of peril and song. She is quite the apprentice." He made a dramatic flourish with his hand, presenting his distinctly intact neck.

"He exaggerates, Sir Galin," Albree cut in demurely, a small smile playing about her lips. "All I do is care for the horses and help pen the occasional song. I have been learning much from him. One day I hope to be a bard as well. This blade is a last resort in case we ever find ourselves in danger."

Milo blustered, about to disagree, when Galin cut in. "I'm sure you can do much more than that, Miss Albree. And there is no need to call me *sir*. I'm a simple man with a simple life, nothing noble about me."

"Then there is no reason to call me *miss*. I certainly require no additional title, call me Albree."

"And a lovely thing Albree is, may I say?" Galin smiled. This time, he saw her cheeks dimple and turn red. Something stirred in his chest, and he wanted to try and make her smile like that again.

Milo popped up between them, and Albree turned away.

"Drinks, anyone?" he offered, jingling a few coins in his hand.

"I know of a place with the finest ale in Wellsford, if you don't mind," Galin suggested. "The innkeeper is an old friend of mine. He may be able to set us up with a room for the night." He looked up to the sun. "They should be open by now. We best go before they get too packed."

The trio gathered their things and headed for the tavern.

When they crossed the threshold of The Pewter Piglet — a name Milo found amusing — they found it was unlike any other tavern around Wellsford. Milo and Albree winced at the wretched odor.

"You better step inside quickly," Galin laughed. "The stench is worse in the breeze. Once we find a table, you'll grow accustomed to it."

They stepped onto a floor of dirt and straw. Quite a change from the tavern Galin drank at when he first arrived. The friends could not tell the difference between clumps of dirt or horse dung tracked in by customers' boots. Despite the dirty building, the atmosphere was quite welcoming.

The walls almost burst with customers drinking ale, guffawing and scarfing down hearty meats and breads. Two burly men shook their table violently as they tested their strength in an arm-wrestling match. There were men and women at another table – warriors by the looks of them – exchanging tales of battle and laughing at each other's victories and defeats.

The innkeeper welcomed the three and slapped Galin on the back.

"Why, if it isn't good ol' Galin! You know I haven't seen you since you rid our town of that Kralle. Nasty thing that was. Frightened my children. Gods only know how it got this far from the cold mountains." He turned to Milo, "But Galin, being the master at killing that he is, ripped one of the creature's horns from its head and stabbed it in its chest." He then nudged Albree with his elbow. "I tell you what, he had all the ladies after him that evening."

"It was actually a swamp Kralle. And I left town that night before any of them could enthrall me," Galin rubbed his neck.

"Maybe, but you need to find yourself a nice lady someday and settle down." The bartender showed the three to their table. "Drinks are on me, the name's Farnsworth. If you need anything, just shout." Farnsworth returned moments later with food and jugs of ale.

"So tell me Galin," Milo asked as he chewed on his meat. "What brings you to Wellsford? Slaying more monsters, I assume? Because I must tell you, I've slain a few monsters myself in the past few seasons. And by monsters, I mean lasses. And by slain-"

"Milo!" Albree snapped. "I know you're with your old friend, but did you forget to watch your manners around a woman?"

"I know what you mean, old friend." Galin interrupted. His eyes rolled to Albree, regarding him with silent laughter. "And yes, I have heard rumors of the dragon. As well you know, it's a bunch of bollocks. It's probably just a cockatrice."

"Do you believe dragons could ever come back?" Albree inquired, sipping on a tankard of ale.

"No, my lady. Though there is no definitive proof, warriors of old speak of the Dracon-esti killing every one of them for good. This nuisance that I have on my hands will be taken care of by midday tomorrow."

"You mean the nuisance *we* have on *our* hands," Albree corrected him.

Galin choked on his ale.

Milo cut back in. "Albree, you have studies this week. We cannot go on a wild goose chase when you..." Milo chuckled. "Hey Galin, what if this nuisance was a wild goose! That would be comical, and I could show Albree how to add humor to our songs. Oh! And Galin, you and Albree should see about getting a room for us before they are all taken."

"That sounds pleasant." Albree gave Galin a girlish smile. "And if they have extra rooms, we can give one to Milo so we won't have to hear his heart-swooning anecdotes all night."

Milo's face went red. "What's wrong with my anecdotes?"

No one answered him.

"I'm quite fine going by myself." Galin stood up and wiped his face. "But why don't you two enjoy yourselves and decide whether or not you want to come with me tomorrow. Maybe you could pen a good song out of it."

Albree diligently dug into her meat.

As Galin departed the table, he heard Milo speaking about him.

"That man can be hard-headed at times. He fears no monsters. The only thing he fears is the dedication a man is sworn to uphold to the woman he chooses to love. He once told me, 'no creature is as complex and unpredictable as a woman. Neither monster nor beast can overpower man with a force like love can. No evil mage or demon can conquer the heart and soul of a warrior like the unwavering grasp of love.' He's never been held down by man nor beast, and I fear he worries a commitment to a woman will weigh him down like an anchor. But don't let that deter you, young Albree. I know you feel for him, and with some probing, I'm sure you will be able to bring him to his knees."

Milo winked and sipped out of the pewter tankard chained to the wooden table. Albree smiled awkwardly, only following half of Milo's speech. The longsword at her hip weighed her down as much as the inescapable feelings she had for Galin.

"Where is Farnsworth?" Galin asked a new face behind the bar.

The man was worn and scarred like weathered stone. His expression was bleak, contradicting the atmosphere of the tavern.

His voice was even less welcoming than his face. "He's in the back."

Galin raised an eyebrow at him and then entered a back hallway leading to the storeroom. Galin coughed. The place smelled strongly of dust.

"Farnsworth, you back here?"

Metal flashed from the shadows. A gloved hand gripped Galin's shirt and forced him against a set of stocked shelves. The monster hunter instinctively tensed to fight back, but the blade to his throat and his unsteady footing convinced him it was unwise. His attacker's face mirrored the one behind the bar. Soot-black hair and dark clothes concealed him in the night. Buckles and straps of all kinds covered his overcoat. His black leather boots were lined with fine metal, and on the outsides of each boot protruded a blade pointing about four inches past the toes. One of them pressed against Galin's shin.

The man's breath smelled of garlic and onions. He sneered at Galin and warned him with a scornful raspy voice, "You best stay away from that woman out there. If I see you lay one hand on Albree, or if you mention this meeting, I will slit your throat and pour the blood down the beautiful mouth of your minstrel friend. Albree is mine, and, in time, we will wed." A dark, obsessive fire burned in the man's eyes, the kind that lights unrealistic fantasies and designs one to die alone.

He had seen the look before. A rabid dog once had its jaw locked around a woman's leg, but Galin aimed his crossbow between its eyes. Moments later, the eyes were dark, lifeless, and bloody. The woman was treated by the town's healer. This time and place, he had no crossbow and didn't intend on being pierced by the teeth of a rabid dog or a twisted blade. He slowed his breathing and remained calm, as all monster hunters are trained to do in times of peril.

"Do you understand?" the attacker asked.

"Got the point." Galin smoothly flicked away the tip of the man's blade.

"I have eyes everywhere. But remember this: I would rather Albree die than waste her time with dirty filth like you."

Galin walked back out into the common area. A cold sweat trickled down his back. The stone face behind the bar glowered at him.

When he returned to the table, Albree was oddly on edge. Galin wondered if she had seen what had just happened, but there was no way she could have seen into the storeroom. Everything had happened so fast. She could not have made it back to the table in time. Her eyes stared blankly at her plate, but her shoulders swayed side to side.

Galin saw his attacker sitting at the table farthest from theirs. His cold eyes haunted their table, but Galin was the only one who could directly see him.

"Do you know that man over there?" Galin spoke softly.

"What man?" Albree replied.

But Galin remembered what the man had said about mentioning him, and he could not put them in danger.

"I do not know him." Her eyes remained lowered. "Can't we talk about other things tonight?"

Milo seized his chance and told tales of old, laughing and drinking for the better part of the hours. Soon after nightfall, customers of The Pewter Piglet exited into the streets while others retired to their rooms. The attacker had left the tavern side by side with the stern man behind the counter, but Galin still felt watched. Milo stretched his arms and queried about their rooms.

"Right! So where are we bunking up tonight?"

"Damn it!" Galin brooded. "I... still have to check on that."

Milo hesitated. "What? You went to get us a room hours ago, what happened?"

Galin avoided the question and left the table. He could never admit he had been shaken by what happened earlier. He soon returned with the tavern master who showed them all to their room. When Galin questioned him about the eerie man behind the counter earlier, the tavern master claimed no one with that description worked for him.

They all filed into a small one-bed room and each made a place to rest their heads for the night.

"Milo," Albree cooed as she lay out her blankets. "Could you play us a song tonight? Perhaps one of your slower tunes will put us at ease this evening."

"That sounds great." Galin glanced at Albree and could sense her uneasiness.

Milo unpacked his handcrafted cittern from a case older than any of the three in the room. The instrument's slender curves wafted into a thin neck fitted with strings. The sound Milo made was angelic, and contradicted his frivolous personality. His notes were slow and precise as he played a rhythm in 6/8 time. The song engulfed the room with thick emotion and a serene atmosphere. His voice was soft, and the very sound of his harmony tugged at Galin and Albree's heart strings.

Twelve set sail
to bridge the billowing seas
Off the west coast of Draston,
most left their women
Some left a child, two or three
And one left their unborn
whom they would never see

When the beaches of Draston faded
Far from our sight
The endless horizon
gave our ship to the night
Sky children settled in the skies up above
They danced around like diamonds
They played in the rough

The waves, they wafted our ship in the sea
Storms came and brought us
to an incongruous beach
But the land, it rose
It punched through the sky
And waters from the heavens
Rained down on that night
With winds of magic, its power so pure
Our ship was lost,
Pushed away from the shore

A warrior strong, so gallant and brave
Held the helm in his hand,
He cut through sharp waves
Then the mouth of the sea
unveiled its fangs
With voices of death,
it cried out his name
The coil, it spoke
Undoubtedly so
And that's when it happened
The leviathans rose

The beasts rang out
Like demons they sang
Six ascended like worms
Thirsty for reign
and behind them, thunder rolled
And thereafter, mountains came
Prodigious monsters surrounded our ship
Four men were struck dead
Six were down on their knees

But the warrior fought on,
his hilt in his hand
And bard by his side,
Crossbow in his hand
Many heads the warrior severed,

much the size of two oxen
Gargantuan beasts surrounded the two
The six men just sat, watching

The warrior battled like light fights the dark
His blade struck like lightning
The bard's arrow made its mark
Cataclysmic events had seen better days
Six leviathans lay dead,
Nothing frightened these lads

Water rushed back to the bosom of the earth
Mountains descended, not a sound was heard
But now the ship was wrecked
on a monster's scaled back
The men swam for refuge,
Six drowned, now dead
Many months afloat on driftwood mahogany
Our rations cut short, only bread, stale and soggy
Two returned home, together side by side
Till we set sail again, we await the high tide

The air was thick. Without comment, the three extinguished the oil lamps and lay in their respective spots. Galin broke the silence. He still had the image of his attacker in his mind.

"Albree,"

"Yes?"

"Are you to be married?"

"No." She paused. "Why do you ask?"

"Just... separating fact from myth. Good night, my lady."

Milo was already snoring, and the other two soon fell fast asleep.

*****

The next morning, Milo paid Farnsworth and the three set off together in search of a creature that was not a dragon. Or a wild goose, as Milo reminded them. Albree seemed much better this morning. She was humming a joyous tune on their way out of town.

Woods lined both sides of the road leading out of Wellsford. The canopies met high above the center to form a natural archway. A flock of birds shot out of the branches to their right. Albree proposed the possibility of wolves close to them, but Galin said there were only goblins in these woods. Albree didn't find it humorous. Milo did.

Suddenly the low branches violently shook as figures appeared.

Albree screamed. She swore that goblins were running out onto the dirt road at them. She and

Galin drew their weapons. Milo crouched behind Albree. When the figures approached, they turned out to be three ruffians dressed in brand new leather armor, though they were nearly as threatening as ogres.

"Stay back, Albree." Galin pulled the young woman behind him, with Milo following her. He turned his attention to the men. "State your intentions at once."

The men continued to march with sinister determination.

Galin grew irritated. "This is your last warning, tell us who you are or have your blood shed."

Without a declaration of their purpose, the three men drew their swords and attacked. Galin parried every attack the two men offered. The third ruffian decided to take on Albree by himself. When she lifted her longsword to swing, he stepped back in surprise at the ease with which she handled her weapon.

Galin quickly disarmed one of the men and severed his hand. While the second ruffian was shocked by the blood, Galin stuck him in the abdomen.

The handless man fainted and fell to the ground. The second man stumbled into the woods, disappearing after a few seconds.

Albree was struggling to fight the remaining man. He was overpowering and her energy was waning. Galin stepped in to help her and the man quickly turned to block Galin's advance. While his back was turned, Albree pierced her longsword directly through his lungs and out his chest. The battle was over. They caught their breath, then Albree went to retrieve her sword from the first man she had ever slain.

"It's no use, my lady. Your blade is now encased in his ribcage. Next time, aim away from it." Galin sat down on a small rock on the side of the road.

Albree checked herself for wounds and bleeding. Besides a couple of bruises, she was fine.

"I can't believe I just killed someone. Who were they?"

"I don't know," admitted Galin. "But if we didn't kill them, they would have killed us. You handled yourself well, Albree. I must say, I was quite impressed."

"Thank you." She hesitated. "I… I think we should keep walking."

"I love that idea. Their bodies are already starting to reek." Milo looked up from his notepad.

Galin sighed. "Alright. Milo, help me with hiding the bodies in the woods. We will report this when we return to town tonight. Albree, are you sure you're alright?"

"Yes, no open wounds. I'm fine."

The two men pulled the bodies ten feet into the woods and covered them with branches. Galin found a lone hand lying in the street and picked it up. It was wrapped in a black leather glove. The palm was well worn, as was the opening at the wrist. A silver insignia was on the back of the hand: a serpent spiraling around its own body, its open mouth snarling at a crescent moon above.

He studied the insignia, trying to remember why it looked so familiar. He pulled the glove off the hand, pocketed it, and chucked the hand into the woods.

"Let's keep moving, shall we? I am willing to bet there are more ruffians inside these woods. Albree, take rear guard. Milo, try to keep up."

Galin pondered the insignia as the group progressed. His temples clenched. He swore he had seen the insignia before, but couldn't say until he knew for sure. Galin never shared information unless he knew beyond a doubt that he was correct.

The farmer's sheep pasture was completely empty when they arrived. They assumed the farmer had taken them all to a shelter while they came to fight the menace. They split up and searched for clues.

Galin talked silently to himself, remembering any facts they had about the monster and deducing possibilities as to what it could be.

They all rejoined at a hill in a corner of the pasture. It was overgrown with thorny shrubs and twisting vines. Albree pulled some branches back and squealed.

"I knew this brush looked funny! No one in their right mind would place these here in this fashion." Albree hugged Galin in gleeful excitement.

Galin hadn't the slightest clue as to what she was talking about, but he was impressed and overjoyed they hadn't run into a dead end on this journey.

"Rather impressive, my lady… I mean, Albree. Who would've known there was a hidden path back here? Now, do you have the bravery of a monster slayer to see what awaits us at the top of this path?"

"Sir Galin, I do."

"And do you know why this is the right way to go?"

"Well, let me see." Albree observed the shrubs. "The branches are broken inward."

"Impressive. Anything else?"

"And, there is something small hanging from the ends of the branches. It looks like dark skin."

"Scales." Galin smiled. "The branches scraped off the scales of whatever ran through here."

Milo shivered.

"Come on, we're on the right track." The others followed Galin up the narrow path.

The trail took them into an area west of Wellsford, an area in Glandstone that hadn't seen human footsteps for many years.

The wall of trees to their left dropped gradually away with the descending land. Albree held onto Galin's left arm as she dared to peek down the steep thirty-foot drop. Milo studied the red cliffs rising up to their right, the tree roots now fifteen feet above them. They had entered the Cliffs of Baghazna.

"I'm confused, are we getting higher or are we going lower?" Milo's child-like eyes opened wide in amazement.

"Where are we?" Albree couldn't stop moving her head in all directions, taking in such a vastly eclectic landscape.

Galin was proud to share his knowledge. "These cliffs were home to a hermit long ago named Baghazna. Have you ever heard the story?"

Both shook their heads.

"Well, in the days of Baghazna, this forest was mostly flat with only small hills, as was the land we just came from. No cliffs existed. He lived as one with nature, sharing in its glory with the animals and plants, and all that hogwash."

"Hogwash?" Albree cut in. "I think that way of life sounds beautiful. Please continue."

Galin stammered. "Uh, I am just retelling it as I had heard it. Um, where was I?"

"Hogwash!" Milo beamed.

"Yes. Baghazna lived in beautiful unison with the world, and his mood was always high.

"One day, hunters came into the forest and killed much of the wildlife. Men with axes cut the trees for lumber. This depressed Baghazna so much that he snapped. He went on a killing rampage and slaughtered every man who entered these lands because of their selfish desire. The creeks running through this area of Glandstone turned red with blood. The cries of the murdered drove away all remaining animals that still dwelled near. The blood tainted the streams. The trees along their banks hung low, for the water was no longer sanitary.

"Baghazna killed every last hunter and axe-man so that he may finally find peace. But when the rage lifted from his eyes, he only saw unhappiness and death. Peace had not been returned. He was now at the lowest point he had ever been, for beauty and life had now left the forest. The tale says that he picked up an axe and took his own life. And when that happened, the only life remaining in these woods were the many trees still outstretched towards the heavens, and the few still hanging onto life sulking by the red water. When the warm earth below his body soaked up his blood, a great earthquake shook the land. The tremors split the ground and raised some areas high above, while other areas sunk low into valleys and caverns.

"Today, the land still remains broken to remind all travelers that even though great evil can attack one's happiness, anger will only enhance the pain. It reminds us that we can both grow and rise above the darkness onto the higher cliffs where happiness still reigns, or we can fall into the gloomy depths down below where the blood of selfishness drains."

Everyone was quiet for a long time after hearing the story of Baghazna. Albree shed a few tears. Milo scribbled in his pad.

Albree broke the silence. "Are you sure we're still going the right way?"

Wind whistled through the leaves, birds and insects sang, but no sounds of monsters could be heard.

The path leveled out again and Galin surveyed the area. Several trees had been slightly bent northward, and decent-sized branches had been broken off.

"It ran through the woods to our right. See the slanted trees?"

"No, I don't see them," Milo confessed. "But I do see a few broken branches where a monster could have run through."

"Good eye, Milo." Galin pointed. "The untrained eye will not see the trees, but if you line those ones up with the straight trees, you will observe a curve to the north. On those particular trees, I spotted a few large feathers as well."

"So it's a giant bird." Albree looked up to Galin.

"Not quite." The monster hunter ran five paces up the path and knelt down. "See these tracks?"

The tracks had three large front toes. The indented tips in the dirt suggested talons. One rear toe sank the deepest – that toe applied the most pressure. The tracks were placed far apart from one another, and disappeared around a bend.

"Yup, I was worried it may be one of these creatures. Damn."

"But what is it?" Milo and Albree implored.

"Simple. Lady and gentleman, please turn your focus to the nest of a greater basilisk."

In a corner of the clearing was a huge thorny nest nearly twenty feet in diameter with walls about four feet high.

"It is so terrifyingly beautiful." Albree approached the nest but jerked her head back in disgust once she was about a foot away. "Yuck! It smells like death."

Galin pulled out a thick blanket from his pack and threw it on top of the edge of the nest to cover the thorns. He drew his sword. Milo hoisted Galin up over the nest. Galin disappeared for a moment before reappearing.

"All clear."

Milo helped Albree up, then her and Galin reached over the edge and dragged Milo over.

Three small, ugly creatures ran up to them with monstrous cries of utter delight.

"Baby Basilisks! Aw, can I keep one?" Albree reached down to embrace the featherless chicken-serpent creature.

"Not if you want to end up like those guys over there," Galin spoke grimly.

Albree and Milo looked across the nest. Underneath hay and branches were twisted grotesque bodies. Two dead humans — both appeared to be male — were gutted like a cannibal's leftovers. Milo covered his mouth and averted his eyes. Albree was fascinated at how many insects were feasting upon the remains.

"You'll see a lot of that when a monster is on the loose. Come on, we have to kill the hatchlings."

"What!" Albree pulled back defiantly. "You will not harm these babies! What did they ever do to you?"

"Nothing yet, but what we hunt today is the very same creature these hatchlings will grow into. They are extremely close to the village and we don't have enough time to relocate them. To save lives, we have to kill them."

Albree's face steamed as she scoffed at Galin's words. Her eyes clenched with each thrust of his sword. She ignored him as he walked up behind her.

"All done."

Galin looked around the clearing for any clues as to where the mother could be. He didn't have to wait long. Blood-curdling screams echoed throughout the forest, bouncing off the high cliffs. It seemed to come from all directions at first, but with each new scream, Galin focused on the location of the source.

"How typical." Milo rolled his eyes. "The scream just so happened to occur at the appropriate time we needed to track down the monster." But he jumped around the clearing soon after in excitement. He had never seen a basilisk in all his journeys with monster hunters and warriors. The description in his song had to be accurate and horrifying. He knew that the ladies always swooned more when his songs struck them with fear.

The screams ceased, and the cracking of fresh wood, or bone, sifted between the trees from the west. Galin pinpointed where the sounds were originating and lunged into the forest. He did not pay attention to his rear to make sure Albree and Milo were following. Pursuing monsters always injected him with adrenaline.

Albree was advancing on Galin fairly easily. Milo fell behind because he was too busy jotting down words in his notepad. The beast was much louder now, so they knew they were all heading in the correct direction.

Galin and Albree exited the forest at the same time and halted when they got to a huge grass field. A few hundred feet in front of them were six soldiers. All were dressed in plate armor. Five of them wielded a sword in one hand and a large wooden shield in the other, the sixth soldier gripped a crossbow. All of them stood in battle stance, encircling the basilisk.

Milo exited the forest just before his two friends could run out to help fight the beast. The bard froze in horror at the spectacle. Any onlooker would have believed the old myth that the basilisk could turn its enemy into stone.

Albree and Milo both hesitated. They admitted they weren't fond of being turned to stone.

Galin assured them he had killed basilisks before, and it was only a myth, nothing more.

After a few of the soldiers had already fallen, Milo snapped out of his hypnotic state and scribbled down words of monstrous horror, describing the gallant battle scene before him.

Milo wrote that there were three known species of basilisk in Draston. Most were rare, one was recently extinct, and nearly all lived in the southern deserts. This particular basilisk was a greater basilisk, deadliest of the species and most common in the Aryan desert.

The monster had the body of poultry, sans feathers. Serpent scales coated it from its giant snake-like head all the way to the sharp whipping tale. The feet were those of a rooster, and their talons were close to those of dragons that thrived many hundreds of years ago. Its wingspan must have covered ten to twelve feet tip to tip. The only feathers on the body were on the inner perimeter of the wing, which helped serve toward a faster running ability.

The tail slashed wildly at the soldiers and Milo's friends as they so desperately tried to avoid its venomous tip. It was that piercing stinger that had ended three of the soldiers' lives. The soldier with the crossbow had his head ripped off by the monster's razor teeth. Two more soldiers were trampled by its poweful feet. The talons had ripped through their armor like an arrow cuts through leaves.

Albree ran to help one of the dying men and retrieved medicine supplies from one of her packs. She took off his helm and begged him to not close his eyes. Albree promised everything would be alright, though she was lying. The blood was flowing heavily out of his right shoulder. She noticed another wounded man was barely holding on. His ribcage was half ripped out of his chest. She had little hope for him.

It was now only the basilisk and Galin, slowly sidestepping, trying to determine each other's weaknesses. The basilisk's hourglass eyes hinted at intelligence, almost as if it could guess the hunter's next move.

"You're a big girl, aren't you?" Galin's blade pointed right between the eyes of the creature. "From the look of your feather pattern on your wings there, I'd have to say you are a native of the southern deserts. What are you doing this far north?"

The female basilisk waited for the man to make the first move.

"That means your scales are the toughest of your kind. No wonder these knights couldn't wound you very easily." Galin sheathed his blade.

Albree looked up worried, and shared her concern with him, but he remained standing strong and proud.

"I have killed your kind before."

The creature feigned an attack.

Galin jumped back, but he regained his composure.

The basilisk seemed to silently laugh. Bored of the man's talking, she made her move.

Her white fangs snapped near Galin's left arm, but he danced around her head, avoiding any contact. Her swift tail thrust toward his legs but he leapt over it. He fell onto the beast's tail and hugged it tight as it thrust like a scorpion's tail. After the ground struck Galin's head several times, he fell off.

Milo gasped as the mighty talons stomped around the big man. Surprisingly, Galin dodged them with impressive speed.

When Galin stood up, the basilisk snapped at him, tearing fabric from his shirt, uncovering his shoulder. The powerful attack caused the hunter to collapse to the ground once more. The monster's fanged mouth opened and it roared in victory. Galin held his breath so he wouldn't inhale the poisonous vapors. He kicked its jaw, giving him just enough time to escape.

Galin pulled his blade from its scabbard. The basilisk stomped its feet and charged. With his arms above his head, the sword dangling behind his back, Galin lined up his shot, and threw the heavy blade over his head.

It flew with greater speed than Milo had ever seen before, almost as if it were guided by magic. But this was no magic, only the experience and skill of a professional hunter.

The sword's point entered the mouth and punctured its way through, straight into the brain.

"By the gods." Milo watched from behind the rock in unwavering respect for the hunter.

The basilisk's eyes rolled back and she fell to the ground, dead.

Galin pulled his sword from the slain beast and cleaned off the mess.

"Galin! Come here, I think this soldier is going to make it."

Galin cut off the basilisk's head and strapped it to his pack. Later he would present it to the farmer.

The soldier was now sitting up on a rock, drinking out of Albree's water skin. His complexion was kind, but aged from many battles. He took the few last sips then exhaled deeply with satisfaction.

"That was damn good fighting out there," he said to Galin.

"Thank you, sir."

"This woman you've got yourself is one hell of a healer." Galin saw Albree really did do a fantastic job.

She dressed the remaining wounds, and began to put her supplies away.

"I'm glad I could have assisted you gentlemen, it was only a magical potion. I wish I had gotten here sooner," Albree said sadly.

"Yes, they were damn good men, but they fought valiantly. We shall get help from Wellsford to return the bodies home and see they receive a proper burial."

The soldier stood upright to gain a better look at the aftermath.

"Pardon me for my lack of manners. My name is Lord Renier, thank you so much for your assistance."

"The pleasure is all ours," Milo abruptly intervened, showing up out of nowhere. "My name is Milo, this lovely young woman who bandaged you up is Albree, and this here is Galin. He's a monster hunter."

"Yes." Lord Renier did not seem amused by the bard. "And I suppose you always spend your time cowering behind rocks while your friends fight battles?"

"Eh, no, sir. I mean, yes? You see, I am a bard." Milo held up his cittern case. "In the days of our children—or your grandchildren—this man Galin will be a legend. It is my duty to ensure him and others like him live on through song."

"And who will tell the stories after you are impaled by a rogue arrow on the outskirts of the battlefield?"

Milo sulked in embarrassment

"And as for grandchildren, I am too young for that, thank you very much. This white beard is bestowed to all my kin early in our years." Lord Renier collected his gear and looked out at the basilisk one more time.

*****

"Well, that was the most disappointing payment I have ever received." Albree crossed her arms as the trio left the farmer's house. "I mean, not even Lord Renier gave us a reward!"

"Lord Renier had to set up arrangements to bring his men's bodies safely back home," Galin reminded her. "Besides, he's not the one who hired us for this job. He's lucky to even be alive."

Galin ignored the fact that he didn't have to share the payment with Milo and Albree, for he was too humble to insult everyone's minor flaws.

He sighed, and explained to Albree, "Being a monster hunter isn't all about the money. Don't get me wrong, it keeps me fed, and I need to make some profit to get by, but I could do much simpler things for more coin if I desired. No, being a monster hunter comes with honor, duty, and passion you don't find elsewhere. This has been my dream since I was a child. I always remind myself that I live for the adventure. That's why I do this. It gives my life purpose. Remember that when you compose your first song. That's if Milo doesn't get hit with a rogue arrow first."

The two laughed. Milo tried to defend himself to no avail.

"You're right." Albree kicked the dirt path. "And you didn't have to take us both along, nor do you have to share the profit. Honestly, I did enjoy this little adventure today. It was one of the best days I've had in quite a few seasons."

Galin smiled. He knew Albree was strong, and she would make an excellent companion during his travels. Never before had he considered bringing a woman into his dangerous life. Yet, something about Albree intrigued him beyond words. His thoughts wandered for a while as he reminisced about his lonely travels. He thought about the endless nights through which he had always slept alone. For the first time in years, he yearned for more.

"Albree, there's something I want to ask you. Would you-"

"Galin, quiet." Milo gestured up the road. "Look up there, at The Pewter Piglet. Are those town guards?"

Five men in armor stood in front of the tavern, questioning Farnsworth.

The guards began viciously accosting the trio as they approached, while Farnsworth continued to curse them. Everyone argued for several moments until the commander walked out of The Pewter Piglet.

Galin knew the bleak expression He knew the black leather and metal-bound boots with blades jutting from the sides.

"Baxale." Albree froze.

"You know this man?" Galin snapped.

"I know of him," she whispered. "He is insane. He's been following me from town to town, saying he is to marry me. At night when I sleep, I see him outside my windows. I had to ward him off with my blade one time, but he cornered me and threatened to take my life. He is a high-ranking officer of some army. I do not know which one, but others I have talked to swear that he would never do such a thing. He has done well at keeping his composure around others, but this has gotten out of hand." For the first time, Galin saw her tremble. "I'm so sorry I never told you, I didn't want to hurt you or Milo."

"I was hoping I would not see you two together again." Baxale stomped around the trio, his breath still smelling of onions and garlic. "You have all committed crimes in Wellsford and are to be sent to the prison immediately. Guards, arrest them. But keep this elegant woman in a cell to herself. I want to pay her a little visit tonight." He stroked her chin with his clammy hands.

Galin could see that Albree wanted to cry, but she was too stoic to let her deepest fears show. The guards fitted all three with manacles and marched them down the street towards the prison cells. When they questioned the reasoning behind their apprehension, Baxale explained that they had attacked guards on the road this morning. Milo denied this and retorted that they had been attacked without warning by thieves that wore no uniform. Unfortunately, Baxale was a high enough authority for the prison guards to believe his story and haul the three off to the cells.

The prison cells were underneath the guards' quarters. The group walked down the curving stone stairs and into a single long hallway fitted with four cells to a side. Galin saw Albree was still trembling, and snuck her a soft kiss as the guard lead him and Milo to the last cell on the right. Albree was thrown into the first cell on the right and was reminded by the guard to be ready for Baxale's visit tonight.

Several long hours went by with the trio not saying much at all. The only comments came from Milo's mouth, attempting to joke about the moments that he, Albree, and Galin had shared earlier. His failed humor was challenged by silence.

The door above crashed open. There was yelling up in the guard house. Milo thought a fight was about to break out but was disappointed when the cacophony settled down, and boots were racing down the stairs.

One guard rounded the corner into the hallway, followed by Lord Renier. The guard began to unlock Albree's cell, then did the same for the two men at the end.

"Lord Renier!" Albree was so happy she embraced the man with an endearing hug.

He backed up awkwardly. "Yes, yes, Albree! Glad to see you. Why, I couldn't believe my ears that you three had been locked up!"

Galin and Milo glared at the guard as he made his way back up the stairs.

Lord Renier continued his story. "'Locked up?' I said. 'Why, that's preposterous!' I said. I told them that you three saved my life and are all heroes. I told them you have lives to live, people to save and monsters to kill. That you would never attack town guards, at least not without reason."

"And you told them we have songs to write!" Milo cheered.

"Uh, yes, and I may have bribed them with a bit of gold as well, but I'm sure it was the valiant story of the battle with the basilisk that convinced them to set you free."

"We thank you for your help, Lord Renier." Albree bowed respectively.

"Now, if it's all the same, let's call us even."

They laughed and agreed with Lord Renier.

Once the four of them stepped out of the guard house and into the streets of Wellsford, their laughter suddenly stopped.

Baxale was far less than pleased to see Galin's arm strong around Albree's waist. His face twisted in rage. His black-gloved hand gripped the hilt of his sword. He wore an overcoat they had not seen him in before, but it was fitted well to his body and had to be his. What shocked Galin was the insignia of a snake about to swallow a crescent moon imprinted onto his coat.

Galin reached into one of his pockets.

Baxale flinched in anticipation.

Galin pulled out a black glove with the same insignia and tossed it onto the ground before Baxale's bladed boots.

"That belongs to one of your men. Be sure that he gets it." Galin stood tall.

Baxale scoffed. He kicked the glove into the dust. "Idiots, those men. I should have murdered you myself. You are far too clever for your own good." He began circling them, like a shark teasing its prey. "Sneaking around with my woman right under my nose. This is punishable by death." He unsheathed his blade and stepped forward.

"Baxale!" Lord Renier stomped in front of Albree. "What is the meaning of this! Have you gone mad?"

"You better get out of this feud, it doesn't concern you."

"You are under my command!" Lord Renier threw his arms to the sky. "In the name of the gods, you are causing a scene in broad daylight. Sheath your sword now or you will be relieved of your duties for the rest of your days."

"No!" Baxale screamed. "I have fantasized of marrying a woman so radiant such as Albree since I had first laid eyes on her in Evesburg years back. I owe myself nothing less than her. Nobody can take her from me!" He threw stones to the ground and kicked buckets and crates throughout the street. "I will not let this man or any other man take the only beauty from my life! They will all die before they have her hand!"

Albree scowled, about to cut in, but the scraping of metal on metal interrupted her as Baxale drew a second blade, leveling it at Galin. Beady eyes glanced quickly at Lord Renier, and he lifted a corner of his mouth in a sneer.

"Galin, the lady thief, you are a dead man." Baxale marched a few steps forward.

Galin's mouth was already ajar, but this time, Albree was not to be interrupted. She stepped forward, stopping Baxale in surprise.

"You wretched rat, you have plagued me long enough! I shall pierce your heart. I give my affection to whom I choose." Her face glowed with power, bravery, and rage.

Galin put his rough, warm hand over hers, staying her from drawing her blade. "Albree," he started, voice quiet as he moved close to her. "Let me take care of him. Not because I do not think you can do it – I know there would be naught left of the man if you fought him – but because this is not a battle you need to fight. Killing this man will not bring him justice, he only needs a reason to remember his place in this world, and that place is not between you and I."

The woman blushed deeply, looking down at their hands. Her momentary rage subsided. "You surprise me, Galin of Darvalon."

He gave her a warm smile, eyes soft in wonder at this woman he was lucky enough to meet. "Fighting a man in anger is not the adventure we aim to seek. He is no monster." Then he turned to the glowering Baxale, and his smile turned mocking. "Now then, Baxale, shall we end this?"

Light flashed as the Baxale instantly dove towards Galin, putting all his weight behind a thrust to Galin's left ribcage. Bracing himself, the monster hunter smoothly swung his sword into an underhanded hold, the point facing down. Screeching echoed through the evening, sparks pinged off into the approaching darkness as Galin parried, then spun around to follow Baxale's momentum, sword transitioning back into a normal position. He moved from one form to another like water running down a hill, with an ease that only experience could give. The flat of his blade swung heavily against the back of Baxale's shoulders, sending the already unstable man stumbling into the dirt.

With a smack of his blade on his opponent's wrist, Galin disarmed him, flicking the sword away. A flurry of small cuts and jabs then fell upon the downed man, leaving his clothing shredded and skin torn.

Baxale, who seemed to have broken his fall with nothing but his face, looked up, wiping blood from his nose.

"You cheating b-"

A sharp sword tip at his chin stopped his words in his tracks.

"Are we done here?" Galin asked calmly, with a look that warned Baxale against saying no.

Hesitating for a moment, the man in black nodded once. The obsession in his eyes was now replaced with anger and humiliation. "Aye."

"And you will agree to never see nor speak to Albree again?"

Another pause, then another affirmative answer.

Galin smirked. "I believe you."

In a flash, Galin swung his blade and severed Baxale's head.

"You won't be bothering anyone any longer."

The crowd whispered. Some rejoiced.

Lord Reneir covered his mouth and exclaimed, "My gods, man. Was that really necessary?"

"Do you oppose?" Galin turned to his friends, offering an arm to Albree and a wink to Milo, whose agape jaw made him laugh. "Shall we make haste to our next adventure?" he asked in high spirits. "Monsters wait for no one."

Albree couldn't help but smile, even though she had experienced more murders today than ever before in her life, she felt free of the burden of Baxale. Milo didn't even notice Lord Reneir order his men to dispose of the headless body at once, nor did he pay attention to the head in the lord's arms as he walked away. His thoughts were with the two closest to him, the rest of the world didn't exist.

"I honestly wish we could all remain together." Milo wiped a tear from his eye. "But Albree still has studies. We must return to Evesburg to finish the song I wrote about our adventure today. Albree has come a long way, and soon I believe she will be ready to write her first song."

"Milo." Albree left Galin's side and put her arm around the bard's thin shoulders. "I have loved our time together. You have taught me much, and you're a fantastic teacher, but..."

"But what?"

"I no longer believe a bard is my calling."

Milo saw her eagerness to travel with Galin. Galin also eyed Milo with affection and understanding. The bard struggled to find the right thing to say. For once in his life, he was at a loss for words. Albree embraced him with the biggest hug she could offer.

"Milo, to go with Galin is something my heart tells me I must do. It feels like a part of me that's been missing. You know I will be safe, and we will all meet up again soon, right here in Wellsford!"

"I suppose I knew this was going to happen." Milo managed to smile.

"Now don't you have a song to finish?" Galin nudged Milo.

"That's right! I must spread the word of your heroism! Oh my, you will go down in history as the greatest monster hunter alive." The bard danced around joyously as the other two laughed once again at his peculiar antics. "I really love you two. Promise we will meet again in four seasons. Life would be boring without our adventures."

Galin repeated the phrase he had spoken so many times before: "Life is all about the adventure."

Galin, Albree, and Milo traveled together until they came to the crossroads. They said their last goodbyes, and Milo went east to his hometown.

Albree looked up at Galin with loving eyes and embraced him in her warm arms. "Where will you take me now, monster hunter?"

"Why must we choose one place in particular? When you're with me, all of Draston is your home."